SLIDING INTO HOME

THE DECKER CONNECTION
BOOK 2

CHERYL CAMPBELL

ISBN: 979-8-9929865-1-8

2nd edition

This book is dedicated to Taylor Swift.
Thank you for creating the soundtrack of our lives.
🤍
Darcy and Swifties everywhere

CHAPTER
ONE

DARCY

———

"I can't believe I just heard your song on the radio!" I scream into the phone.

"Yeah, it's pretty wild. I can't believe you heard it since it's not Taylor Swift." Cole responds with sincere modesty and a good hearted jab. He's humble about his music. His baseball career? Not as much.

"I branch out occasionally, but you could learn a thing or two from her," I chide.

He laughs, knowing better than to get into a Swiftie debate with me. "I'm sure I could. But how are you doing, Darcy? Did you secure an internship yet?"

Ugh. Thanks for the reminder. I'm in my last year of college, and this senior project is the only thing standing between me and graduation. This assignment looms large, and as a design student, it's important to build my portfolio and get a passing grade. All the interior design studios I applied to already had interns or weren't interested. I only have a few days to secure the project, or I won't be graduating this year.

"Not yet, but I'm sure something will work out." I let out an enormous sigh.

"Sounds like you're driving. Where you heading?"

"I'm on my way to The Wreck to see if I can pick up a few shifts until I find something. I could use the cash. Besides, you know I never turn down free food."

The Wreck is a local seafood restaurant in Charleston with great food and even better people. I've waited tables there on and off since I was sixteen, primarily for clothes money and extras.

"Darce, you know if you need money..."

"No way, rich guy. I'll never be a kept woman." I laugh at the idea. Cole and I grew up solid middle class. Mom always provided for us, but I lean towards trendy taste in fashion, and I know it. Granted, I'm a thrifting extraordinaire too. But Cole's new circumstances have changed his bank account to the extreme.

My brother is living the dream. Drafted by the New York Liberties this summer, he's working his way through their minor league system. He's living with his love, Ashleigh, in Nashville, where he plays baseball, and now, a song he wrote is playing on the radio, sung by one of today's hottest country stars. He's living a charmed life.

"You know if you need anything," he says for the hundredth time.

"I know. And I appreciate it. But you've done enough. You paid off my student loans and Mom's mortgage. Cole, that's too much already. Save your money."

"It's my job to take care of my family." His words are laced with love and devotion for us. Even though Mom is a kickass single mother, Cole has always been our protector. Our dad left when we were kids and never looked back. But Cole? He's the best guy I know, with a heart of gold and a commitment to people he definitely didn't get from our father.

"And you have. Now, focus on your new family. Have you and Ashleigh set a date yet?"

"No, we're just enjoying the engagement for now, but we're trying to find a date that works for everyone. She's establishing her company, and who knows what next season will bring." I hear a door slam, and a muffled sound comes through the phone.

"Ugh. Are ya'll making out while you're on the phone with me? Knock it off!"

"Hi, Darcy!" Ashleigh says through giggles. "Got that project lined up?"

"Hey, girl. Nah, not yet." I try to sound upbeat but know I can't fool them.

"Well, I might have an idea. Let me see what I can do," she says.

"Oh, please don't worry about me. I'll make it work."

"Are you kidding me? After the great job you did at our house? I'd give you five gold stars, six if they'd let me."

Cole yells, "Hell yeah," in the background.

"Hey, have you heard from Matt lately?" Cole asks as he gets closer to the phone again.

"Matt? No, why?" Matt Hartman is Cole's best friend and my gold standard for guys. He's like Captain America and the boy next door wrapped up in one. Think of the guy in Taylor Swift's music video "You Belong with Me," only brunette. With a killer smile and kind eyes. And a total panty melter in baseball pants. Just like in that video, I've harbored a crush on him since, well, forever. But unlike that video, I didn't walk into prom and sweep him off his feet. I mean, Matt is my brother's best friend, and I'm the annoying little sister. So why would I be hearing from him?

"I asked him to reach out now that he's back in Charleston. If you need anything, ask him like you would me. You know, a surrogate big brother," Cole says innocently.

"Ugh," Ashleigh says. "Sometimes, those are the worst. Leave her alone, trouble."

Cole mumbles something, but I hear lips smacking, and I know Ashleigh has his attention now.

"Thanks. Look, I'm gonna let you two go and do whatever you do. Love you guys!" This conversation is making me uncomfortable. They're living their best lives, and I'm, well, not.

"Bye, Darce. Love you," Cole says before we disconnect.

I envy their relationship. It's sickeningly sweet, and they're perfect for each other. I'm not sure I believe in soulmates, but if they exist, then Ashleigh and Cole are examples.

My relationship with my on-again-off-again ex-boyfriend, Ryan, is nothing like what Cole and Ashleigh have together, and unwittingly, they make me reevaluate what a relationship could be. Should be.

Ryan and I were too hot and heavy to start, and then he took advantage of my kindness. He'd flake on dates, cancel at the last minute, or call me late at night for a booty call. I was a little slow to catch on, but now I'm done. I'd rather be single than used. We are officially off again. Us getting back together? Never! Taylor Swift's songs are the soundtrack of my life.

I park in the gravel parking lot, wave to Eddie, one of the cooks, and wait for Jeff, the manager of The Wreck. I sit at a picnic table overlooking Shem Creek and smile wistfully at the scenery. The boats return home loaded with fresh seafood while seagulls circle for the chance to steal a snack. The smells of marsh, saltwater, shrimp trawlers, and restaurants compete for my attention.

I've worked for Jeff for the past five years during summer breaks and holidays at this locals-only shack with the freshest and best seafood in the area, bar none. It's nothing fancy, which I'm convinced is what keeps the tourists away. The tips aren't as much as one of those tourist hot spots a few doors down, but I know almost everyone who comes in, and it feels like home. If we aren't friends when you sit down, we are when you leave. The connection is as valuable as the money.

Jeff greets me with an overloaded paper plate of extra crispy fried shrimp, just the way I like it, and an ice-cold sweet tea. He knows my order without asking, and the gesture warms my heart. After a quick chat, I'm signed up for a few peak shifts over the next two weeks. Bonus because tonight's dinner and probably lunch tomorrow sit in front of me.

"I've gotta run back in," Jeff says as he stands up. "Enjoy dinner and the view. You know I love having you here. Tell your mama to swing by sometime. It's been too long." He gives me a wink.

"Thanks, Jeff. I will. I'll see you Saturday. And thanks for dinner." I hold up my cup in a mock toast and give him my biggest smile. Free food is unnecessary but always welcomed by this college girl.

My phone buzzes with a text from an unknown number.

> Hey Beautiful! This is the patron saint of senior projects.

I read the message through several times and have no idea who this could be. They must have the wrong number. Several minutes later, I get another text.

> Darcy? You busy? I've got a proposition for you.

> Ummmm, who is this?

> Sorry. Shit. I thought Ash gave you my number. It's Chance. Didn't mean to creep you out. Super sorry. Call me 😉

I breathe a sigh of relief. It's not some weird stalker. No, it's even more bizarre. Chance Fuller, professional hockey player for the Raleigh Renegades, absolute god on the ice, and one of the most gorgeous men on the planet, is texting me. And he called me beautiful? And has a proposition? I swear, my life continues to be more surreal each day.

The first time I met Chance was in Nashville while visiting Cole and Ashleigh. I totally thought he was a male stripper. With his body, he could be. Chance is Ashleigh's brother, Julian's best friend. Tangled web, right? I practically need to put an organizational chart on the wall to keep up with all of Ashleigh's people. My little circle of friends has expanded into a list of Who's Who since Ashleigh joined our small family.

I save Chance's number in my contacts and hit the call button. He picks up on the first ring.

"Darcy, I'm sorry. I hope I didn't freak you out or anything. I bet my texts were strange out of context. Are you okay?" He rushes through all that without taking a breath, and I'm not sure I caught every word.

"Hi, Chance. Yeah, um, I'm fine. A little confused, but it's great to hear from you."

"I've got to head to the arena in a minute, but Ash told me you need a senior project. I'm not sure if you knew I was her senior project last year."

This I did not know. I admit, I'm curious. "Dare I ask?"

Laughter is his primary language, and as he chuckles, his low rumble comes through the phone. "She completely took over my social media and increased my followers by an insane amount. She got her project, and I got a body wash contract. It was wild."

"Wow. That is wild. But I don't do social media. I'm a design major."

"Yeah, yeah. She told me that. Look, I don't have much time to go into details, but I just bought a house on the Isle of Palms. It needs a refresh. New kitchen, decor, furniture, the works. I want it to make Tripp's Cancun place look shabby. But I need someone to oversee it and do the interior design. That's you, right?"

"Chance, that's an enormous project. Don't you want a professional?" My stomach flips, thinking about the massive undertaking. It would be amazing and certainly get me an instant portfolio. But a student managing a hefty six-digit project? My advisor won't believe it. Hell, I don't believe it.

"Nah, if you're up for it, I want you to do it. We can talk details later, but I'll give you carte blanche. If Ash's house is any indication of your style, I like it. Besides, you're practically family now."

Ashleigh tried to explain how protective her brothers and their friends are with her, and, I guess by association, me, too. That's something that will take a lot of getting used to. She told me it was futile to fight it. These guys will smother me with love and protection, and apparently, a senior project, whether or not I want it.

"I'll be down there in a few days when we play the Sharks, and we can connect. I'll give you the keys and my credit card and introduce you to the contractor. How's that sound?"

"Um, yeah, sure. Let me know when you're here." This is too good to be true. "Are you sure about this?" I still can't believe he would trust me with such an expensive project. Even if I had landed an internship at a design studio, my job would be to get coffee and run errands for the most part. Maybe pick out fabric for the drapes, but a senior designer would still sign off on that.

But this? Carte blanche? No one to oversee me? No one to take credit for my work? Wow. This project could launch me. Or sink me. I swallow hard, thinking about failing.

"Like I said, beautiful, I'm the patron saint of senior projects. I'll text you the details later."

I'm still in shock at Chance's generosity. "Sounds good." I remember he said he was headed to the arena. I saw him play when we were in Nashville and totally loved it. Growing up around baseball, I never watched other sports. Hockey is exciting. And physical. Chance doesn't hesitate to slam someone into the boards. "Hey, have a great game tonight. Be safe."

"Don't worry about me, beautiful. You just stay out of trouble, and I'll see you soon. Bye!" He hangs up, and I stare at my phone.

Is Cole's charmed life rubbing off on me? Yes. Yes, it is. I can say this with total certainty. I don't deserve it, but I'm not mad about it either.

Who would imagine Chance Fuller, NHL superstar, would be my fairy godmother? Certainly not me.

CHAPTER
TWO

MATT

———

I'm never more alive than when I'm at the beach. I love the feel of the water pulling against my ankles as I stand in the surf. The smell of the salt air brings life to my lungs. There aren't a lot of waves this morning, so I decide to go for a run. I need to clear my head anyway.

My life has been a whirlwind lately, what with finding a place to live, meeting my new team, playing ball, living in hotels on the road, and thinking about my next step. Then the season ended three weeks ago, and it's like slamming on the brakes. I went from busy and chaos to nothing to do in one day.

I've never had this kind of downtime, and it makes me uneasy. Spending this much time with myself isn't something I'm used to, and it's made me rather philosophical. I wasn't a liberal arts major, so being in my head is a whole new level of mind-fuck for me. I was a physics major, for god's sake. This existential crisis shit is not something I'm used to, and it's got me a little freaked out.

I'm wired for action. I do things. Go to school. Study. Play ball. Hang with friends. There's always something on the calendar demanding my time and attention. But now, there's not.

I've also always lived with teammates, so when the time came to move into this new role, I got my own place because I thought it'd be nice to live alone for the first time. And now that I'm doing it? I don't like it. It's so quiet. Too quiet.

I admit being back home in Charleston, where I was born and raised, is comfortable. Most guys would kill to be in my shoes, but I haven't really lived here for the last four years since I went away to college. I didn't even come home for the summers because I was playing for the Savannah Pajamas, a college summer league that created some of my favorite baseball memories. It all was more time away from home. So, being back here? It's confusing. I don't know if I belong in Charleston anymore, but I'm grateful for the familiarity when I see specific landmarks. It's home.

Mom and dad like having me over occasionally, but they've grown accustomed to the empty nest. I love my folks, but I'm twenty-three and should be living my best life, not hanging with my parents. I mean, I'm living my dream. I'm getting paid to play baseball after being drafted in the third round with the Carolina Reapers, my childhood dream team. Most guys would give their left nut to be in my shoes. Now I'm assigned to their triple-A team, the Charleston Ghost Peppers, which brings me here. Home.

So, what the fuck is wrong with me? I don't know how to process this uneasy feeling settling in my chest.

My rental house is on the Isle of Palms in a year-round, primarily locals, residential part of the island. This morning, I run down the beach further than usual because I have extra steam to let out, and I find myself in the expensive vacation home part of the island.

I stop and put my hands on my knees to rest and catch my breath. The wind burns my lungs as I take a few deep gulps of air. The weather in October can be unpredictable in Charleston, and this morning, it's cooler than expected.

I check out the mansion behind me while I steady my breathing. It's hard to believe these ginormous places are vacation homes and not someone's primary residence. There are three levels of porches spanning the width of the house and the entire side is made of glass, giving amazing ocean views, I'm sure. Its imposing size dominates the dunes. Why would anyone need this huge house?

As I survey this monstrosity, movement on the upper porch catches my eye. These houses are usually closed up in the off-season, so seeing a beautiful girl in a baggy Raleigh Renegades Hockey sweatshirt captures my attention. She leans against the rail, warms her hands with her coffee cup, and stares off into the horizon, watching the sunrise. I do a double take because if I didn't know better, that girl looks like Darcy Davidson, my best friend's sister.

What would Darcy be doing at this big beach house so early in the morning? Maybe she spent the night with a friend? A *girl-friend*, my head tries to convince me. Darcy may be a senior in college, but I can't imagine she'd be with a guy old enough or rich enough to own a house like this.

Maybe my brain is playing tricks on me, and it's not even Darcy. I can't deny she's been on my mind since Cole's housewarming in Nashville a few weeks ago. And I promised Cole I'd check in on her and haven't done that yet. Fuck. Some best friend I am.

I automatically walk closer to the dunes to verify whether I'm going crazy. A tall, bearded guy walks out on the porch to join her. He leans his athletic body against the rail and bumps her shoulder. She laughs and takes a sip of her coffee. He reaches over and tucks a piece of dark hair behind her ear that has blown out of her messy bun.

I'm stuck, frozen in place, watching this interaction, and I realize I've become a fucking peeping tom. I'm watching my best friend's sister get cozy with Chance Fuller, NHL superstar, at the literal crack of dawn. My stomach rolls, and I feel like I might throw up.

Yeah, they were friendly when we were all together a few weeks ago in Nashville. I wasn't a fan of their playful banter, the way he tossed her over his shoulder, and I absolutely don't like what I see now. Could they be together?

There's no way. He's at least ten years older than her, and Cole would have a stroke to think they're hooking up. And honestly, I don't like the idea much at all, either. Darcy's relationship with Chance differs from Ashleigh's, so could she be fair game? After all, Ashleigh is the little sister of Chance's best friend, and we all know you can't be with your best friend's sister. It's rule number one of the bro code. The problem here is there is no bro code between Chance and Cole.

Chance puts his arm around her and leads her inside.

I don't like this in the slightest. Nope. Not at all.

Add it to the growing list of things making me uneasy. The real question is, what am I going to do about it?

CHAPTER
THREE

DARCY

———

I can't believe Chance asked me to meet him before sunrise. He flew in late last night and needs to return to his team this afternoon because they have a game in town tonight. He promised me gourmet coffee and breakfast. How could I refuse? Not to mention, he's gifting me with this project. Meeting at six-thirty? Sure, no problem.

Chance greets me at the door with a full-faced smile, a light beard on his chiseled jaw, and a friendly hug. His six-foot-three frame swallows me whole, and his warm brown eyes twinkle with excitement. He picks me up, my feet leaving the ground, and I'm embraced in his hug. He gently places me down and welcomes me into the house.

We go directly to the kitchen, where he makes my coffee and gives me a tour of the downstairs living area. When he notices I'm chilled, he refills my coffee, tosses me a sweatshirt, and sends me upstairs to look around while he throws a breakfast casserole in the oven.

This house is fantastic. Sure, it's a little dated and too "beachy" for my taste, but it has excellent bones. I never understood why people decorate a beach house with so many items that portray beach life. I mean, open the windows. Hello, beach. No need to bring it all inside, too.

There are three levels of living space, with the garage and pool at the ground level. After checking out the seven bedrooms on the upper floors, I make my way to the large upstairs living room that overlooks the ocean. The French doors open onto the porch that stretches across the entire width of the house. I slip out the door and lean against the rail, my coffee cup warming my hands.

The sound of the waves rolling onto the shore is the white noise I need while my mind races with ideas to make this house stunning. The magnitude of this project is equally energizing and paralyzing. I can't believe Chance is trusting me with his house.

Lost in my creative mind, sorting through all the possibilities, I'm startled when Chance joins me on the deck.

He bumps my shoulder with his. "Didn't mean to startle you. You okay?" He leans down against the rail, mirroring my body language. His tall, muscular body has to contort a little more to meet my five-five frame, shoulder to shoulder. He gives me a warm smile, and I instantly relax.

Chance is a friendly guy. He's kind. And fun. And hot as hell. And saving my ass with school. I'm grateful.

"Yeah, I'm good. Already thinking about ideas. The house is amazing, and the views are spectacular."

"I thought so, too. I've always loved the beach and wanted a place close enough that I would use often. Tripp has an extraordinary house in Mexico, but I wanted something more accessible."

"What's your overall goal for the house? How do you want it to feel?" My aesthetic is all about connection, how it makes you feel. Adventurous? Relaxed? Stimulated? On vacation? Or warm and cozy like a home?

"I want it to be a retreat for me and my friends. I want a comfortable, relaxed vibe. But nice, you know. Chill."

"You want hygge." He wants an escape where he find peace from the high stress of being a professional athlete. Hygge is a simple, serene, relaxed environment that is perfect for this house.

"Hygge, like from *Frozen*?" He smiles like we've bonded and I get him. Which I don't, because he's always full of surprises. Who would have thought Chance would make a reference from a Disney movie? This guy has layers.

He earns a full out laugh for that comment. "Yes, exactly. But I don't think neutral is the way to go here. We'll add some pops of color, too. Have a few unexpected elements. It'll be nice, posh, I promise."

"But not too nice where a spilled glass of red wine makes anyone uncomfortable or upset." Chance doesn't want this house for show. He wants it for people, connection, fun. Maybe a little love too?

"Do your friends spill wine often?" I quirk my eyebrow at him, challenging him regarding his choice of hot female friends.

"You'd be surprised. Tripp may be a Cy Young award-winning pitcher, but he's clumsy as fuck when he drinks his expensive red wines."

We both laugh. The wind picks up, and my messy hair whips across my face. Chance reaches over and tucks the errant strand behind my ear. Kindness and caring oozes from every pore. He can't help it. I know he isn't romantic or flirty with me. He's just Chance.

"Tripp?" I wasn't expecting that. My mind immediately went to sexy women, red wine, and candles. I mean, Chance is a handsome, wealthy, professional athlete. Surely, he has women lined up outside his bedroom door.

"Yeah, Tripp Stevenson. He's a pitcher for the Reapers. We hang out a good bit because we tend to run in the same friend group. Since our seasons only overlap for a few months, we can support each other at games." Chance's friend group is star-studded.

"Oh, I know who Tripp Stevenson is. His rookie card is one of Cole's most treasured possessions. Cole's a huge Reaper fan. Or was? Still is?"

He laughs and it resonates across the porch. "Yeah, I forgot Cole wanted to be a Reaper. Sometimes, the universe knows better than us. What we want isn't always the best. We're better off getting what we need, and it's so much better."

"Wow, that's deep." I yawn. "Especially at seven o'clock in the morning."

Chance chuckles. He throws his arm around my shoulders and pulls me toward the doors. "Come on, sleepyhead. Let me get you some breakfast, and let's talk about this house and how you're going to finish school with a bang. Jayden, the contractor, will be here in an hour, and I want to make sure you're prepared. He may do the heavy lifting, but to be clear, you're in charge. This is your project."

We return to the kitchen, where Chance scoops up a casserole on two plates. The creamy grits and perfectly cooked shrimp are delicious. This guy never ceases to amaze me. Is he part Martha Stewart too?

We eat and get to know each other better over breakfast. We've been together several times, but always in group settings. This is the first time it's been one-on-one, and he's easy to talk to. Of course he's relaxed. I'm the one about to take on a project I have no business leading.

Chance asks about my family, friends, and school experiences. His genuine desire to get to know me is sincere. He tells me his friends and family are the most important things in his life. Hockey is second. Apparently, I'm one of those friends now. Chance is a great guy and will be an even better friend. He's one of the sexiest men in America, and I'm not even tempted to flirt.

I'm as comfortable with Chance as if I were hanging with Cole. It's a total friend zone, and it feels right. Another big brother.

Jayden, the contractor, arrives a short time later. I was expecting a middle-aged white guy with a beer gut. Was I way off base! Jayden is young, probably a few years older than me. He's a few inches shorter than Chance, but his body is just as toned as the professional hockey player, if his muscular arms are any sign. His caramel skin and baby-blue eyes give him an exotic look. His jeans and work boots look is sexy and rugged, but I'd bet he could also rock a business suit or walk the runway in New York.

I remind myself we need to work together, and technically, I'm his supervisor. He's in the *look but don't touch* category. It may be cold outside, but the temperature in this house is hot.

After spending several hours with Jayden, sharing rough ideas, a general budget, and a timeline, he leaves. I've filled up twenty pages of notes and rough sketches of ideas for this house. Most of the construction work will revolve around the kitchen. It feels like a massive project, one I hope I can pull off.

"Chance, are you sure you want me to do this? You can hire a professional, and I can be their assistant. It's a lot, and I don't want you to—"

He shakes his head and looks me square in the eyes. "Nope. I want you to do this, Darcy. I know you can do it. If *you* need an assistant, hire one. I love listening to your ideas. You come to life when you sketch and I'm excited to see what you come up with. Remember, this is *your* project." He pulls out a black credit card with my name and hands it to me. "This is to cover all expenses. I got this one with your name, so you won't have any issues. Use it for furniture, paint, subcontractors, appliances, or whatever you need. Keep the refrigerator stocked with food and drinks for you and the workers. I'll be upset if I don't see regular meals on there for you." He hands me a set of keys on a Renegades keychain. "Here are the keys to the kingdom. Make yourself at home. If you want to crash here, bring friends here, whatever, I'm cool with it. You're in charge. Mi casa es su casa."

"Oh, I couldn't...."

"You can and you will. Got it? We're making this house a retreat for me and my friends. And that, dear Darcy, includes you." He gives me a wink and a full smile.

I'm officially the president of the Chance Fuller fan club.

An Uber picked Chance up an hour ago to get him to the arena, and his parting words were, "Have fun, you'll do great, I'm sure I'll love it, and let's shoot for a great New Year's Eve party here. Doable?"

New Year's Eve? That gives me precisely ten weeks to get this done. Jayden assures me the kitchen renovation will be the project's most challenging and time-consuming part. Still, he can have it done before Christmas, provided I can get him the tile, countertops, cabinets, and appliance choices quickly.

I review my notes and prioritize what needs to be done first. Based on what I wrote, the answer is simple. Everything. I need to make the color and style selections in the next few days. The enormity of what I've committed to sinks in, and my heart races. I've done nothing like this before, and now Chance gives me a Black Card and tells me to have fun. What I thought was kindness and generosity was actually cruelty and evil, wrapped in a charming smile.

I'm about to lose it, but I don't want to come across ungrateful. With a deep breath, I swallow my fears and anxiety and focus on the task at hand. Unfortunately, this is not my strong suit. I'm more of a fly-by-the-seat-of-my-pants, go-with-the-flow kind of girl. I know I'll need some help, but right now, I need to get to work at The Wreck. Waiting tables and taking care of people, I can do well. This project? Time will tell.

CHAPTER
FOUR

MATT

———

"I appreciate you volunteering to help with our fall ball camp. Now that you're a big-time professional baseball player, it's nice to know you still remember your roots and have time for your old high school." Dad grabs me around the neck and pulls me in for a knuckle rub to the head. I may be twenty-three and over six feet tall, but I'll always be a kid to him.

"Quit busting my balls, Dad. You know I'll never be able to repay you for all the camps and coaching you gave me over the years. I wouldn't be where I am without you." I throw my arm around his shoulder and walk up to the field.

"I get to brag that two of my alumni are professional ball players now. As your coach, but especially as your father, I'm bursting with pride. But you did all the hard work. I just encouraged you along the way."

Yeah, life is pretty amazing these days. In the past few months, I graduated college, signed with my dream baseball team, and played the rest of the season in Charleston on their triple-A team, the Ghost Peppers. Now, I'm officially in the off-season, the first one I've ever had in my life. When my father, who is also my former high school baseball coach, asked if I could give him a hand as a batting coach this fall at my old school, I couldn't say no.

Honestly, I didn't want to say no. This off-season is the first time I haven't had a baseball in my hand since I was six. Helping Dad keeps me on the field and off my couch. Sounds like a win-win to me.

"Got any hot prospects this year?" I ask. Our school has always had a solid team. Dad is one hell of a good coach. It's common for several players to make it to college ball, with a few even playing for Division One schools. Cole Davidson and I are the first two to get the call into the big leagues, and Dad isn't shy to let everyone know.

"I've got a junior pitcher that has serious potential. And our catcher can knock the leather off the ball. There's one kid I'd like you to mentor if you can. He needs to focus and get his head straight, but he won't listen to me."

"Sure, just point him out, and I'll see what I can do." I'm used to being the father figure on the team. In college, I always kept tabs on teammates, ensuring the grades were there, monitoring study hall, and offering relationship advice. That role was ingrained early. The guys dubbed me Captain America. I'm not sure I'm all that, but I'm a clean-cut, do-the-right-thing kind of guy.

It's the curse of the coach's kid. I have to be better and work harder because everyone thinks I got the starting spot because of my dad. Little do they know, he'd pull me faster than any other kid on the field. His standards were high, especially for me. I'm not complaining. Because of him, I've developed a strong work ethic, a healthy level of responsibility, and excellent baseball skills that'll take me far. I plan on playing baseball at the highest level for a long time. My dad gave me the foundation for my future, and I'll always be grateful. But to say it was easy because I'm the coach's kid is flat out wrong.

My phone buzzes in my pocket. I pull it out, and Dad says, "Make it quick. We have a strict no phone policy and no special rules for the coach's kid." He gives me a wink and steps toward the field.

"Don't I know it," I mumble.

Without knowing who's calling but having a father's sixth sense, he adds, "And tell him if he can make the time, I'd like to see his sorry ass down here soon." He laughs as he walks away.

I answer the FaceTime request. "Hey man, what's up?" Cole's face fills my screen.

"Matt, where the hell are you? Did the Reapers knock you back to high school already?" He laughs at his jab. We spent so many hours at this ball field, he knew it as soon as he saw it.

"Nah, man. About to help Dad with fall practice. He says to get your ass down here and help, superstar. Or are you getting soft in the off-season?"

"I'm not complaining about this downtime." He glances to his right, a smile lighting up his face. "You know what? Send me the schedule, and I'll see if I can't get down there in the next few weeks."

"Really? That would be great!"

I'm trying to find my way as a solo act, but truth be told, I miss my best friend. We've been inseparable since third grade. Until now. It's the first time we haven't been on the same team, in the same city, in fifteen years. I visited him a few weeks ago, but it wasn't enough time.

A beautiful girl wraps her arms around his neck and puts her head on his shoulder. Ah, the reason for the momentary distraction and smile, Ashleigh.

"Hey Matt, what's going on with your hair? Looks like you just rolled out of bed." She wiggles her eyebrows suggestively. Well, she attempts to be suggestive. This girl cracks me up.

"Seriously, have you met me? Like I've got time for a hookup." Unfortunately, that's not exactly the truth. I've been busy, but I have more time on my hands than ever right now. If I wanted to date, now would be the time, but why bother? The season starts back up in a few short months, and I could move at a moment's notice. Nah, now is not the time to start a romantic relationship. Besides, being back home has made the dating pool seem small, and I can't stomach cleat chasers.

"Well, now that it's the off-season, make time," she says. She kisses Cole on the cheek and disappears from the screen.

"Just because you two are blissfully happy doesn't mean we all have to be subjected to it, you know." I'm happy for them. It's just hard to watch sometimes.

A chuckle escapes his lips. "I can't complain about the life-style, my friend. You should give it a try."

"Look, I gotta run. No phones at practice. But quick question. Have you talked to Darcy lately?"

"Um, not sure I like that transition. I tell you to get laid, and you mention my sister?"

I turn red as a tomato. "No, no, not what I meant. Just wondered what she's been up to. I haven't checked on her since we got back from Nashville."

"She's busy with her senior project and picking up a few shifts at The Wreck. I don't know if she's on or off with that d-bag Ryan. I know I promised to let her live her life, but I don't like that guy. But I think she's good. Just a lot going on. I bet she'd appreciate food or something fun."

Do I mention her getting cozy with Chance yesterday? I didn't realize Ryan was still in the picture. That's even more confusing. "Yeah, I'll shoot her a text or something."

"Thanks, man. I know Leigh will disagree with me, but she needs an older brother, whether or not she knows it. And you know, since I'm not there, you'll have to do." Cole's right. Darcy is family, and it's my job to ensure she's doing well.

My dad blows his whistle to call everyone in from warm-ups.

"Gotta go. I don't want to get fired from my volunteer coaching job." Cole and I both laugh.

"Sounds good, man. I'll check my calendar and see about getting down there soon. Peace, brother."

I disconnect the call and pocket my phone. Damn, I miss my best friend. I'm trying to stay busy with practice, going to the gym, and hitting the surf most mornings, but it's not the same without him. This adulting thing kinda sucks.

————

Dad and I finish up practice and decide to grab dinner. Mom has a book club or something, so we make it a guy's night out. It beats grabbing fast food and eating it alone while I watch Sports Center.

Even though I've been back in Charleston for a few months, I've been busy with the team traveling and haven't been able to hit my favorite places. Pulling into the familiar parking lot transports me back to when Dad would bring Cole and me here for dinner after a big win.

It's a warm evening, so we sit at an outside table and watch the shrimp boats come in from their day. Shem Creek is fresh seafood, colorful sunsets, and family. I smile at the memories, and peace and tranquility wash over me. With a deep exhale, I relax into my seat.

"That's a rather ominous sigh," Dad says.

"Nah, it's good. I'm just thinking about when we came here after games. It's nice to be home, that's all." And it is. I relax for the first time in years. Maybe ever. It's a foreign feeling, but one I'm willing to explore.

"Hey Coach, what can I get ya'll tonight?" I look up when I hear a familiar voice, her slight southern drawl wrapping around me like a warm blanket on a chilly night. She looks tired. Her dark hair is pulled up in a high ponytail, but her hazel eyes sparkle, even with the circles underneath. She's wearing a baggy sweatshirt that fits like a micro dress, with her cut-off denim shorts peeking out from under the hem. Her red Chuck Taylors, her signature waitress shoe since she was sixteen, complete the outfit that is totally Darcy. She makes eye contact with me and smiles.

"Hey Matt. Fancy seeing you here."

"I didn't know you still worked here, Darce. I thought you'd be swamped with your senior year."

"Oh, trust me, I am. But Jeff's let me pick up a few shifts for shoe money. You know, a girl can never have too many shoes." She gives me a quick wink and blushes.

"Hey, if you need money," I start. Dad tilts his head with an amused look. He's always teased me about my relationship with Darcy. She's the little sister I never had, that's all.

"Don't be silly. I'm good. I signed up for these shifts before my sugar daddy made me a kept woman. So, I won't be doing this much longer, anyway." She giggles, her laugh light and airy.

"Um, excuse me?" My voice is a little louder and harsher than I intended. "Sugar daddy? What the hell, Darcy? Are you trying to give me a heart attack here?" That fucker. Chance Fuller.

Dad laughs at the incredulous look I'm giving her.

"A girl's gotta do what a girl's gotta do. Isn't that right, Coach?" She gives him a wink.

"As long as the girl is happy," he says, smiling back at her. WTF, Dad?

"So, what can I get you guys," she says, shifting back into business mode.

"I'll take the flounder and a Blue Moon," Dad says.

"Gotcha. Matt?" She's looking at me, waiting for my order. I've lost my appetite.

"Same." I glare at her, trying to figure out what's happening.

"Great, I'll bring that out in a flash."

She turns and walks away, her hips swaying under her baggy sweatshirt.

"Darcy sure has grown into a beautiful young woman, hasn't she?" Dad asks. He pulls my attention from the retreating figure of my best friend's little sister. "I always liked her. I admire the way she marches to her own drummer. She has a unique sense of style."

"Um, yeah." Darcy is unique. She's stylish and a trendsetter, putting her stamp on everything she touches. She has a way of making everything around her more beautiful. I'm sure she could be a social media influencer with minimal effort if she put her mind to it. She has that magic touch to make beauty seem effortless and natural. It's a gift.

"What's got you rattled?"

"I didn't like the sugar daddy comment," I answer honestly, not thinking how Dad might interpret it.

"I noticed, but I'm sure she was teasing. Darcy's smarter than that. She's independent. The last thing I could imagine her doing is relying on a man for anything."

Was she teasing? I would've taken that comment as a joke, too, if she hadn't been on the deck of a multimillion-dollar beach house with a professional hockey player this morning. Now I'm not so sure.

"Maybe." Another waitress brings our beers while Darcy serves other tables outside. Dad and I take a big pull from our bottles. He watches the boats, and I watch Darcy.

She connects with her diners, many locals like us, and chats with everyone. Her infectious smile makes everyone around her feel at home. A little boy, probably about two or three years old, is wiggling in his chair, causing his mother anxiety. Darcy scoops him up and puts him on her hip, bouncing him while she talks to the parents. She takes him with her inside while she places their order. I assume they must be regulars or friends because she brings him back a minute later with a coloring sheet and crayons. She puts him in his chair and whispers something in his ear. He grins up at her and earnestly draws something for her. She rubs his head and walks off to her next table.

She's a natural with people. Easy going. Friendly. Kind. Beautiful. Sexy. Wait? Where did that come from?

"She's the real deal, isn't she?"

"Um, what?" Dad's comment catches me off guard.

"Darcy, she's the real deal. An extraordinary young woman." He takes another draw on his beer, his attention shifting from the boats to me.

She approaches our table with our food.

"Here ya go. The best flounder caught today for the best baseball guys in Charleston." Dad chuckles at the comment.

"Thanks," Dad says. "Looks great."

I stare, trying to figure out what's going on with her. Dad kicks me under the table.

"Yeah, looks great. Thanks."

"Well, let me know if ya'll need anything else." She walks away.

"What time do you get done tonight?" I call out.

She turns her head and looks back at me. "Huh? We close at nine. Why?"

"I want to catch up. Let's grab a drink or something."

"Um, I'd love to, but I can't. I'm meeting someone after work."

Shit. Is Chance still in town? I make a note to check his team schedule. When did I become a puck bunny? Damn. "Oh, okay. I'll text you. Let's catch up soon."

"Sure, that would be great." I watch her walk back inside.

"You think drinks with Darcy is a smart move?" Dad asks casually and begins to eat his dinner.

"I promised Cole I'd watch out for her. Something's going on. Did she look tired to you?" I don't wait for an answer. "She looks tired. I just want to make sure she's doing okay." I want to find out what's going on with Darcy because I'm Cole's best friend. It's what he'd want me to do. I'm doing this for Cole. And Darcy.

"You keep telling yourself that," Dad says under his breath.

He gives me a strange smile, like he knows something, but I have no idea what.

I pick at my dinner. This food is delicious, but my mind is racing with scenarios of Darcy and sugar daddies. When I can't stand it anymore, I pull out my phone and find the Renegades schedule. They have a game tonight against the Charleston Sharks and don't have another one for the next three days. Chance could stay in town, I guess.

"Since when are you into hockey? I know you met Chance Fuller a few times. Are you in his fan club now?" Dad nods to my phone as I lay it on the table.

"Trust me, I'm most definitely not in the Chance Fuller fan club. Not one bit."

I need to go. Tossing plenty of money on the table to cover dinner and an extra hundred for Darcy's tip, I grab my phone and head to my car. I may not have NHL-level money yet, but if Darcy Davidson needs money, she'll get it from me, not Chance "Sugar Daddy" Fuller.

Dad laughs as I walk away. I'm glad he thinks this is funny because I don't see any humor in it. Nope. None at all.

CHAPTER
FIVE

DARCY

————

After a quick and very profitable shift at The Wreck, it's time to work on the house. I need reinforcements, so I sent out an SOS on my break. It may be late on a Saturday night, but I know who to call.

911

SAMMIE

What?!?! Did you already succumb to the charms of your benefactor? 😜

Worse! I need to make a week's worth of decisions in days. Help!

Wow. I don't think I've ever heard you ask for help in all the years I've known you. Sounds like you need a crash course in triage.

> Exactly. I'm desperate. Please come help me. I'm headed back to the house to get started after my shift. Pack an overnight bag for each of us.

Wait, you're serious?

> Dead. 💀 I need you, Sammie. Please hurry.

———

I text her the address, knowing she'll come because that's what your ride-or-die does. We've been best friends since sixth grade and have gone through everything together. First love. First heartbreak. Mean girls. High School. College decisions. All the milestones of my life involve Samantha, aka Sammie. This project will be no exception.

We couldn't be more opposite. Her skin is dark and flawless. I'm so pale I could pass as a vampire. My dark hair is long and straight, and she has gorgeous natural curls. I'm more bohemian, and she's structured. She had an almost perfect SAT, and I got into college with average grades and the power of extracurriculars. She's practically OCD, and I'm a bit of a mess. But somehow, our opposites mesh. We make each other better.

We moved into a small apartment above Mama Kim's on King Street the summer before our junior year. It was time to practice adulting. Admittedly, Sammie is much better at it than me. Kinda like how I'm always waiting until I'm out of underwear to do laundry. Sammie has her chores scheduled and listed on a color-coded chart. Yep. Total opposites. My favorite thing about Sammie? She never judges or lectures me about my opposite behaviors, which I'm sure drives her insane.

She's not only book smart but also has high emotional intelligence. She understands the importance of my 911 text. I'm stubborn and proud. It's a terrible combination of character traits. I tend to take the road less traveled, and may find myself in predicaments of my own making, but I never ask for help.

I'm like my mom in that way. She taught me to stand on my own two feet because you never know when the person you depend on, the person who you pledged your love and future to, who you had children with, might up and walk out on you, leaving you to do it all for yourself. That's what happened to my mom. My dad left when I was three, and we never heard from him again.

Me asking Sammie for help? Yeah, it's a big deal. She shows up forty-five minutes later, overnight bags in one hand, a bottle of vodka in the other.

"Wow, this place is incredible," she says as I open the door.

"Right? It's fantastic. I can't believe he's given me the keys to a multimillion-dollar home and says have fun. Have fun?" I throw my hands in the air. "What kind of sick person does that? I'm freaking out!" I enter the open living room and throw myself onto the couch. It's not very soft, so I stop instead of the dramatic bounce I was going for. Add comfy seating to the priority list.

Sammie drops the bags in the foyer and enters the kitchen. She puts the vodka in the freezer and pulls out her laptop.

"We drink later. Let's tackle this first. I'll set up a spreadsheet to help you track everything, including timelines, costs, and follow-up. I'll even color code it for you." She gives me a knowing smile. I love things with colors.

"I don't know how to use a spreadsheet," I sigh. I took more art classes than business, and now I'm questioning all the college decisions I've ever made.

"I'll teach you. It's not hard. And I know you love your colored pens and notebooks. Unfortunately, this project is going to require something more. But girl, you got this. You're going to make this place go from nice to amazing."

"Yeah, in ten weeks," I squeak out. Ten short weeks. Jayden

seems confident on his end, but it all depends on my timely deci-
sion-making.

"Okay. Ten weeks. Got it. Then, you prioritize and work
backward. Easy peasy."

"Says you. You know I'll get bogged down in the details and
freeze."

"Then don't. It's like eating an elephant."

"What?" I think Sammie has officially lost it. Eating an
elephant?

"Yep. How do you eat an elephant? One small bite at a time.
Let's walk through it. Give me your vision. I know you're good
at that. Then, we'll break down the details on the spreadsheet for
each room. Easy peasy."

"Would you quit saying that! It's not easy peasy." I pull at my
hair and grab a hair tie from my pocket. I throw it up in a sloppy
ponytail as I feel my anxiety rise.

It's not easy. It's not about new cabinets. It's about colors,
style, hardware, functionality, and how they make you feel when
you see them. It's about emotion, comfort, connection. It's not
easy peasy.

"Take a deep breath. I'm about to show you what asking for
help looks like. And maybe you'll even learn how to do it
again." I give her a skeptical look. "You'll see. Before you know
it, you'll be reaching out for help from your friends who love
you dearly, and it will honor them to give it. Asking for help can
bless both the receiver and giver."

Tears fill my eyes, and I'm overcome with emotion. I hug
Sammie hard, willing my tears to recede. I'm a crier. When my
feelings overwhelm me, I cry. I can't help it. I leak emotion.

Sammie pulls away and puts her hands on my shoulders.
"Okay, one shot. Then we get to work." We start in the kitchen
and toast to senior year.

We go room to room, and I ramble. Somehow, Sammie turns my
word vomit into a list of everything needed in each room. She asks

questions, making me look at it in more detail. Colors, theme, style, feeling, what needs to be purchased, timeline. She leaves spaces for measurements, fabrics, dates ordered, prices, etc. It's taken us hours when we finish, but the spreadsheet gives an organized picture of what needs to be done. I feel better. Sammie's organization and triage skills give me confidence I can complete this on time.

"It's like eating an elephant," I mumble. I can admit when she's right, which is most of the time.

Sammie gives me a knowing smile. "Told ya."

"Sammie, you're the best! I don't deserve you."

We return to the kitchen and toast with a few more shots just as our midnight pizza arrives.

As we devour our late-night dinner, I search for the perfect sectional for the living room. Replacing this uncomfortable furniture is at the top of the priority list.

Jayden sent his list of preferred vendors earlier this evening. I appreciate his openness to work with me, especially given my inexperience. While we didn't talk about it yesterday, I'm sure it was clear I don't know what I'm doing. He offered to meet me on Sunday to make sure we're on the same page. This will be my first meeting without Chance and my opportunity to be the project leader, and I'm nervous as hell.

We get a few hours of sleep before I take on this project tomorrow. Or is it today? I have a feeling time will be a blur for a while. Might as well get used to it.

———

Sammie is lying by the pool, her Kindle propped up beside her. It's a perfect fall day at the beach. I wish I could relax with her, but I have a lot to do.

"Whatcha reading?" My shadow blocks the sun, getting her full attention.

"This fun sports romance. The main character is a hockey

player who reminds me of Chance or what I imagine him to be like. A great guy, but unlucky in love."

"I'm not sure how unlucky Chance is, but he's a pretty great guy." He'll make some woman very happy someday, and she'll be the lucky one. I hope he finds it. Hell, I want to find it eventually, too.

"You know what this space needs?" Sammie breaks me out of my romantic daydreams.

"What? Pool boys in Speedos feeding you grapes?"

"While that would be fantastic, it needs a bar and food storage, so you don't have to go upstairs whenever you need something. And a bathroom."

"You know, you're right. I can picture a bar over here. I can give it a total resort vibe. But maybe with some whimsy? And there's already an outdoor shower. We can punch that up a notch and add a bathroom there. And an outdoor kitchen in the corner with a grill and brick oven for pizzas. It'll be unique and have everything they need. They'll never want to go inside. I'll conceal a space over here for storage and games." I close my eyes and picture the space, the colors blending, and the joy they'll create. I can practically hear the laughter from Chance and his friends. "This is the cherry on top. Chance and his friends will love this when I'm done."

"There's the excitement I needed to see! I knew you could do this. I can't wait to see it when it's finished and has the Darcy touch. It'll be the best house on the East Coast."

I know Sammie means well, but her comment causes my chest to tighten. This project is everything. My graduation. Chance's house and money. Being a disappointment and embarrassment to my brother's friends makes my pulse quicken. I take a cleansing breath and calm myself. Now is not the time to panic.

"Jayden's going to be here soon. Do you mind helping me with the spreadsheet and stuff when he gets here? I'm afraid I'll delete it or mess it up or something."

"Of course, I'll help. But you can't break it. And I have it automatically backed up every few minutes to the cloud. I made it Darcy proof." She gives me a smile and a half-shrug, conveying she gets me. Sammie totally has my back. That's why she's my person.

"Hello! Anyone back here?" A deep male voice calls from the side of the house.

I get up from the lounger and meet Jayden as he walks around the corner of the house.

"Hey Darcy, I rang the bell and took a chance you might be back here." His eyes move from me to Sammie and a slow smile appears. His eyes brighten as he checks her out from her bouncy curls to her neon green painted toes.

"Yeah, maybe we need to figure out something so the doorbell alerts back here, too? We were talking about this being a central entertainment spot." I watch him as he blinks a few times and scans the area, taking his eyes off Sammie for a moment.

"It's gorgeous out here. What were you thinking?"

I tell him my ideas for the bar, bathroom, outdoor kitchen, and storage area.

Jayden nods his head in approval. "Those are great ideas. We'll incorporate a weatherproof video system so he can watch sports or movies. And we'll tie it to a video doorbell. Let's include a killer sound system, too. His neighbors will either join in the party or call the cops. Good to give them options." His eyes drift back to Sammie.

I'd better do the introductions. "Jayden, this is my roommate, Samantha. Sammie, this is Jayden."

"Nice to meet you," Sammie says, not hiding her scan of him from head to foot and landing back on his light eyes. "You seem pretty young to have your own construction company."

"I took over from my dad. He still runs the business side of it, but I prefer to be the hands-on guy," Jayden says. He shifts uncomfortably. Today, he's not rocking the contractor vibe. A worn, long-sleeve t-shirt from The Windjammer, a local beach bar, covers his muscular arms. His broad shoulders fill every inch. His dark wash jeans hug his narrow hips, and Jordans finish the look. He has no ball cap today, so I notice his dark hair is a little long on top with a fade that gives him an edge.

Sammie is paying attention to Jayden, too. As much as I'd love for them to flirt and get together, I must stay on task. Maybe I can attempt to accomplish both?

"Sammie has put together a spreadsheet to help keep us on task. She's not only beautiful but has brains, too." I glance at Sammie and watch a blush climb to her cheeks. He gives an approving smile. "So, let's sit down and go over everything, add the outdoor kitchen to the project, and see if we can still stay on schedule."

Jayden looks at me, pulls his phone out, and types something in. "Yep, let's look at that spreadsheet and get to work. Are you joining us?"

I smile. "Of course, she's my assistant this weekend until I can find a permanent helper. Come on, let's dazzle this guy with your brilliance. Then we'll treat him to dinner. That is unless you have plans with your girlfriend or something." Being subtle isn't what this situation needs.

Jayden shakes his head. "Nope. No plans. Or girlfriend. And please, my friends call me Jay." He smiles at Sammie, and good god, he has dimples. His hotness factor just skyrocketed. "I think we're going to be good friends." He gives her a wink. "Hey, let me grab something from my truck, and I'll meet you in the dining room in a few minutes." He turns and walks around the house.

"Who needs dating apps when you live your life?" Sammie asks accusingly. "You've got them eating out of the palm of your hand." She raises one eyebrow, giving me the I dare you look.

"Are you kidding me?" I laugh. "That guy was all about you, my friend."

"What?! No. No way." Sammie never sees herself as the rest of the world does. Then again, do any of us?

"Yes, way. So come on, let's go upstairs and show Jay, with no girlfriend but sexy dimples, how smart you are. I've got a project to complete and college to graduate. You've got a handsome as hell guy to flirt with and a spreadsheet to teach me how to use."

We finished reviewing the changes, and while Sammie and Jay talk about who knows what, I'm shopping online like a fiend. I ask for room sizes and opinions, and Jay occasionally challenges me to think about something differently. He makes me reconsider my ideas, which makes them better. Getting help is new, but I like it.

Jay measures where the cabinets will go while Sammie enters everything, both giggling when I make changes to my changes. Most contractors would be fed up with me by now, but Jay seems to find me amusing. I think it's my roommate he finds even more delightful, but I'm happy as long as he's not mad at me. I can't afford to get on Jay's bad side.

I think the lesson this semester might be learning the advantages and hopefully not the consequences of asking for help.

CHAPTER
SIX

DARCY

_____

I'm beyond grateful for Chance and this opportunity. But damn. These early morning meetings are killing me. I'm working around Chance's schedule, but I will never be someone who can function before nine in the morning. Even then, I can only promise to be civil, not necessarily coherent. Thank goodness Chance wants to meet in the city today, not on the island. That saves me time and gives me a few extra minutes not to look like I just rolled out of bed. Which is a total lie because I did.

"Hey, beautiful," he says as I approach the booth he's tucked away in. Chance may not be a star in Charleston, but fans know him well enough. His Reapers hat is pulled down, hiding his eyes a bit, but his smile is instantly recognizable. His choice of disguise makes me smile. Trading a Renegade hat for the Reapers isn't exactly going undercover. Although I'm not sure he cares. He'll never turn a fan away.

"Hey. Sorry, I'm late. Mornings." I shrug like the word mornings explains everything, which it basically does. He's already seen me more times at this hour than my own family. I think he gets it now. And how can he call me beautiful? I'm in an extra-large college sweatshirt and leggings, with my hair in a clip. Beautiful, I am not.

"Never apologize. Ever. You're worth the wait." Chance gives me a mega-watt smile that exudes charm. He slides a cup of something coffee and sugar-related my way. I love how he remembers.

"You know, you may not be from around here, but you've got that southern charm thing down pat." I take a sip of the super sweet, caffeinated goodness and smile and sigh. My insides warm, and the sugary beverage will kick in any minute and give me the strength I need to start the day.

Chance gives a hearty laugh. "Contrary to popular belief, mamas teach manners to hockey players in the north too. Especially if their mother is from Georgia."

"Good to know. I'll put that away in my don't make assumptions' file." I take a bigger sip and allow the caffeine to work its magic.

"So, how's the project coming? Jayden's given me a few updates, but nothing major."

"Yeah, um, it's good. Jay is awesome. Easy to work with. He told me how you found him. You really are mister nice guy, aren't you?"

When I confessed Chance was a friend of a friend helping me with my senior project, Jay wasn't judgmental or condescending, only supportive and encouraging. He told us about his difficulties being young in a good old-boy club of high-end construction. We make an interesting partnership, given our age and obstacles.

Chance found Jay through the Boy's and Girl's Club. Jay and his dad partner with local kids who need mentoring or direction. They teach them a trade, give them a leg up, and help them succeed in school and after. This is the largest project Jay has led.

"Nah, just doing my part." He gives me a once-over, concern

creeping across his face. "How are you, really? Do you have everything you need?"

Being honest is all I can do with Chance. He still has time to hire someone qualified that won't mess up his investment and vacation home. "Well, Sammie has been getting me focused when I was overwhelmed. Jay asked brilliant questions and helped me think about a few things differently. I think you'll love what I've come up with for the outdoor area."

"I'm sure I will." He gives me a genuine smile. "Who's Sammie? I think Jay mentioned that name, too. Boyfriend?" He looks puzzled. So, Jay mentioned Sammie? That's cute.

"Samantha," I say slowly and clearly to clarify, "is my room-mate and best friend." I lean in a little to whisper conspiratori-ally. "Between you and me, I think Jay may have a thing for her." I give him my best attempt at a wink.

Chance leans forward. "You don't say. Well, I'm all for a good love story."

Our waitress comes and takes our order. I'll never get over athletes and their in-season diets. Chance gets enough for four people while I order a waffle with fresh strawberries. I figure the fruit might give the appearance that I eat somewhat healthy, which I do not.

I pull out my phone, share the few items I've purchased for Chance, and discuss the plans for each room. As we review the details, he focuses on me and makes sure I have everything I need. He seems more concerned about me than his house.

Our heads practically touch as we lean over the table, scrolling through my phone, that I don't notice when someone approaches our table.

"Hey, Darce." The deep voice startles me and I look up to find Matt giving us a disapproving scowl.

"Oh, hey, Matt. I'm sorry I didn't get back to you. I've been super busy." He texted me after our encounter at The Wreck, but I've been too busy to respond. I can't imagine that would

warrant the evil eye he's giving me, but then again, he's probably not used to girls ignoring his texts.

"I can tell," he says while glaring at Chance. "So, is this your
sugar daddy?" His tone is dripping with disdain.

"Oh, for god's sake," Chance says under his breath. He sighs
and sweeps his hand to the empty spot next to me. He mumbles,
"Sugar daddy, please," to himself and then says firmly, "Sit
down, Matt. You baseball boys are all the same. Your game is so
long your imagination gets the best of you. Let's save some time
here, shall we? Yes, Cole knows all about us, and as a matter of
fact, this," he says, motioning between us, "is all his and
Ashleigh's idea."

Matt continues to glare at Chance. Chance laughs as he
stands up, puts his hand on Matt's shoulder, and encourages
him to sit down. Matt shrugs his hand off, his sour expression
darkens. Their moods are polar opposite. Chance appears
amused, and Matt looks pissed. "You're ridiculous and making a
scene. No, Darcy and I aren't together. She's way too awesome
and amazing for a guy like me." Chance gives me a half smirk
and a wink. I roll my eyes at his ridiculousness.

The heat rises in my cheeks. This guy. There is some lucky
woman out there for Chance, and when he falls for her, she
won't know what hit her.

Matt shakes off some of the tension, but still appears
skeptical.

I attempt to be the peacemaker for a disagreement I don't
even understand. "Come on, join us." Sliding over in the booth
and throwing my bag on the other side, I make room, while
giving him the best before nine o'clock smile I can muster.

His eyes soften when he looks at me, so I pat the seat, encouraging him to sit down. "We just ordered. I know you love the
waffles here." Matt has a sweet tooth like me. I bet he can't say
no to the powdered sugar and syrupy goodness.

Back in high school, Matt drove Cole and me to school. We
used to eat breakfast here every Friday, and Matt always got the

waffles. Even though it's been years, I'm banking on his love for sugar to still be an integral part of his food pyramid.

"Damn, I love those waffles. You sure I can crash this, um, whatever it is?"

Chance speaks up. "Absolutely. And it's a, what would you call it, Darcy? A business meeting? Nah, that seems too formal."

I smile at Chance as he attempts to defuse Matt. "It's like a school project advisement? Or more like a wellness check-in because of how overwhelmed I am."

At that confession, Matt sits down and pulls me into a side hug. "What's wrong, Darce? What can I do? Just say the word."

Chance chimes in before I can. "She needs an assistant. I don't know, say a person with time on their hands, who can help her with the little things so she can focus on the big picture and graduate with honors." He doesn't break eye contact with Matt.

Matt looks between us, still not knowing what we're talking about. I put my hand on his thigh to stop his leg from bouncing, and he turns to me, eyes wide. He gives me a look that says I did something wrong. My head is yelling, retreat, retreat, but my mouth always had a mind of its own.

"What the fuck, Matt? What's your problem?" I snap.

"My problem?" he shouts.

I slide toward the wall, pulling away from him.

Chance's cheerful smile is gone. "Maybe this was a bad idea," he says more seriously than I've ever heard him. His chest puffs up and he becomes larger, if that's even possible.

Matt has my attention, so I barely acknowledge Chance's change in tone. "Yeah, you come in here with all kinds of PMS mood swings, and I don't appreciate it. Now, if you're going to be an asshole, just leave." Seriously, what's his problem?

A few people look at us. We're getting more attention than Chance probably prefers.

Matt focuses on Chance. "What are you and Darcy up to, exactly?" His tone is sharp and accusatory. They're in a stare down and I'm still clueless why.

The waitress brings our food and asks Matt if he wants anything. I can see his mental debate about whether to stay or go. He orders coffee and a waffle and turns back to Chance, ignoring me as if I'm not involved somehow. I shrug and dig into my food after smothering it in warm maple syrup. Manners be damned at this point.

Chance takes a bite of his omelet and pauses Matt's inquiry. After what seems like minutes of eating, he proceeds. "Well, Darcy needed a senior project, and I am the benefactor of senior projects. It seemed like a win-win." He sips his orange juice and continues the stare-down with Matt.

I take a bite of my warm, fluffy waffle. The perfect ratio of buttery syrup, whipped cream, strawberry, and waffle melting in my mouth causes me to let out an involuntary moan.

Both heads swivel in my direction. Chance looks amused. Matt looks constipated. "What? It's a perfect bite." I swear, I'll never understand these guys. A minute ago, they acted like I wasn't even sitting here.

"Please don't do that," Matt says under his breath.

"Do what?" I'm bewildered. Matt is acting so strange, and it's too much for me this early in the morning.

Matt takes a deep breath and exhales. He looks back at Chance and says through gritted teeth. "So, she's doing what, exactly, for you?"

Chance looks at me, his expression asking if I want him to answer. I give a half-shrug and take another bite. Whatever this male posturing that's going on is not my problem. My waffle and I are pretty content for now.

"She needed a project to graduate, so she's designing my beach house. It's extensive." Chance turns his attention to me. "But I don't want you to be overwhelmed, Darcy. I'm serious when I tell you to hire an assistant. Please don't overwork yourself. I can ask Jay if he can do more or give you a guy."

"Nope," Matt interrupts. "I've got it. I'll be her assistant. Tell me what you need, Darce. I've got you."

"Wait. What?" My waffle is no longer the focus of my attention. I look at both of them and rejoin the conversation. "Matt, you have things to do. I don't even know what kind of help I need. I'm figuring it all out. But Chance, I won't let you down. I know it's a lot of money and..."

Chance reaches across and grabs my hand. "Girl, you got this. I'm not worried at all. I'm only worried about you. Let Matt help you. Make him your bitch." He gives me a smile and another wink. Matt stiffened as soon as Chance reached for my hand.

"I'll always be here for Darcy. She's family." His tone is harsh and final. He turns his body to me. "So, when do we start?"

Yep. Got it. Family. Good reminder.

CHAPTER
SEVEN

MATT

———

The pieces fall into place. Darcy is decorating Chance's beach house. His hockey schedule is packed, so early morning meet-ups make more sense. Probably explains her being there with him at dawn. Maybe. They looked pretty cozy that morning.

Chance seems like a genuinely nice guy. He was there for Ashleigh when she needed help. Maybe Darcy is his next damsel in distress? It was innocent with Ashleigh, and he didn't seem interested in Darcy that way and even admitted she was too good for him. That's the truth if I've ever heard it. Hell, no guy is good enough for her.

Darcy is top-shelf. Unique. Amazing. Beautiful. Funny. Sexy. Hell, there I go again. Where did that thought come from? She's my best friend's little sister. So, by default, she's like my little sister. And no one thinks their sister is sexy. At least, I hope no one does.

After breakfast, Chance got a call from Julian, his agent and best friend, and said he had to get back to his team, cutting the meeting short. I assured Chance I would be Darcy's assistant and make certain she doesn't get overwhelmed. Chance seems satisfied with our new arrangement and leaves an envelope with cash for Darcy's expenses. Since she technically can't get paid for this school project, Chance is taking care of her rent and other bills so she can focus. As much as I hate to admit it, he's a stand-up guy.

"So, where do we start?" I ask Darcy.

"Matt, you don't have to do this. Sammie has set me up with this great spreadsheet to keep me organized. I need to order everything, so it's just a lot of shopping. I know how much you hate that." She smiles at me, and her eyes sparkle with mischief. She's baiting me. Yes, I hate shopping. I do it for necessities and I don't labor over the right shoe or a specific color of blue like she does. Going to the mall with Darcy and Sammie was only entertaining because Cole and I gave snarky color commentary over their selections. We were total assholes to them, even if we secretly thought they were fantastic.

Darcy has a panache for finding the perfect thing. She has an artistic eye and knows how to take the ordinary and make it extraordinary. That takes time and thought. Time. It's something I have now. I can do this for her. I mean, how hard can this be?

Even though she always appears relaxed and casual, her mind is on a mission to find the special touch. Her shopping ventures are intense. With the Darcy magic, everything is elevated. Hell, it practically sparkles.

"Darce, make a list, use that spreadsheet, whatever. I'm in. I'll take you where you need to go, carry the bags, whatever you need." Even though I know she doesn't need it, I reach out for her hand to help her out of the booth. I want to show her I can be supportive.

Her hazel eyes come to life. The tiredness fades a little, and a smile grows at the corners of her perfect lips. "You're sure about this? I know you have other things to do."

"I'm sure. Let's go." I pull her up, and she wraps her arms around my waist, embracing me with a clinging hug.

I chuckle at her enthusiasm, hold her tight, and kiss the top of her head like her big brother's best friend would do. Her friend. But right now, my body doesn't feel friendly. I react to her touch, and my dick wakes up. Her messy hair tickles my cheek. She smells like vanilla and sugar, and I take a quick inhale. Putting some space between us, I pull her back and motion to the front door.

What am I doing? This is Darcy Davidson. I shake my head to clear my wayward thoughts. "Your chariot awaits."

Her giggle is all it takes to bring those thoughts right back. Making Darcy smile and laugh is my current life goal. It's the best sound in the world, and makes me feel things I've never felt before.

I'm seriously screwed.

CHAPTER
EIGHT

DARCY

———

This is a bad idea. Unfortunately, I'm nothing but a string of bad ideas right now. Taking on this project, for one. I may be full of positive vibes and grit with Chance, but the truth is, I'm in way over my head. I can use all the help I can get, even if it's someone to keep me from jumping off the Cooper River Bridge. After all, I'm sure keeping me alive is the bare minimum of Matt's obligation as Cole's best friend. But being my assistant? Above and beyond.

Matt's offer is generous. Kind. Maybe even noble. Helping his best friend's kid sister is typical Matt behavior because he's a good guy. A great guy. Ah, hell, who am I kidding? He's the guy I measure all other men against. There. Sammie would be proud of me. I admitted it to myself. The first step to solving a problem is acknowledgment, right? So, like step one in a twelve-step program?

Admitting it isn't the problem. The problem is that Matt is a great catch, the guy who lives in my head rent free. The bar is set so high no other guy comes close. I mean, I've dated. I go out with a guy, and there is always something wrong by date two. The problem? They aren't Matt Hartman.

It's more than his downright adorable kindness and his clean-cut charm. Mix in his tall, lean, muscular frame, and then add his thick, luscious, dark hair that I want to run my hands through. Combine it with his expressive brown eyes framed with long, full eyelashes that make me reevaluate my mascara. Whoa, is it warm in here? Top it off with a perfect smile that lights up a room, and he's lethal. He's gorgeous and dare I say, enchanting. And totally off limits. Not that he'd be interested in me.

Matt and Cole are a year older than me, but you'd have thought I was a different generation by how they treated me. I never dated in high school, waiting for the day Matt would notice me. I had notebooks full of my practice signature - Mrs. Darcy Hartman.

Granted, I was a late bloomer. I didn't get boobs until my senior year in high school, and by that time, Matt was off to college.

Sammie says I like Matt because he's unavailable and, there-fore, unattainable. He's my brother's best friend, which makes him a no-go. He'll never see me in *that* way. Not the way he saw Penny Lewis, his high school girlfriend. When he asked her out, I cried for days. My mom was so distraught at my sudden depression she stayed home from work for two days to hang out with me because my behavior was so erratic. When he came home at Christmas during his first year in college with news they broke up, I thought he'd wake up and see me. He didn't. He threw himself more into baseball. I'm sure he hasn't been celi-bate, but Matt hasn't had a girlfriend in years, that I know of anyway.

A therapist would tell me I have unrealistic ideals and this crush is an unhealthy infatuation. Matt can't be all I make him out to be in my head. Except he is. Case in point. He just offered to be my assistant on this project, which has me so overwhelmed

I agreed to the crazy idea. Yeah, this is bad on so many levels. Even though I've accepted that Matt is a nice guy who will never be interested in me romantically, a spark of hope ignites. Maybe?

I get into the passenger seat of his Toyota FJ, the same car he's had since his junior year in high school. I close my eyes and breathe in Matt. There's a hint of leather from the baseball gloves in the back, a lingering scent of his cologne, and coffee. This car smells like Matt.

I shake my head to clear all the errant thoughts and focus on the task at hand. I need to get to the designer's warehouse to review the fabric samples and complete the furniture orders. Matt's going to be miserable. I shudder at his torment and think of something to make it up to him.

Matt gets into the car, and when he turns on the ignition, the blast of the radio jolts me out of my jumbled thoughts with a startled squeak. Matt looks at me and smiles while he turns down the volume.

"Okay, Darce. What's first on the list today?" His fingers are ready to enter our destination into his GPS.

"Really, Matt, you don't have to do this. I need to pick out fabric for the furniture and bedrooms. I imagine getting a bikini wax would be more enjoyable for you."

Matt visibly shudders at the thought. "Damn, girl, can you not make me think about that? Nothing can be worse, can it?"

"Me wading through fabric samples? I'd wager I'm accurately describing the level of pain you'll be in."

"I'll take that bet. I've got time. And a male perspective. I mean, you're putting together a guy's house. That should count for something." He cocks his head to the side, giving me a half-shrug. "My helpfulness will amaze you." He gives me a little wink, and the butterflies in my stomach take flight. My reaction to his gesture is far different than when Chance does the same thing. Oh yeah, I'm in trouble.

"So where to, boss lady?" He hands me his phone to enter the address. With a shake of my head and a resigned sigh, I take it and tap away. He can't say I didn't warn him.

Matt looks at the directions, pulls his sunglasses out of the console, and then covers those beautiful chocolate eyes with his Ray-Bans. He turns the music back up, puts the windows down, pulls away from the curb, and drives toward his own circle of hell. As we cruise through downtown, Matt drums to the song with his thumb on the steering wheel, a genuine smile on his face. I've seen him do it a million times before, but something about it now makes me anxious. How much is Matt the same and how much has he changed over the past few years we've been apart?

I've studied Matt for years. Take his smiles, for instance. I know his fake ones from his polite ones. The smile he has now reaches his eyes. He's happy. It's the same one he has after a good batting practice. And in his prom photos with Penny. I assume he means it when he says he doesn't mind doing this with me. He's happy. For now.

"So, tell me about your vision for Chance's house?"

"You should see it. It's an enormous house with amazing potential. I'm mostly focused on updating the kitchen and the decorating. Jay, that's the contractor, is handling the heavy lifting. I'm most excited about the outdoor space. Chance wants a place where he and his crew can relax, so nothing fancy. Comfort with a masculine style. Not frat house chic, but something that allows guys to relax. His challenge was to make it better than Tripp Stevenson's Mexico house. That's a huge ask. I've seen pictures of that place."

"I've heard stories about Tripp's place from Cole. It's like a private resort, complete with house staff."

I gulp. That's my competition? A place with staff. Great. I fidget with my hair, taking it down and wrapping it back up in a messy ponytail. How am I going to top that?

I focus on Matt instead of the resort house. "Cole is lucky to have a friend like you."

"Nah, I'm the lucky one. Cole's like a brother to me." His smile fades, and he concentrates on the drive.

The change in mood is too noticeable not to comment on. "Something going on with you two?"

"What? No, I don't think so. Why?" He glances at me and looks back at the road.

"You just flinched when I mentioned him."

"No, I didn't."

"Yeah, you did. What's going on, Matt?" I let the silence sit between us.

"I miss him, that's all. We've been together for so long. Honestly, these last few months have been tough. I haven't bonded with anyone on my new team. That's not uncommon when new draftees come in mid-season. Baseball is all about competition, and most of the guys had to work up to where I am, taking them years. I took Frankie's position, who was on third for two years when I came in, and it's just awkward."

"Cole's experienced a little of that, too," I add.

"Yeah, but he has Ashleigh to come home to. It's an adjustment I wasn't prepared for. I always knew it was a possibility we wouldn't play for the same team, but I was hopeful, that's all."

"No, that's not all, Matt. Don't dismiss it. I can't imagine not being around Sammie. It's a huge life change for you. I know I'm not Cole, but maybe I can be your surrogate Davidson? You know, friends?"

It pains me to say friend, but I'll take any piece of Matt I can. Knowing how lonely he is for friendship, I offer that. It's more than I had of him a month ago.

"Well, you're the prettier Davidson, that's for sure," he says with a smile.

"Oh, I don't know about that. Cole is a pretty boy, after all." A blush fills my cheeks.

We pull into the parking lot, and Matt parks the car. He takes his sunglasses off and turns to look at me.

"I may not know much, but Darcy Davidson, you are by far the prettiest girl I know."

My face doesn't hide the look of shock at Matt's statement. He reaches over and puts his hand under my chin to close my mouth, which is literally hanging open.

"Come on, pretty girl," he says as he opens his car door. "Let's get this done so you can graduate."

CHAPTER
NINE

MATT

———

I stop just inside the door and assess the place that Darcy called Design Heaven and Ballplayer Hell. There are books upon books of fabric swatches, rows and rows of furniture samples, and more throw pillows than even Ashleigh could handle. The outer ring of the room is full of cabinets and a separate wall of nothing but cabinet handles. This warehouse is the size of a baseball field and is arranged in organized chaos. It's not a place for the faint of heart.

So, Darcy is partially correct. This place is my circle of hell. But when I look at her, she lights up with excitement. I smile at her and reach out for her hand. She gingerly puts her small hand in mine, glances down at our clasped hands, and gives me a questioning look.

"What? I don't want to get lost here. It looks like the labyrinth that housed the minotaur. It's scary." I give her an exaggerated shudder.

She rolls her eyes and pulls me toward the center of the warehouse with all the bookshelves and large tables. She points to a stool and tells me to sit. Like an obedient Labrador, I do. She pulls her computer out of her bag and opens up a complex spreadsheet.

"You did this?" A cover page summarizes approaching deadlines, compiling information from multiple tabs. It's quite an impressive project management file.

"Are you crazy? This is all Sammie. I'm terrified to use it, but she assures me it's Darcy-proof." She spins around slowly, getting her bearings. "I need to pick fabric for the duvets, and then we can walk around and look at furniture. Unless you want to wander on your own and make a short list."

"I'm not sure I'm qualified for that. I'll stick with you if that's okay."

"Suit yourself." She turns to the bookshelves and starts stacking them, creating a pile in front of me. The pile gets so high I lose her when she goes around to the other side of the table.

I shift in my seat to watch her handpick fabrics that seem different but somehow coordinate. She has a vision that I don't understand but appreciate, nonetheless. Once she decides on a piece of fabric, I enter the information into her spreadsheet, along with pricing, timelines, and each designated room.

My personal circle of hell isn't that bad after all. I'm amused as I watch her face light up, she squeals, and then holds the fabric to her heart. That's when I know she's found the perfect combination—her words, not mine. My chest warms watching her, and I wonder what else I can do to keep that smile on her face.

"I notice each room seems to have a name. Is this place so fancy that the guests will stay in named suites?"

She laughs, and it echoes in the large warehouse. "No, that's just my way of keeping each room straight. Chance wants this to be as much for his friends as for him. I'm kinda designing a room for each of them. When we met about his vision, he talked about it being a refuge for them to gather as a group or individually whenever they needed to relax or escape. He told me a little about his core group, and I asked a few questions about each. It might be a little ambitious, but I think they'll like it."

"Who are his core people?" I know a little about this circle of friends, but even less about Chance.

"Well, there's Julian Decker, his best friend, of course."

"Obviously. And I'll assume Alexander Decker, Ashleigh's other brother?" I quirk an eyebrow at her. Alexander is the General Manager of the Carolina Reapers and, technically, my boss. I'm represented by Julian Decker's sports agency, too. Yeah, this circle is one I'm all wrapped up in. *Come into my parlor said the spider to the fly*, I think to myself.

She nods. "Yep. Since the house has seven bedrooms, one will be for Ashleigh and Cole, too. It's a romantic space in a house full of testosterone. Trevor and Tripp each get a room, too. You know Trevor from Savannah?"

"Of course." Trevor is Alexander's best friend and owner of the Savannah Pajamas, a summer college league Cole and I played in for years. Trevor is a character, a modern-day P.T. Barnum of sorts, and my summers playing with the Pajamas are some of my most fond baseball memories. "But Tripp Stevenson?"

"Yeah, apparently, Chance and Tripp are tight. They support each other since their seasons don't overlap much. Chance is quite the baseball fan when he's not on the ice, regardless of what he may say." This time, she gives me a little wink, letting me know she's giving me privileged information.

Chance loves to cut on baseball players, and his chirp game runs deep. He has some good ones, and now I know why. Good information to file away for later.

"Hmph. Is that so? That's an elite circle."

"Yeah, it's a little intimidating. I'm more of a design-on-a-dime person. These guys have lots of dimes." I watch her confidence drop as she thinks about the money.

"Yeah, but at least from my interactions, they're down to

earth. Flashy cars, maybe, but they aren't looking for that here, just comfort. Personal will mean so much to them. You're on the right track."

"You think so?"

"I do. So, let me guess, the reader's retreat? That's Julian's room?" He's an avid reader and started a book club with Ashleigh and her best friend, Emma. They're always talking about romance books and new authors they support.

She bounces excitedly. "Exactly! He enjoys unwinding with a good book, so I wanted his room to feel like a cozy reading nook. Maybe with a little spice." The twinkle in her eye has a hint of mischief.

"Ugh. Don't tell me you're a member of his Smutty Romance Book Club?"

"Um, how do you know about that?" Her blush darkens her cheeks.

"Cole's told me all about it." I laugh, remembering when I caught him reading some baseball romance book on his phone.

"Yeah, well, it's fun. And I prefer spicy, not smutty. Our book club Zoom calls are a blast. We even talk about the book a little. But we mostly drink and drool over the swoony book boyfriends. We're planning a book club and ski weekend in February. Maybe you should join us to learn about the fairer sex."

"Yeah, I'll pass. I don't need to get hot and bothered over a book."

How long has it been since I was hot and bothered? Yeah, it's been too long if I need to think about it. I haven't been with a girl in almost a year. Between baseball season and the move to Charleston, I've had little opportunity.

"Well, if you don't get hot and bothered, it's not spicy enough, now, is it?" Her innocent flirting is giving me a half-chub. She needs to stop, and I need to change the subject.

"So, each of the bedrooms has a theme. I like it. If you designed a room for me, what would mine be?" I say it before I catch myself. I'm not sure where this is coming from, but I want to know what she thinks of me.

"Your theme?" She twists her lips into a half grin while she thinks. "Well, definitely masculine. Nothing trendy. Solid furniture. But comfortable, you know. Like home. I'd fill it with memories for you. Maybe a picture wall of your family and friends? You value people and relationships above everything, even baseball. Even though they're intertwined, you'd see them as the same."

"Wow, Dr. Phil, that's deep. You think you have me figured out?"

She gives a slight shrug of her shoulders. "I've had years of practice."

That makes me pause. I've known Darcy most of my life. After all, she's Cole's little sister. But do I really know her? I know facts about her life. She's a senior, twenty-one, and her birthday is in December, right after Christmas, I think. She and Sammie are inseparable. She has style, and sometimes I don't like how guys look at her. But isn't that the big brother's best friend's role?

But do I know her? Have I really noticed her?

Of course, I noticed her. But now? I'm seeing her. And I like what I see. I've grown up around Darcy, but I've never spent this much time alone with her. She was always tagging along with Cole and me, or we were driving her and Sammie around to places because neither of them had cars. She was the giggling girl in the back seat, or the one cheering loudly from the stands. Not just for Cole, but for me, too. She was always there in the shadows. Now I see her in the light, and she's beautiful.

"What color?"

She's quick to answer. "I'd use forest green."

"Why?"

"Because it's your favorite color." She says it like a fact. Which it is.

"How do you know it's my favorite?"

She smirks and shrugs. "Practice."

I feel very humbled and ashamed I don't know these things about her. That's about to change.

"What's your favorite color?"

"Mine? Orange. The shade changes with my mood."

"What shade is your favorite right now?"

"Tangerine."

I'm unsure of the differences between tangerine, pumpkin, and crayon orange to take this further. "Why orange?"

"It's composed of red and yellow. It's a give-and-take color. Sometimes more vibrant, sometimes less. I adore the spectrum. It's less aggressive than red, but more expressive than yellow. It can be happy, bold, vibrant, or more subdued."

"Wow, I never knew there was so much thought into color."

"There's a whole psychology around it. How it impacts moods, how it makes us feel. You can tell a lot about a person by their favorite color."

"Is that so? What does green say about me?"

"Well, generally, green ties to nature. But in your case, I think it's tied to the baseball diamond. It's also calming, invokes memories, and represents relationships. All qualities that are very Matt."

"I never thought about it like that, but maybe you're right. Green can also be about greed and money. Maybe I'm just a money-grubbing guy." Her insights about me are humbling, and a little unsettling.

She laughs like I just said the dumbest thing ever. "True, it can represent money, but you're not about money. If you were, you'd have bought an expensive new car by now. No, that's not you. Green has its emotional ties. Like you can also be green with envy or jealousy. So, tell me, Matt, are you a jealous guy?" She says this with a twinkle in her eye and a knowing smile.

Her hazel eyes captivate me. Those might be my favorite shade of green now.

I think about what she said for a moment. I'd describe myself as laid-back and easygoing. I'm the caretaker of the group. But am I jealous? My initial answer is no. Then, I think about how I felt when I saw Darcy and Chance together. What was that emotion?

Something about this conversation with Darcy makes me feel the need to confess.

"I can be about some things. You're right. Relationships mostly. As much as I like Ashleigh, I was a little jealous of her hold on Cole at first. But it's complicated. Because I want nothing but the best for him. And trust me, that girl is the best thing in his life. When I was with Penny, I didn't like other guys looking at her. I guess that's jealousy?"

"I'd say a little less jealousy and a little more protective of relationships. But yeah, I can see that about you. You value people, and it shows." She's looking at me like she's unlocking all my secrets. I can't let her unlock the deepest and darkest secret I have. I'm starting to like her. Maybe more than a brother's best friend should.

"Well, this therapy session just got deep and slightly uncomfortable. What do I owe you for your services, ma'am?" I give her a quick smile to lighten the mood and take a drink from my water bottle to break the connection.

She wiggles her eyebrows in an attempt to be seductive. "Let's go test mattresses?"

I spit water across the table, garnering glares from several people around us. "Excuse me?!"

Her laughter is louder this time, and the others return to their discussions, giving us scathing looks before they do.

"Come on, silly, let's go pick out furniture." She grabs me by the arm and pulls me off the stool.

After what seems like an eternity, we select furniture for most of the house. I'm chilling in a recliner with more options than a spaceship.

"I think you need a few of these." I turn the massage option on, and my body melts into the leather. "Trust me. Nothing feels better than a massage after a workout."

"Noted. Let's get, um, two or four?" She pictures the space and screws her mouth up as she thinks. I can practically see the wheels turning. "Two, I think. There needs to be room for the sectional and the big chairs, too."

"Two it is." I enter the information into her order sheet. "This is fun spending Chance's money." Someday, I hope I'm signing the big contract, too.

Darcy chews on her bottom lip. "Did I say something wrong?" Her face has worry lines between her brows. I start to reach out to rub them away and catch myself mid-reach. I let my hand rest on the arm of the recliner instead.

"No. It's just so much money. What if he doesn't like it? My god, what am I thinking? I can't do this." She sinks into the chair beside me and buries her face in her hands.

I lean over, turn her massage chair on, and let it work its magic. I reach over and hold her hand. Her tiny fingers grip mine, and I relax into the comfort of it. Honestly, it's more relaxing than the expensive massage chair.

"Darce, look at me." She peeks at me through her fingers. "You're a natural at this. I love what you've done, and I haven't seen the finished product. It's amazing. And Chance has more money than you can imagine. That lucky bastard just signed a sweet three-year contract worth over fifty mil, so stop looking at the price tags. He wants you to do this, and he'll be blown away. It will be a show stopper, which he asked for."

"You think so?" Her voice is small. The confidence she had earlier is stripped away.

I kiss the back of her hand. My lips on her skin send a spark through my body, warming my chest. When her eyes meet mine, a look of surprise crosses her face. I meant the gesture to be reassuring, comforting. It has the opposite effect on me. If anything, it makes me uncomfortable in a warm, gooey kind of way. Again.

I give her a rally smile, the one I use when the team is behind and has one inning to win the game. "I fucking know so. Come on, hotshot designer." I pull her up from the chair, and my brute strength forces her into my chest. I look down at her and take a step back. "Let's finish up here and grab some food. I need to keep you fed so you can continue being brilliant."

"Hey," she says hesitantly. "Thanks, Matt."

"For what?"

"For, just, um, everything." She hugs her bag to her chest and walks towards the front doors.

When she's a few feet away, I whisper, "No, Darcy, thank you."

CHAPTER
TEN

DARCY

———

MATT

I watched that show last night. I can't believe
you liked it.

What? You didn't?!? Do you have no heart?

That girl was manipulative and shallow. How
can she kiss both brothers?

Because she loves them both. Duh.

Selfish if you ask me. She's totally messing with
their dynamic.

This is a typical exchange with Matt. The banter never ends. And
I've never enjoyed arguing more.

Three weeks into this project, and the demolition is daunting.
I have to check out the big kitchen install today. I'm overwhelmed and stressed because this is a sizable piece of the

project. It looked good on paper, but what if it doesn't work in reality? My confidence is on thin ice.

Jay assures me everything is going well, and he wants me to bring Sammie so they can compare spreadsheets or some silly excuse. She's driving us over the bridge to the island while I text Matt. I giggle and Sammie glances at me. I can't believe he watched more episodes when he got home.

> You just don't get it. The heart wants what the heart wants.

> Still don't like it. See you at the house later.

"Matt is meeting us when he finishes up with baseball camp."

"So, what's going on there?" Sammie asks.

"What do you mean?" Matt and I have spent almost every day together. We work, run errands, and argue about TV shows and music. It's become our thing.

"You two are pretty chummy. I'm worried about you."

"Why are you worried about me?" I glance over at Sammie and see her quirk her eyebrow at me. "What?!"

"Girl, I know you. You've always crushed on Matt. Now, I'm afraid it might be more than that."

She's right. It's more, at least for me. "Don't be silly. He's just being a good friend."

"Nah, that smile you get when he texts? You didn't do that when Ryan texted. Girl, I see it. You're falling for him."

I've never been in love before, not even with Ryan. I'm not sure what that feels like. Being with Matt feels different. He calms my nerves and gives me confidence when I don't feel it. I feel accepted for me, just as I am. Do I love Matt? It's just that childhood crush manifesting into my crazy reality. Love? It doesn't matter.

"He's Cole's best friend, and that's a line Matt will never cross. He would never jeopardize his relationship with Cole, and

I would never want him to. So, it's a non-issue. Now, you and Jay, there's something to talk about." I laugh at her blush. Better to deflect than reflect.

"He is pretty great. I wouldn't mind getting to know him better."

"Samantha Chapin, you like him," I say in a sing-song tone. "Sammie and Jay sitting in a tree...."

"Stop it. He's just interesting. Driven. It's impressive."

"His hot body and mesmerizing eyes are impressive, too," I tease.

"What? I hadn't noticed." Sammie tries to act like it's all about character. I know she sees past the physical, but damn, Jay's physical attributes are nothing to look away from.

"Well, tonight is your chance. We'll order dinner, and Matt and I will leave you two alone. Maybe sparks will fly?" I attempt to wiggle my eyebrows at her, which makes her giggle and snort.

"Sparks with who? Me or you?"

"Hey, if we're lucky, both."

———

When Sammie and I arrive, Jay shows us around the house, pointing out what's still pending. He has me start a punch list to follow up on items that aren't finished or need touch-ups. The kitchen is almost done, and several bathrooms are ready for wall coverings.

"Jay, this is amazing. You guys have worked hard," Sammie comments.

"Thanks, Sammie. It's been inspirational. The design is fun and unique. I can't wait to see it all come together."

I know I said I'd never been in love, but that was before I saw these cabinets. Picking teal was risky, but they really pop with the gray marble countertops. I snap a few pictures and send them to Chance. My excitement and insecurity well up. What if Chance hates them?

The doorbell rings, and Sammie offers to get it.

"You're pretty quiet over there, Miss Designer. Everything okay?" Jay asks.

I'm overcome with emotion. I'm happy and relieved it's coming together, and I think it's perfect. But what if? Hot tears fill my eyes as I nod my head that I'm okay. Jay puts his hands on my shoulders, and a panicked look crosses his face. Some guys can't handle a crying woman, and apparently, that includes Jay.

One thing I hate about myself is that I'm a crier. I hate my overactive tear ducts. My eyes and tears betray every emotion I have, making me look like a crazy person most of the time. My potent emotions always seem to evoke a physical response.

I close my eyes to pull myself together and the next thing I know, I'm wrapped up in muscular arms and pulled against a broad chest. Hmmm, Jay smells good.

"There, there, pretty girl. No crying on my watch." He kisses the top of my head, and his hand gently rubs up and down my back.

It takes a moment to register it's not Jay, and I put my arms around Matt and hold on tight. I will my tears to stop, but it's no use. The exhaustion, the panic, the joy, the uncertainty, the happiness, the love — it's all coming out at once.

Matt holds me tight, comforting me. How did he get in the kitchen so fast? He must have sprinted through the house. I relax into his embrace, letting his powerful arms hold me against his hard chest. My mind wanders, and I will my hands not to do the same.

"Come on, Jay, let's give her a minute," Sammie says. "Show me the upstairs."

Matt holds me and puts his cheek on the top of my head. I'm very aware that my five-five frame fits perfectly under his chiseled jaw.

"Why are you so nice to me?" I whisper between sniffles.

"You make it easy, pretty girl. Now, what has you all teary?" He puts me at arm's length, and I immediately miss his warmth.

"Would you believe me if I said cabinets?"

He looks around the kitchen, nodding in appreciation. "They are pretty fantastic. I'm feeling a little emotional myself." He twists his face like he's trying to cry.

His teasing makes me laugh, and I swat at his chest. I leave my hand resting on his heart. The steady beat grounds me.

"Are you making fun of me?" I feel foolish, and the heat of embarrassment rushes to my face.

Matt looks down, his thumb wipes away an errant tear, and says, "Never." His eyes search mine, looking for something. We stay like that longer than is appropriate, looking at each other, searching for answers to unspoken questions.

My phone buzzes with a FaceTime request, breaking the moment. I pull my phone from my back pocket.

"Hey Chance, what do you think?"

"Girl, they're amazing. You're rocking it. Everything okay? You look like you've been crying?"

"No, I'm fine. Just," a slight hiccup escapes, and I laugh at my ridiculousness. It's replaced by a smile. "Had an emotional moment."

"I'd hug it out with you if I could, but I'm in Toronto."

"Don't worry. I've got her," Matt says, interjecting himself into the conversation. His tone is serious and firm.

Chance laughs. "Hey Matt, glad to hear it. I knew you were the man for the job."

I smile at Chance's easygoing personality. "Do you want a quick walk-thru since you're here? It's amazing."

"Sure, show me your awesomeness."

I walk Chance through the house, showing him everything on FaceTime. Matt holds my hand and never leaves my side while I'm on the call. He adds a comment when he thinks I'm leaving out a detail, telling Chance what a great job I'm doing.

The realization that he was paying attention to my color psychology makes my heart flutter.

We make our way to the top deck, and when we step out, we find Sammie and Jay swinging in the hammock together. "Looks like I should rename the house the Love Shack," Chance says when he sees Sammie and Jay cuddled up.

Chance's voice startles Jay, and he jumps, causing Sammie to fall to the floor. I drop the phone to help her, and Jay apologizes to Sammie, Chance, and anyone who can hear him.

"Sammie, you okay?" Jay asks.

"I'm fine, I'm fine," she says, pushing everyone away. She blushes from embarrassment. It must be contagious today.

"Hey, can I chat with Jay for a minute?" Chance yells from my phone on the floor.

I pick up my phone and see Chance laughing at us.

"Sorry about that," I mumble as I pass the phone to Jay.

Sammie brushes past me and goes back into the house. I hear a door close and assume she needs a minute. I smile at the idea of her and Jay because they make a cute couple. At least one of us can be on the path of a happily ever after or at least happy for now.

"What's got you smiling, pretty girl?" I roll my eyes at Matt's new nickname for me. I know it's a reaction to Chance calling me beautiful. As professional athletes, their competitive spirit never stops. These guys can lay off the flattery, especially when I'm make-up-free, hair barely brushed, and wearing an over-sized sweater and ripped jeans. This is not the look of a girl that is beautiful or pretty.

He catches my eye roll and puts his fingers under my chin, forcing me to look at him.

"I'm not sure I'm keeping up here, Darcy. Are you okay?" Matt's face is full of concern. His eyes sweep my face and seem to focus on my mouth.

My lips suddenly feel dry, and I wet them with my tongue. His intense gaze causes my breath to hitch, which he returns with a slight upturn of his mouth. We stare at each other for a long moment. His head leans toward mine. Is Matt about to kiss me? I close my eyes and wait, and Jay comes in from the deck. Matt steps away, and the moment is lost. If there was an actual moment.

Jay hands me the phone and extends his hand to Matt.

"We haven't officially been introduced, but I'm Jay, the project manager."

Matt shakes his hand and smiles at Jay. "Hey man, I'm Matt. I'm Darcy's, um, assistant."

Jay laughs. "Then I guess we both work for this girl. She's quite the visionary, isn't she?"

"Oh, please," I sigh. "I'm a blubbering, anxious, in over my head, hot mess. I know it. You both know it. Chance knows it. We all need to get on the same page." I drop down on the over-stuffed chair in the upstairs rec room.

"You are none of those things," Matt says.

I give him a look that says get real.

"Okay, I'll give you anxious." He pauses until I smile. "At times, you might be anxious. But you're not a hot mess."

"And you're not in over your head," Jay interjects. "Chance was very impressed with the work. He said something about Tripp's place not holding a candle to this one. Does that mean something to you?"

"Yeah, it does." I find my confidence and feel much better. I exhale loudly and pull myself up from the very comfy chair.

"You guys get to know each other and order dinner for us, okay? Whatever you decide. It's on Chance so, by all means, order dessert. I'm going to go check on Sammie." I toss the black card to Matt. He examines it and frowns. He's seen me use it to buy house stuff, but he acts like the card is poison or something.

Jay blushes and looks down at his shoes. "Should I go check on her?" he asks quietly.

"Nah, this is a job for her bestie. I've got her. She'll be back better than new. You guys just be prepared to feed us when we come back. And use the card, Matt. Chance gets mad if I don't use it for food."

"I don't care if he gets mad. I can buy dinner." Matt's pride seems to be wounded too.

"I know you can, slugger." I walk by and punch him in the arm. "I don't care who pays for dinner as long as it's here soon. And there's something sweet. Surprise me."

I leave the room in search of Sammie. Boys and their stubborn pride.

———

I find Sammie downstairs by the pool. It's a little chilly, so I grab a few throw blankets and join her in the double lounger.

"You okay?" I ask.

"Yeah, I'm fine. Just embarrassed."

"You sure looked cozy with Jay up there." I wiggle my eyebrows. I can't do it right, and it always makes her giggle.

"It was nothing. Just staying out of the way so you could have your moment with Matt."

She gets one of my eye rolls. Now those I've perfected.

"Seriously, if you could've seen him practically tackle Jay to get to you. If I weren't afraid for Jay, I would've swooned. He saw him reach out to comfort you, and it became his mission to be the one to do it."

Is that what he did? "It's not like that. He's just protective, like Cole."

"Nope, not like Cole. Trust me."

"He's my brother's best friend. I'm like his kid sister." These are facts. I wish they weren't, or that they didn't make a difference, but they do.

"Yeah," she drags out. "Not gonna lie. I don't think he was looking at you like a sister."

I stare at Sammie with dismay. I thought we had a moment

upstairs. Was he about to kiss me? That spark of hope takes root in my heart. Could Matt see me more than Cole's sister?

I look out over the dunes and watch the waves gently breaking at the shore. It's so peaceful here. Sammie and I watch as the sun dips down below the horizon.

I lean in and bump her shoulder, knocking us out of our errant thoughts. "I asked the guys to order dinner. It was a test to see how well they could feed us. They were arguing over who was going to pay when I left. I threw Chance into the mix for fun." I laugh at the absurdity of the male ego. "How about we embarrass them with a little friendly game night challenge? Girls versus boys?"

Sammie lights up at the idea. "Absolutely. We need to make sure they know who's in charge."

"Well, I'm the boss, after all."

"Hell yeah, you are." Sammie high-fives me, and we head inside to prepare for a fun night of reminding them who's the boss.

CHAPTER
ELEVEN

MATT

———

I almost kissed Darcy Davidson. I wanted to kiss her more than anything I've ever wanted. I wanted it more than being a Carolina Reaper. When I saw her tongue sweep across her lips, nothing mattered more on this Earth than my lips connecting with hers. If Jay had stayed outside five more seconds, it would've happened. Then what would I've done?

There's no stepping back from crossing that line. I can hear it now. 'Yeah, Cole, about your sister, the one person you asked me to look after and protect. Yeah, I kissed her and didn't want to stop there.' Fuck no. That conversation will not happen.

After I came to my senses, we had dinner and a rousing game night where the girls kicked our ass in every event: Jenga, Scattergories, Heads Up. Nah, we didn't have a chance playing against those two. They've been linked for years and know each other better than themselves. Jay and I just fumbled through and let them have their fun. We reverse Uno'ed them and made them drink when they won instead of us drinking when we lost. Jay and I agreed we needed to be the responsible ones. I can tell he cares about the girls, too, especially Sammie.

The kicker of the evening? The more they drank, laughed, and mocked us, the more fun I had. I enjoyed watching them high-five each other and wiggle their butts in celebration. Hell, even with my competitive spirit, I was cheering for them to win to watch the dances and brace myself for the smack talk.

I admit, watching Darcy laugh freely and let loose did inexplicable things to my chest. Working with her these few weeks, I'm watching the stress and worry chip away at her usual carefree spirit. She smiles and acts like she's fine, but she's not fooling me. The pressure is getting to her. Tonight was good because she let loose and relaxed.

Darcy and Sammie are doing some TikTok dance in the living room as they celebrate their latest win in Pictionary.

"We have a situation," Jay tells me in the kitchen.

"What? That we can't draw for shit?" I chuckle at my last attempt to draw pickle juice. You can only imagine what it looked like. The girls were in tears as Jay yelled every euphemism for ejaculation Urban Dictionary has to offer.

"Well, thank god that situation is over. No, you know they can't drive?"

"Of course," I growl. Jay implying I'd let either of them drive kicks in my protector mode, and I stand a little taller. "I figured they could sleep it off here. It's not the first time."

Jay's slow smile is one I've seen on guys when they recall an excellent female memory. I don't like the idea of him thinking of Darcy like that. With that, I step a little closer. I like Jay, and he seems like a good guy, but if he's seen Darcy in an inappropriate situation, I'll have to hurt him.

"Down, lover boy." His words catch me off guard, and I quirk my eyebrow at him.

"Dude, it's obvious you like Darcy. You track her every movement around the room like a man possessed. She's a great girl, and I'd never do anything to hurt her. She's safe with me, I promise. But them staying here tonight is not a good option."

Like a man possessed? I let his words sink in but decide not to address them. Avoidance is the best tactic here. I will admit watching her cry, and Jay reaching out to comfort her, set off alarms in my head I didn't know existed. I damn near tackled him to get to her.

"Yeah, why not?"

"First, Sammie has an early class," Jay starts.

I interrupt before he can get to the second point. "You know her class schedule?"

"Yeah, we've, uh, been hanging out a lot." Jay gives me a shrug.

"Okay, she can drive back before class."

Jay looks back at the girls as they giggle and fall into an oversized, comfy bean bag chair. He's right. They're wasted. I smile at their connection and think back to when we were younger, and they would be in the back seat of my car, their giggles floating into the front seat, overtaking the radio, while Cole and I would drive them to a friend's house or the movies so many years ago.

"No, the water is getting cut for some scheduled plumbing work first thing in the morning. I was going to offer to take them back to their place tonight if that's okay with you."

I think about his offer. Jay has proven trustworthy and cares about the girls, especially Sammie. Like me, he only had two beers, and that was hours ago. He's good to drive. Sammie is tipsy, but Darcy is leaning more toward drunk. I recall Darcy's schedule tomorrow and remember she has a meeting back at the house in the morning.

"Why don't you take Sammie back and I'll take Darcy to my place? It's on the island. That way, she can be back here early enough for her meeting and get maximum sleep. That is, if the girls are okay with that idea." Even under the influence, consent is everything.

Jay arches his eyebrow, questioning my motives.

I chuckle. "Trust me. She needs sleep. And Cole would kill me."

"Who's Cole?"

"Her brother." I sigh. "And my best friend."

Jay lets out a low whistle. "Oh man, I hate that for you, but it explains a lot. The best friend's little sister is a no-go zone." He pops me on the shoulder. "That bro code is sacred. But I don't know." He shrugs his shoulders and smirks at me.

I give him a skeptical look. "I'll go see what the girls want to do. Do you mind finishing the cleanup?" He smiles and grabs the trashcan, scooping the takeout containers into the bag. I have my answer.

When I return to the living room, the girls are still in the bean bag chair. Darcy's eyes are closed, and she looks peaceful. Sammie is scrolling through her phone.

"So, what's the plan?" she asks.

"What makes you think there's a plan?" I ask.

"Because I know you, Matt Hartman. You're a protector and planner if there ever was one." That's what I get for not expanding my social circle. I'm with people who know me, down to my soul.

"Well, safety first. Are you comfortable if Jay takes you home? I don't think either of you are in any shape to drive, and Jay says this house won't be habitable in the morning."

"Yeah, that's fine." She gives me a mischievous grin. "I'll keep my finger on your number if that would make you feel better."

"Sammie, I trust your judgment. I just don't want you to be uncomfortable."

She sighs and glances at the kitchen. "He's one of the good guys, Matt. Just like you." She gives me a wink. "What are you going to do with sleeping beauty here?" Darcy is sleeping with her head on Sammie's shoulder.

"She has an early morning meeting back here, so I'll just take her back to my place down the road, and she can get a good night's sleep. I'll get her back here ready to go in the morning. Do you think she'll be okay with that?" I mean what I say about consent, but I don't want to wake her when she looks so peaceful.

"Yeah, hang on a minute, and I'll pack her a quick bag. We've both left some overnight items here." Sam gently extracts herself from the chair and is a little unsteady.

"You sure you're okay?" I question, grabbing her by the upper arms to steady her.

"Yeah, probably shouldn't have done that last round of shots, but I'm good. Able to pack a bag but not enough to drive good. I'm sleeping more than Darce most nights, though. She's just wiped out."

Sammie rushes upstairs. She returns and hands me a floral backpack as Jay enters the living room. I watch Darcy sleep, a small smile gracing her face. She's content, exactly how she should be at this point in her life.

"We good?" Jay asks.

"Yup, looks like you're my Uber driver. I hope you have five stars," Sammie teases Jay.

"Yes, ma'am." Jay jingles his keys and makes his way to the door.

"You need help?" Sammie asks as she looks at Darcy.

"Nah, I've got her. You guys be careful and let me know you got home, okay?"

"Yes, Dad," she says condescendingly and pats me on the arm. "I'll lock up behind you."

With the bag over my shoulder, I lean down to get Darcy. I gently pick her up and pull her toward me, holding her tight. She fits easily in my long arms and snuggles against my chest without opening her eyes. I kiss her gently on the top of the head.

"Come on, pretty girl, I've got you," I whisper as I carry her to the car. Jay opens the passenger door for me while Sammie locks up the house.

After buckling her up, I check with Sammie one last time. "You think she'll be okay with this? I can always bring her back to your place."

"Yeah, but then she won't have her car. She'll be fine on your couch. Remember, coffee first thing in the morning. She'll be good as new." She gives me a wink and loops her arm in Jay's.

"Text me," I say directly to Sammie. She may not be my best friend's sister, but she's family, nonetheless.

I get in the car and glance over at Darcy. Her long dark hair slips out of her messy bun, softly framing her face. I reach over and put the errant strand of hair behind her ear. When she pulled her hair up during our heated Jenga game, I saw a competitive streak that wasn't typical of Darcy. I have to admit, it was sexy. She's changed since I've been away, but she's still sweet, adorable, kind Darcy at her core.

I drive a few minutes to my beach rental and carry Darcy inside. There's no way I'm letting her sleep on my couch. I take her to my bedroom and gently lay her down.

I debate with myself about her sleeping in her clothes, but waking up without clothes will upset her. Instead, I take her shoes off and tuck her in. The small bag Sammie packed sits on the nightstand within her reach, and I step out of the bedroom to lock up the house. With a blanket in hand, I make my way to the couch.

Every attempt to get comfortable is futile. I can't settle down. Darcy is on the other side of that wall and she's occupying my every thought.

Sammie texts to let me know she's home. I respond, telling her to have sweet dreams. She sends a "you too" and a winky emoji. What does that mean?

I check on Darcy and see she's curled up on her side, a sweet smile on her lips. Leaning on the door frame, I battle with myself. What if she gets sick or needs me? What if she wakes up scared because she doesn't know where she is? My protective side is laughing at me, knowing she doesn't need me, but I need to take care of her. As a friend? As a surrogate big brother? Cole wouldn't be here having this internal debate. He'd be snoring on the couch without thinking twice about this. And he's a grumpy, overprotective bastard regarding his sister. Yeah, but he's not here right now, and she's on my watch. Staying by her side is for her safety.

I give in and lay next to her. I can stay on this side of the bed and care for her. After all, that's my job.

CHAPTER
TWELVE

DARCY

———

I've always had vivid dreams full of color and fantasy. I keep a notebook by my bed to write them down. But in all my dream journals, I don't recall any being so realistic that I remember smells or textures, so this one feels different.

I inhale the scent of sandalwood, fresh air, and bubble gum. The smells remind me of Matt. I snuggle into the warmth of the dream and feel muscular arms holding me tight around my waist, a calloused thumb absently rubbing circles on my stomach. There's a slight tickle at my ear that I reflexively swat at, coming into contact with something solid. The body behind me moves, and I hear, "Mmmm, I could get used to this," mumbled in my ear.

"Me too," I reply to my dream.

"Good morning, pretty girl." Wow. My dream speaks. That's odd, but I'm willing to roll with it. I don't want to wake up and lose this feeling of contentment.

I wiggle my body against the solid one that's the big spoon

and hold on tight to the large forearms wrapped around me. The warmth feels so good, I barely notice the headache forming.

"You make me feel so good," I respond to my dream.

"Same," the deep voice responds.

I open my eyes slowly, and the dream fog begins to lift. When I suddenly realize it's not a dream, I start to freak out. I'm in a strange room with arms wrapped around me. My mind panics, my body stiffens, and I think backward to the last thing I remember: Chance's beach house. Game night. Sammie. Jay. Matt. Shots. Then nothing.

Without moving, I look around. This is not one of the bedrooms at Chance's. Where am I? Strangely, I'm not afraid, even though I should be. Waking up in an unfamiliar room is not part of my usual behavior pattern. I should be terrified, but if anything, I feel comfortable and content. Safe.

"How ya feeling?" my dream asks. I still want to call him my dream, even though as my brain puts the pieces together, I realize I know this voice.

I don't know how to respond, so I stay silent for a few more seconds. My head is pounding, but it's secondary to my heart racing.

"Oh," he says and pulls away. His sudden departure is like a slap to the face, and a wave of disappointment and sadness fills me. He knows we're a mistake. I'm just a silly girl with a child-hood crush. I curl into myself, embarrassed and hurt.

"Right, caffeine," he mumbles. I feel the bed move as he quickly gets out, tossing the covers aside.

My body shudders at the sudden lack of warmth. I blink several times, allowing my eyes to focus and take in my surroundings. I want to close them again and shut out the embarrassment and rejection wrapping around me, but I need to pull it together.

The room is basic beach house with white walls and blue accents. Why do these houses have to look the same? There are a few seashell pictures on the wall. Blah. The furniture is light pine. Boring. Then I notice a familiar floral bag on the nightstand and smile. Sammie.

The clock says it's still early, and as much as I want to pull the blanket over my head and snuggle up in bed, my bladder says something else. I grab the bag and shuffle my way to the ensuite bathroom.

I feel somewhat normal after a quick shower, an abbreviated morning routine, and fresh clothes. My towel-dried hair goes up in a clip. That's the best this is going to get for now.

I need to figure out how to escape this situation with as much dignity as possible. Then, I need to research how to change my identity and start over because Darcy Davidson has officially died of embarrassment.

I cautiously open the bathroom door and find Matt sitting on the side of the bed with a steaming cup of coffee and a tentative smile. He stands up and comes toward me with arms outstretched, handing me the mug like an offering.

"Good morning, pretty girl. I was told coffee first, so here." He thrusts the mug in my direction.

"Thanks," I mumble, taking a small sip and smiling as the dark roast and ample sugar hits my tongue. "Who gave you those instructions?"

"Your girl, Sammie. She packed your bag and gave me strict instructions."

"She's the best." I feel the heat rise in my cheeks. I'm feeling very awkward, but hope blooms as I realize she can help me out of this predicament. "Where is she?"

"Jay took her home so she could get to class this morning." He rocks back on his heels and keeps his hands in his pockets. This is awkward for him, too. Leave it to me to make him uncomfortable in his own home.

Shit. I need to come up with another plan. I'm sure my car isn't here, so I'll need to call an Uber, but getting one on the island during the off-season will take some time. I glance at the nightstand for my phone. I don't see it, but that doesn't mean I should give up on my exit strategy. My phone is probably in my purse, which is, um, where? I need to think. Ugh, my head. Too much vodka for my brain to function. And then there's Matt.

It's hard to concentrate with this distraction right in front of me. I take a moment to appreciate the man watching me while I consume another hit of coffee. His dark hair is mussed and messy, contrasting his typical put-together look. The wrinkled Reapers t-shirt is tight around his biceps. His jeans sit loose and low on his hips, and his hands are shoved in his pockets. And he's barefoot. What is it about this morning casual look that hits me more than usual? Yep. He's pretty damn sexy standing in front of me. This might be a reality, but just rolled out of bed Matt is my dream. Unfortunately, that's a place he'll need to stay.

"I'm sorry about this," I say, motioning to myself up and down. "I didn't think I drank that much. I promise I'm not in the habit of passing out and waking up in strange surroundings."

"I'd hope not," he says as he smiles and winks at me. "You didn't drink that much, but I think the exhaustion caught up with you. Sammie says you haven't been sleeping well?"

"Lots to do. I'll sleep when I'm dead."

His look softens, and he reaches out and puts his palm to my cheek, his thumb gently rubbing my bottom lip. He looks sad.

"No, I won't allow that," he whispers.

I lean into his hand and close my eyes for a moment. The flutter in my chest catches me off guard. When I dare sneak a glance at Matt, he looks conflicted. Apparently, I misread the situation and his attraction. Here I go messing things up again. He's just fulfilling his surrogate big brother role.

Embarrassed, I step away and take another sip of my coffee. I turn and walk out of the bedroom in search of my phone so I can escape and lick my wounds. I find my purse on the kitchen counter, quickly retrieve my phone, and groan because it's at ten percent charge. Hopefully, it's enough.

Quickly I order an Uber, and just like I thought, it'll be a twenty-five-minute wait. I'll have to put on my fake smile for a bit. I finish my coffee and rinse the mug in the kitchen sink, my mind racing with ideas to salvage my dignity.

Matt told me he was renting a small beach house, and this is small compared to Chance's monstrosity. The traditional floor plan opens to a large deck that overlooks the ocean. It fits Matt's style: simple, only the basics. Will he ever get the fancy car or mega-mansion when he makes the big show? Matt's motivation was never money, but I wonder if that will change once he really has it. I hope not.

Outside on the deck, the cool fall air slaps me fully awake.

"You've always wanted to live near the water," I say, sensing he followed me outside.

"Yeah, it's great. I'm enjoying the surf in the morning." Two boards lean against the rail next to a wetsuit.

"I hope I'm not keeping you from your routine." It's not like I haven't already stolen his off-season, but now I've kept him from something he loves.

"Nope. Not at all."

I feel incredibly awkward and contemplate taking the surfboard to escape. Twenty-five minutes feels like forever, so I swallow my pride and devise a quicker way to end this situation.

"Um, do you mind taking me back to get my car?"

"Of course not. Let me get cleaned up, and we'll grab breakfast on the way." He says it like it's an item on his to-do list, with no room for discussion. He turns to head back inside.

"You don't need to do that. I've burdened you enough." This is a bad idea. "Abort, abort," my heart screams. "You know what, I'll just wait outside for my Uber."

I sense his movement halt. The stillness travels down to my bones. Even the surf quiets. "What the hell are you talking about? You called an Uber?" he says gruffly.

"I just," I start. How do I say that I've had a schoolgirl crush on you my whole life, and you don't see me that way? That all guys are measured against Matt Hartman, and none have measured up. How do you admit you are turned on and morti-fied at the same time?

"Look, you have a life, Matt. I've highjacked enough of it. It's not that I'm not appreciative. I am. So grateful for everything. But you don't have to babysit me anymore. I'll tell Cole you fulfilled your best friend role."

Matt moves back beside me and puts his hands firmly on my shoulders, turning me from the rail and the ocean to look at his beautiful, dark, soulful eyes. I look down, unable to bear the humiliation of unrequited feelings.

"Is that what you think this is?" His tone is angry, very unlike the easygoing Matt I've always known.

I try to pull away from his grip, and he tightens his hold. He releases one hand and puts it below my chin, forcing my eyes to his.

I can't speak, words are stuck in my throat. I nod. The hot tears well in my eyes, and I will them to go away. I will not cry in front of Matt. Yet one more embarrassing thing to add to the list of reasons I need to leave.

Yes, this is Matt being the noble best friend, the good guy that is part of his DNA.

"Oh, pretty girl," he says on the exhale. "I wish I knew what was going on in your beautiful head right now."

I turn my eyes down again. My cheeks flush with heat, morti-fied by the slightest possibility he could hear my thoughts. My thoughts are more like fantasies of the adult variety that are a secret I'll take to my grave.

His hand slides from my shoulder to my waist, pulling me closer.

"Look at me, Darcy." I move my eyes back to his. His eyes search mine, looking for something, but I won't allow my secret to be known to him. "God, you're so fucking amazing. I have the hardest time keeping my hands off you. I want..." He pulls me even closer. His thumb caresses my cheek, and his warmth spreads throughout my body, making me feel like it's a hot summer day instead of a crisp fall morning. My blush rises up my neck to my face.

My phone blares "Shake It Off," and we both step back. It's Cole calling on FaceTime. I answer, keeping the beach in the background and Matt in front of me.

"Hey, Darce. Sorry to call so early, but hey, are you already at the house? This early?" His head cocks to the side like he's trying to figure out my view and where I am. He would flip if he knew I slept in Matt's bed last night.

"Um, early meetings with contractors," I hedge. "What's up with you?"

Matt looks at me with wide eyes. I try to ignore him, but his glare is severe.

"Wanted to let you know we're coming down tomorrow. Leigh was hoping you could do a little shopping with her while we're in town. That is, if you can spare the time. Hey, you look wiped. Are you okay? I thought Matt was watching over you?"

"Thanks, just what every girl wants to hear. You look horrible." I try for sarcasm, but it comes out a little too sincere.

"I didn't say that, and you know it. You've been busy, and this house renovation is a huge project for you."

Matt gives me a death glare. Does he agree with Cole? That I look horrible?

"It's a big project, but I'm enjoying it. And you can check it out when you're here. Where are ya'll staying?" My stomach is rolling, from last night's vodka or nerves, I'm unsure. Either way, I hope I don't throw up. I feel guilty talking to Cole and I'm not sure why. It's not like anything happened between us, but I feel like I'm lying to him. Hell, the only one I'm lying to is myself.

"I thought I'd treat Leigh to a little romance downtown at one of the bed and breakfasts. I was hoping you could hang out with her while I work with Matt at the baseball clinic on Saturday. And then brunch with Mom on Sunday, of course."

"Of course. That would be great. We'll have a full girl's day."

"I appreciate you doing this on short notice. And invite Sammie too. Leigh will love her, and it's been too long since I've seen that girl."

"Sounds great. I'll take care of her, Cole."

His eyes soften. He's changed since he's been engaged to Ashleigh. She's his everything, and my heart tightens a little. I wonder if I'll ever have someone love me like that. "I know you will. Now we need someone to take care of you," he teases with a wink.

"I'm good. Don't need anyone taking care of me," I grumble.

"Not what I mean, and you know it. You're a rockstar. Gotta run. Love you, Darce."

"Love you too. See you tomorrow."

I look back at Matt. "Sorry about that," I say to his retreating figure. A door slams, and a horn honks out front. My Uber must be here.

I grab my purse and head to the waiting car. I've got contractors to meet and plans to make. This girl's day might be the distraction I need.

CHAPTER
THIRTEEN

MATT

———

After Cole's call with Darcy, I knew I'd be next and didn't want to have this conversation in front of her. Could I ignore his call and finish what we started? Sure. Was it the right thing to do? Probably not.

In frustration, I slammed the door harder than I'd meant. Then the horn honked, and before I could reach the front door, Darcy was down the stairs and headed to the car waiting in the driveway. The thought of her in a stranger's car fills me with panic. I open the door, and the older gentleman gives me a friendly wave as he backs out of the driveway with Darcy in the back seat. She's clutching her purse and looking down, probably running scared from me and my slamming doors.

"Fuck!" I shout and slam the front door.

My phone buzzes. And just as I predicted, Cole is calling.

"Hey." My frustration barely contained.

"Hey, what's up, brother?" Brother. Oh, that's fresh. I almost kissed his sister. FML.

"Um, not much. What's new with you?"

"Just wanted to let you know I'm coming down tomorrow. I already texted your dad, and he's excited about having the dynamic duo back together."

"Yeah, it'll be great. I know Leigh will have fun with Darcy, and your mom will be excited to have you guys for Sunday brunch."

"How did you know those are the plans?" Oh shit. Thank God we aren't on FaceTime.

"What else would they be? It's not like you'll leave Leigh alone, and your mom would skin you alive if you missed Sunday brunch." Fuck. My stomach churns. I hate lying to Cole, but I can't exactly say his sister was at my house this morning because she was drunk, and I woke up with her in my arms. Nope. Can't go there.

"Yeah, you're right about that. But Saturday night, let's get everyone together for dinner and drinks downtown?"

"Sounds good. It'll be fun. You bankrolling this party, superstar?"

Cole lets out a hearty laugh. "You stuff your mattress with that signing bonus? I thought Julian got you a pretty sweet deal."

"Oh, I'm fine. But I'm not rocking a music career in my off time and engaged to a billionaire's daughter, either." I honestly have more money than any twenty-three-year-old needs at this point. Busting his balls about being a kept man is one of my life's little pleasures.

"I'm living the dream and I'm not complaining one little bit."

A girl's voice says, "Hey, trouble," and I hear lips smacking. Another reason I'm grateful we aren't on FaceTime.

"Okay, that's enough. I've gotta run. Tell Leigh I can't wait to see her this weekend. You know she likes me best."

"I do, Matt!" she yells, and the phone floods with giggles.

"Later." I hang up before I hear any more of their love fest.

A weekend of their happiness while I use all my willpower to stay away from Darcy. This should be fun.

―――――

I head to my old high school to work out and spend time in the batting cages. I need to ground my thoughts and figure out what to do.

"What's got you rattled?" My dad's comment startles me. I step away from the box and let the next ball fly by. I give him a curious glare. How does he know I'm rattled? Is that what I am? Have my thoughts about Darcy rattled me?

He gives me a knowing smile. "You always dip your shoulder when you're working through a problem."

Do I? My dad has been my coach for twenty years now. I guess he's noticed a thing or two about me. The last thing I need is a tell. Catchers notice those things, and there goes your batting average.

I hit the button to stop the pitching machine, remove the helmet, and run my fingers through my hair. With a deep sigh, I look at him and nod slightly.

"Want to talk about it?"

Not really. I can't confess to my dad what I almost did with Darcy. He usually gives good advice, so I take a different tactic. "How do you know whether to do the right thing or the right thing for you?"

"Wow. Philosophy so early in the morning? That sounds like a question Cole likes to debate over Fruit Loops." He gives me a warm smile, encouraging me to continue.

"Yeah, can't talk to him about this," I mumble.

"Everything okay with you two?"

"Yeah, yeah, we're good. It'll be good to see him. It's just...." I don't know what to say. My dad and I are close, and we talk about a lot of things, but never about girls.

"It's hard moving on to the next chapter, isn't it?" I'm not exactly sure what he means.

"Even though you both knew you'd go in different directions, it's hard to make your way through that. But the secret to any good relationship is open and honest communication. You guys hold on to that. The life of a ball player isn't easy. You'll be frustrated, lonely, uncertain, and a million other things. Having someone who's on the same journey is special, and someone who knows how you tick? Even more rare. Don't let that go. Because even when baseball is over, that friendship will last a lifetime."

Dad's right. My friendship with Cole is valuable and, if I'm being honest, part of my DNA. If I lost Cole, it would crush me. But what I feel with Darcy is special too. I know his words were meant to help me, but I'm more conflicted now than ever.

"What's wrong?" Dad's question breaks me out of my thoughts.

I shake my head. "Huh? What? Oh, nothing. Just thinking about how Leigh has changed Cole, for the better, of course."

"The love of a woman does that for us. Makes us practically human." He winks and claps my shoulder. "You'll see. Once she captures your heart, you'll do anything to hold on to that feeling. She becomes your home base."

"Yeah, I guess." Anything? Like risk a lifetime friendship?

"I'm proud of you." My dad's a lot like me, not used to talking about feelings and such, so when he says this, it hits me hard. "But the question about doing the right thing versus what's right for you? What if it's both?"

"Huh?"

"You'll do the right thing, son. You always do." He goes to leave and turns the machine back on. "Get out of your head and square your shoulders. Don't practice bad habits."

"Yeah, sure." What if it's both? I don't think Darcy and I can be both, can we?

I hit a few more balls, paying attention to my shoulders. Focus on what you know. Women are distractions. That's why I haven't had a relationship in years. Focus on the goal. And that has served me well. I'm a professional baseball player now. With hard work and focus, I'll play for the Reapers soon. That's what's important. But what if it's not?

CHAPTER
FOURTEEN

DARCY

———

"I'm headed to the school," Cole says as he gives Ashleigh a chaste kiss. "You girls have fun," he says as he kisses me on the forehead and slips a credit card in my hand with a wink.

What is it with guys slipping me credit cards? While I appreciate it, I don't like that they think I can't pay my way. Yes, I may be a struggling college student, but once I graduate, I'm looking forward to working and having adult money that I earn. I have money from waitressing, and since Chance is paying my rent, I've barely spent any of my money. Today might be a little splurge day after all.

"What, no kisses for me, Cole?" Sammie teases from the couch. He grins, walks back into the apartment, leans over the back of the couch, and gives her an upside-down Spiderman kiss, catching her off guard.

She pops up and barely misses falling over the coffee table. Ashleigh and I double over, laughing.

"You should know better, Sammie," he says with a chuckle, kissing Ashleigh again and walking out the door.

"Gah, he drives me nuts," Sammie says.

"Me too," Ashleigh and I both say simultaneously. We all erupt in laughter.

Ashleigh settles on the couch next to Sammie, and I drape myself over my reading chair. "I like your place," she says. "It's exactly what I imagined your apartment would look like. Too chic for a typical college apartment, but bohemian enough to say cool."

"That's all our girl," Sammie says. "She's just got that *je ne sais quoi* about her. Wait until you see what she's done with Chance's house. It's incredible."

"Well, it's easy when you've got money." Spreading my arms around the apartment, I say, "It's a little more challenging when you don't."

"Well, I love what you've done with the place. Sincerely. You have a genuine talent," Ashleigh says. She directs her attention to Sammie. "So, you're pre-med. That's pretty amazing."

"Yeah, it's not bad. I'm working on my applications, but fingers crossed, I get into school here in Charleston."

"Then you can keep seeing Jay," I say in a teasing, sing-song tone.

"Ohhh, who's Jay? Gah, I miss the girl talk," she sighs. She hugs a throw pillow and settles in for the tea.

I smile at Sammie and fill Ashleigh in. She blushes but denies nothing. I'm happy she's enjoying her time with him. He's a good guy. I shoot him a text and invite him to dinner tonight. I'd love for Cole and Ashleigh to meet him. He's become a good friend and an important person in my life in this short time. And in Sammie's, too.

"So, what about you, Darcy? Who makes your heart stutter?" she asks.

I feel the heat rush to my cheeks, betraying my response. "No one, really. I'm too busy to date."

Sammie cocks her eyebrow, and Ashleigh gives me a questioning look. "Seriously?" I glare at Sammie. She better keep her mouth shut. I trust Ashleigh, but can't risk her saying something to Cole. I can't live with myself if their friendship is ruined because of me.

"I don't believe you," Ashleigh says.

I give a slight shrug. "Believe what you will. I don't know what to tell you."

"Okay," she says, her tone sad and disappointed.

I get up and hug her. "Honestly, there's no love interest in my near future. I'm holding out for an epic love story like yours."

"I don't know if I'd say epic. It was hard. But so worth it. Love is worth the struggle, I promise."

"I don't know. It shouldn't come at a price."

"Everything worthy comes at a price. And to prove my point, let's go shopping! I love your style. I might even want to try on a wedding dress or two." She gives me a wink.

I squeal like a sixteen-year-old at a boy band concert. "Really? I know this adorable boutique. Does this mean you've set a date?"

"No, but we're thinking about next fall, after the season, of course. But I want to wait and coordinate with Chance's schedule, too. I can't imagine him not being there. He's like another brother to me. You know, like Matt is to you?" She arches her eyebrow at me.

Nope, not cracking. Especially after the door slammed. I made a fool of myself and haven't spoken to him for two days. He sent a text asking if I needed him to do any assistant duties. I said no and haven't heard from him since. I'm sure he'll be at dinner tonight, but I'll deal with that later.

"Well, girls, let's hit King Street." I hold up Cole's credit card. "We have some shopping to do."

CHAPTER
FIFTEEN

MATT

———

I'm awash in memories as I throw the baseball to Cole on our old school field. I'm taken back to a simpler time when we weren't complicated. Our lives were baseball and the team, with a bit of school thrown in for good measure. Dad talks to the team about our connection on and off the field, and how that connection can be developed and nurtured, how a team becomes a brotherhood. It results in wins. And bonds that can't be broken, even if you wear rival jerseys, like us now.

I reach up and knock the brim of Cole's Liberties hat down below his eyes and the group laughs. Cole hits me with a fist bump and tosses my Reapers hat behind me. We personify Dad's inspirational speech, and while Dad looks at both of us with pride, he still shakes his head at us. You can make it to the big leagues, but we're still boys at heart. With grown up issues.

Um, Dad. Want to know how to break those bonds? It's not team rivalries. Nope. Those come and go. They're fun. You make silly bets over rivalries. Those bonds get broken, no demolished, when you want to kiss his sister. Which I almost did. Two days ago. If Cole hadn't called Darcy, I would have. No doubt about it.

The coward that I am, I've avoided her ever since. We're all getting together for dinner tonight, and I pray Cole doesn't pick up on our awkwardness. Assuming it will be awkward. Hell, she may not even speak to me. Or maybe this is all one-sided and I need to get over myself. I have no idea how she's feeling and this could be all in my head.

After we help Dad pack up, we head back to my place to clean up and chill. After showers, we crack open a few beers and settle into our old routine. The setting may be different, but our friendship slips back into our typical comfort zone. It's like we haven't missed a day.

I needed this. I admit this off-season has been unsettling, and I miss Cole and the team's brotherhood. But I can't deny I've enjoyed working with Darcy, too. Maybe too much.

Cole checks his phone and smiles.

"Ashleigh?"

"No, Darcy, actually. Apparently, my girl tried on her first wedding dress." He's beaming like a lovesick puppy.

"I didn't know you'd set a date."

"We haven't, but we're looking at this time next year. After the Liberties win the World Series."

"Pretty cocky of you to say that." He gives me a huge smile and a shrug. "What can I say? All my dreams are coming true."

"Remember when your dream was to be a Reaper?"

"Yeah, and that would've been great. I miss playing with you. But the universe had something different in mind."

"Wow. You're being all philosophical after one beer. You've become a lightweight."

"Love has a way of changing you. Speaking of love and weddings…"

"Not sure that sentence has anywhere to go, man."

"It does, actually." Cole takes a long pull of his beer and puts it on the table. He turns to look at me, the playful mood zapped from the room. "Matt, you know I love you like a brother. You're the most important man in my life and have been by my side for all the significant and insignificant moments. There's no one in my life I trust more than you. You're by far the best man I know. I want you standing beside me as I commit to Leigh. So, will you do that for me, Matt? Will you be my best man?"

His words touch me. They ring in my head. Trust. Brother. I hadn't thought about the wedding, but of course, I'll be there for him.

"Wow. Of course. Absolutely. I was kinda hoping you'd write a song to ask me, but there's still time, I guess." Maybe this will be Cole's next chart-topping hit. It's not outside the realm of possibility.

Cole gives a hearty laugh. "Damn, I miss you." He gets up and pulls me into a tight hug. Cole's affectionate side is amped up. Love must do that to a guy.

"I'm thrilled for you, man."

Cole lets me go and grabs his beer, nearly draining it. "What about you? Any girl in your sights?"

I grab the near-empty bottle from Cole and take mine into the kitchen to get another one. I should talk to him about Darcy. I don't think I need to ask his permission, but maybe I should tell him how I feel and that I'd like to see where this leads us.

But what if she doesn't feel the same way? What if we don't work out? Am I willing to take that risk with my relationship with Cole? What about his relationship with his sister?

I change the subject. "What time are we meeting the girls?"

"Darcy made reservations at seven, so we probably need to call an Uber soon."

I bring Cole another beer and pick up my game controller. Cole picks up the other one and charges forward, me covering his six. It's our way.

"How's Darcy doing?" Cole asks. "She looks tired."

"She's working her fingers to the bone on the house. But it's incredible. Her vision is amazing. The way she sees details and understands the psychology of colors. I mean, who even knew that was a thing? She fucking Sigmund Freuded me because I like green. That girl has mad skills."

Cole laughs. "Sigmund Freuded you?"

"Yeah, she took my favorite color, tied it to my memories, dug into my soul, and explained it away because I like green. It was scary shit." Thinking about that day brings a smile to my face.

Cole gives me a suspicious look. I suppress my smile and look back at the game.

"Is she okay?" he asks again. His tone is quiet and filled with concern.

I hit pause and look at him, giving him a slight nod. "She's good. She's driven, and this project is a lot for her, but she's got Sammie, Jay, and me. We won't let her fail. I've been watching out for her." I look him in the eye and say with heartfelt sincerity, "You know I'd never let anything happen to her, right?"

Cole takes another drink before responding. "I know. I'm glad you're here when I can't be. I'm grateful you're watching out for her best interests. I just worry about her, you know? Her fatal flaw is being overly trusting and maybe a bit gullible. Hell, she gave that d-bag Ryan so many chances because she believed what he said. I'm glad she's done with him." He picks his controller up and looks at me. "But she's done with him?"

"Well, it's not like we sit around braiding each other's hair and talking about boys, but yeah. Last I heard, she's done with him. I think Sammie is over him too, so if he comes sniffing around, he'll have to go through her and me."

Cole nods in appreciation. "Thanks, brother. I know you'll always do right by her. That's what family does."

CHAPTER
SIXTEEN

DARCY

———

Shopping for others makes me incredibly happy. Ashleigh and Sammie were my poor victims as I dragged them into stores and pushed them into dressing rooms, but their smiles at the outfits I put together made it totally worth it for all parties involved. It was exactly the distraction I needed to push Matt out of my brain. I may have gone a little overboard with my purchases, seeing all the bags. Whoops.

I toss them all down on the couch and pull a few things out, throwing them at Ashleigh and Sammie. "Ashleigh, you have to wear this red dress we got today. Cole will love it. With the black booties. And Sammie, if you don't wear those leather pants we got, I'll never speak to you again."

Our shopping spree was an overwhelming success, and I relaxed and just had fun. I put all my other worries aside for the day and it was nice. Sammie and Ashleigh hit it off, just like I knew they would. Ashleigh snapped tons of pictures of looks I helped pull together and posted them on her Instagram, tagging me as her stylist and, one of the three of us enjoying hot chocolates at a cafe near campus.

Ashleigh is a social media genius, using it for good and not for evil. She manages several high-profile athletes accounts, like Chance, helping them hone an image and get sponsorships. She manages Cole's accounts and helps promote his love of baseball and music and even helps Matt since he's not much of a social media guy.

My phone is buzzing like crazy at the notifications for likes and comments on her posts since she tagged me.

"How do you deal with all these notifications?" I ask Ashleigh. "My phone is blowing up."

"Simple - turn them off," she responds with a smile and shrugs. "I look at them when I want and only read them when I'm in the right frame of mind. Remember, it's a job for me." She gives me a wink and looks at her phone. She smirks and nods like she knows a secret.

"What's that look for?" Sammie asks.

"Hmmm, what?" Ashleigh looks up from her phone, laughs, and shakes her head like she just heard a bad dad joke. "You're feeling the Chance effect."

"The what?" Sammie asks.

"The Chance effect. Chance commented. See? Here." She points her phone to us, and we both lean in to see it. And there it is. A comment by Chance Fuller with almost eight thousand likes. *Three of the most phenomenal ladies I know.* He started and ended the comment with heart-eye emojis.

"And that's called the Chance effect?" I ask.

"Yup. Looks like I might have to change his password again. He knows I hate the attention. But honestly, I'm not mad about it this time. Hmm, how many new followers do you have, Darcy? They can be helpful as you establish yourself as a designer and your brand. Don't mock the power of the influencer."

"Ugh. I hate those Instagram girls who look for the next post." I drop down in my favorite chair, kicking my shoes off and pulling the throw blanket over me. I pull up my Instagram to see almost five thousand new followers. This morning I only had six hundred. Wow. That's the Chance effect.

"Me too, but strategically using posts is a great way to launch a business. Look at the Home Edit team. They started grassroots as two women who liked to organize. Their only advertising was on social media, and now they have a Netflix show, their own product line, and everyone clamoring for their services. Think about it. When you're ready, let me help launch you. Please?"

When I'm ready? Launch me? I don't know what my future holds after graduation in May, and it's been something that has kept me from sleeping recently. I thought I'd work for an interior design company, but I kind of like doing this independently. But starting my own business is scary. What if I don't have any clients? Or people don't like what I do? And it takes capital to start a business. Thinking about the future terrifies me.

"If that's my direction, you'll be my first call."

She gives me a warm smile. "You're going to do great things, Darcy Davidson. I know it."

"Hell yeah, she is!" Sammie shouts.

Everyone is much more confident than I am about my talents and my future. "Let's get ready for tonight. I'm ready to have some fun. And I can't wait to watch Cole and Jay's reaction."

If I'm honest, I'm ready to see someone else's reaction, too. I know it'll resolve one of my decisions, one way or the other. Do I have a chance with Matt? It felt like he was going to kiss me before we were interrupted. Or was it my wishful thinking? Maybe I'm reading it all wrong? I'm hopeful tonight will tell me if I was wrong about the door slam as a metaphor for us.

CHAPTER
SEVENTEEN

MATT

――――

The beers and bourbon have me loosened up, but keeping my eyes off Darcy is increasingly difficult. Her black, off-the-shoulder sweater shows off her creamy pale collarbone and shoulders in a way that should be illegal. The black mini skirt barely has enough fabric to make up a skirt. If Cole wasn't so captivated by Ashleigh, I'm sure he would kick my ass for the looks I'm giving her.

Our group of six is seated in a private nook of the restaurant, allowing us to relax and cut loose. Jay has his arm around Sammie and throws his head back as he laughs at something Cole said. Ashleigh is tucked into Cole's side, and he casually kisses her temple. Darcy and I sit at opposite ends of the table and enjoy the food and company, but when our eyes meet, we both freeze like statues, staring at each other.

I envy Cole and Jay's freedom to touch, kiss, and publicly claim their dates. I, on the other hand, don't have a date. Even if

I wanted to date her, I couldn't. The more I think about that fact, the crankier I get.

Cole leans over and punches my arm. "What's wrong with you?" he stage whispers.

"Nothing," I mutter. "Not used to three-hour dinners."

"You know what, you're right!" He claps his hands and announces his idea to the table. "I think it's time to move this party. I want to dance with my fiancé. What do ya'll say?"

Sammie looks at Jay with goo-goo eyes. "Ohhh, I love dancing. Let's go to that new club on Market."

"Sounds good," Jay says, practically entranced by the look Sammie gives him. Hell, if she suggested they jump off the Cooper River Bridge, he'd go with it at this point. Bastard.

Darcy looks down at her lap, and Leigh reaches over and touches her hand. "You okay?"

"Um, yeah. Fine." She twists her lips as she sighs. "Let's go."

Her response has my full attention because she is anything but fine.

Cole tells us they've already paid the bill, and we head out. I was giving him hell about money, but he's been very generous with picking up the tab. Having money is new for both of us, especially Cole, and he enjoys sharing it with his loved ones. He's like me because we both take care of our people.

It's a short walk from the restaurant to the club. Sammie and Jay lead the way, holding hands and bumping shoulders as they walk. Cole and Leigh wrap their arms around each other's waists with their heads leaning toward each other. Darcy and I trail behind, the closest we've come to being alone in days.

Although it's a mild November night, the wind coming off the river is brisk. I slip my coat off and put it around Darcy. I'm sure she's cold since she's not wearing much fabric. My coat swallows her up and covers those tempting shoulders.

"Thanks," she whispers.

"Sure, no problem." I'm a fucking blue-ribbon conversationalist at this point. "You feeling okay? I can take you home if you'd rather not go out."

"Nope." She pops her P. "I'm fine. I haven't been dancing in ages. Looking forward to it."

I nod my head, knowing she's lying.

"Look, I'm sorry about the other day. I was out of line. I shouldn't have...."

She pauses and turns to me. The other four walk ahead, oblivious to us.

"Shouldn't have what, Matt? Shouldn't have said really confusing things? Shouldn't have given me hope? Shouldn't have slammed the door? What exactly shouldn't you have done?" Her tone is angry as she whisper shouts. Her eyes are laser-focused on me, and even though she's tiny, she's a force to be reckoned with. I retreat a step under her glare. I'm reminded that Darcy is a strong woman, and I've never wanted her more.

"Yeah, all of it," I admit with a shrug.

I look up the street as Cole's laughter carries back to us.

"Whatever. Forget it ever happened," she says as she storms off down the street.

––––––––

The club is busy, and we're lucky to find a table near the dance floor. The girls drop their bags and coats and dance away, just a few steps from us. They're having fun, and Darcy's smile makes me happy. Even if I'm a broody bastard, I want her to have fun. She deserves it. She's young and beautiful and talented and kind and so fucking awesome. Hell yeah, she deserves the world at her feet.

Darcy heads towards the ladies' room, and Sammie and Leigh head back to the table. They're laughing and enjoying themselves. Cole puts his arm around my shoulders and pulls me towards him. For once, I'm grateful for the loud music that makes conversation difficult. The last thing I want to do is talk.

"Bro, you okay? You don't seem to be having fun."

"Yup. All good," I respond in a clipped tone.

"Bullshit. You never lie to me. Why now?" Cole's right. We never lie to each other. About anything. Even the simple things like he just asked. But that's the thing. His simple question isn't that simple.

Yes, I'm fine. Physically fine. I'm probably the most sober in the group, which is typical behavior for me. You can't take care of your friends if you don't control yourself.

"Not lying." I give him a smug grin. "I'm really glad you're here." I give him a half hug, and he seems appeased for now.

I scan the room, looking for Darcy. I nod toward the restrooms and head in that direction. Cole acknowledges my nod, and the conversation is over.

When I get to the hallway leading to the restrooms, I see a guy leaning against the wall with a girl caged in his arms. As I get closer, I realize it's Darcy, and her eyes are shiny, full of unshed tears. I put my hand on his shoulder and give him a firm squeeze.

"You need to step back," I command.

He shrugs my hand away and mutters, "Go away."

Darcy's eyes meet mine. A tear slips down her cheek, and her mouth makes the O shape of surprise.

Firmly, I pull him back and put myself between him and Darcy. I wipe her tear away with my thumb, and she shies away from my touch.

"Hey, what the hell!" The guy grabs at my arm, but no amount of strength can stop me from touching Darcy.

I turn towards him, anger filling my body, keeping Darcy behind me. "I don't know what you did to her, but you better walk away, buddy," I growl.

"It's okay, Ryan," Darcy says.

Ryan? This is the d-bag she's dated on and off these past years. This frat boy is the one who's touched her, kissed her, and possibly fucked her. Red fills my vision. I hate this guy.

I turn my whole body towards him and shove him away. "Back the fuck up and stay away from her." My body is like a coiled spring, ready to snap. My fists ball at my sides, ready to beat this asshole to a pulp.

Darcy's hand wraps around my wrist, and my blood instantly goes from a boil to a simmer. "Matt, stop." Her tone is pleading. What? Does she want to be with this guy?

I don't take my eyes off him as I stare this asshole down. His nostrils flare like he's a damn bull ready to charge. His eyes are glassy, obviously drunk. Another ten seconds go by before he steps away.

"Forget it. She's not worth it."

"Are you as dumb as you look? Stay the fuck away from her. Do you hear me?" My intention is obvious. I'm not the fighter in the group. I'm usually the one pulling Cole out of altercations. Now? I've never wanted to hit someone as much as I want to slug this motherfucker. Not worth it? Are you kidding me? She's worth everything. I pull back to throw a punch, and her grip tightens around my wrist, her body pressed against my back.

"Don't," she says firmly. "HE'S not worth it."

Ryan smirks, turns, and walks away, leaving us alone in the hallway.

I focus on Darcy, making sure she's okay. She shoves both hands against my chest, but I don't move.

"What the hell was that alpha bullshit?" She's yelling, her eyes full of anger and rage.

"What?" I snap. "You WANT to be with that dickhead?"

"You have no right to come in here and act like that! I'm nothing to you. Nothing!" Her shout is a dagger to my heart.

Does she really think that? Nothing? Her words are more effective than a slap to my face. Nothing? That's so far from the truth, I laugh.

"Great, now you laugh at me!" She pushes at me again. This time, I grab her hands and hold them against my chest, over my heart. Her eyes look at mine in surprise.

I lean down and look her straight in the eyes and attempt to speak to her, soul to soul. "Pretty girl. You. Are. Everything." I practically growl the words to her. She needs to hear my words loud and clear. I don't want her to misconstrue anything. She's fucking everything. Everything.

We stay locked in the stare-down, silently trying to ask questions, seeking unspoken answers.

"There you are," Cole says, grabbing me by the shoulder. He notices Darcy in front of me, our hands together, and we quickly drop them like teenagers getting caught by their parents. He looks confused.

Darcy rolls her eyes, shakes her head, clearly irritated, and steps around us. She stomps down the hall, back towards the bar, and we watch her storm away.

"Something going on with you two?"

"Nope." Great, another lie. But is it? Nothing is going on. Do I want there to be something? Absolutely. But I'm not about to confess that to Cole, at least not now.

"I found her back here with Ryan. I don't know what was going on, but she was crying. I stepped in, but she didn't appreciate it." There. Truth. Every word spoken is the truth.

"Where's that asshole?" Cole focuses his anger on Ryan, not me. That's the Cole I know.

"If he's smart, he left."

"I'd better not see him, or I'll make him regret the day he ever touched my sister." Cole will fight for his people. "I swear, I'll punch any asshole who makes her cry."

"As you should."

No truer words have ever been spoken.

And if I make her cry? Then I deserve it. One hundred percent.

CHAPTER
EIGHTEEN

DARCY

———

A hot shower never felt better. I attempt to wash all the alcohol, regret, and disappointment down the drain from last night. Unfortunately, there isn't enough shampoo in the world for that.

From the sizzling looks I got from Matt at dinner to the growl that filled his voice when he confronted Ryan, he acted like he wants me. And his words? *Everything.* That word echoes in my head as I wonder what that means to him.

I can't believe I ran into Ryan last night. I haven't seen him in months, not since the last time he stood me up and I've ghosted him ever since. I don't have time to be strung along by someone that doesn't have the courtesy or kindness to treat me with respect. Sure, Ryan's cute, and we have fun at parties. He is also self-absorbed and doesn't consider how his actions impact others. Honestly, I've outgrown him.

Ryan is like my old pair of middle school Chuck Taylors. They're comfortable, and you know they aren't the best, but they're yours. And then they fray in all the wrong places. And then you hit a growth spurt a few years later, and they just become uncomfortable and unwearable. For sentimental reasons, you keep them tucked in the back of your closet, reminding you of the good times you had in them. Eventually, the sentimentality doesn't balance out the need for room for new shoes, and you toss them out. Yep. That's Ryan. It's time to toss him out to make room for someone new.

He caught me coming out of the bathroom and thought that tear was actually for him. As if. The alcohol weakened the wall around my heart, and I needed a break from Matt. Watching him come to life around Cole and tamp it down around me cut me deep. Matt and Cole are brothers. They need each other, especially now with all the changes they're going through. They haven't spent more than a few days apart since they were eight. Matt misses him and needs his friend. I can't get between them.

I've distracted Matt, keeping his mind off his new life. And if I'm honest with myself, I serve as a small link to Cole. He keeps me close as a duty to his friend.

Everything.

Shortly after that hallway encounter, Matt asked Jay to make sure I got home okay and made his excuses to leave. He hugged Ashleigh and Sammie, giving them both kisses on the cheek, me a half wave, and left.

Unfortunately, now is not the time to dissect last night. It's Sunday brunch at my mom's. I'm not in the mood to make an effort, so I wear an oversized Liberties sweatshirt, leggings, and my new Chuck Taylors. My shoe choice makes me laugh to myself. A clean face and messy bun complete the Sunday morning, I was out late last night, would rather be in bed, look.

Sammie is at the kitchen table typing away at her computer, her look similar to mine.

"Coffee's still on," she says, glancing at the counter.

"Thanks. Wanna come to brunch this morning?" Sunday brunch at mom's has always been an open invitation since I can remember. Sometimes, it was just Mom, Cole, and me. Other

SLIDING INTO HOME   109

times, we'd have six or ten friends join us. No need to RSVP. Show up and come as you are. I always liked the surprise of who might show up. Today, I'm anxious about who might be there.

"Can't. I need to finish this paper and start my final project for Organic Chemistry."

I lean against the counter and take a sip of my coffee.

Everything.

The typing stops, and I glance at Sammie, who is staring at me.

"Want to talk about it?" She cocks her head and gives me a knowing look.

"Talk about what?" I ask innocently.

"Matt."

That's the problem with having a best friend. They know. Everything.

I shrug. "Nothing to really talk about. He's Cole's best friend."

"And?"

"And nothing." I drink my coffee and wipe at a non-existent spot on the counter.

"The looks at dinner last night were not nothing. The sexual tension was so thick, I was practically uncomfortable."

"I don't know. You and Jay were pretty cozy." I give her a lazy smile. "I like you two together." I sip my coffee and avoid making eye contact.

"Don't deflect. We're not talking about how awesome Jay is and how he's a great kisser. No ma'am. This is about you." Her eyes soften. "You've carried a torch for that boy since we were kids. And if I'm reading the room correctly, he's finally noticed you in that way, too."

Tears well up in my eyes as my heart flutters. Her words allow another seed of hope to plant itself. Was he looking at me like that?

Sammie comes into the kitchen and wraps her arms around me, and I hug her tightly. This girl is my rock. My person. I would shatter if I ever lost her. That's what best friends are, the glue that holds us together. I think about Matt and Cole. I can't be the reason Matt shatters. Not when he needs him more than ever.

I speak my fear. "I can't be the reason he loses Cole."

Her shoulders bounce as I pull away and wipe my tears.

"Are you laughing at me?"

I'm so shocked at her reaction that it stops my tears.

"Gah, you're your own worst enemy. What makes you think Cole would be mad? Don't you think he wants you with a great guy? And don't you think Matt is at the top of that list? I think he'd be happy for you two."

I shake my head and grab my purse. "Sammie, I thought you were the smartest person I knew. But that's one of the dumbest things I've ever heard."

———

Only Cole's rental car is parked at my childhood home. Looks like it's going to be a small brunch this morning. I take a deep breath and pull my armor up. I can show them I'm fine. I can do this.

Walking in, the smell of applewood bacon and pancakes reminds me I'm home. Voices drift from the kitchen, Mom reprimanding Cole for something, and Ashleigh giggles.

"Not fair, two against one," he whines. "I think you like her best." I lean against the door frame and take in the sight. Cole has flour in his hair and looks like he's on the losing side of whatever's going on. A smile fills his face. I've never seen him happier. The kitchen blurs as tears fill my eyes.

"There's my baby girl," Mom says when she notices me in the doorway.

"Hey, Darce," Cole says.

I give him my "I'm fine" smile, and he comes and holds me by my shoulders.

"Hey, hey, what's wrong?" His radiant smile gone, replaced by a look of concern. Mom and Ashleigh hold their breath waiting for my response.

I sniffle, wipe at my traitorous tears, and shake my head. "Nothing. I've never seen you look so happy. You've smiled and laughed more this weekend than in your entire life. I'm so happy for you."

I wrap my arms around him and give him a hug that conveys just how much I love him. He kisses me on the top of my head and hugs me back.

I hear Mom sniffle and peek at her. She's hugging Ashleigh, and they're both crying.

"Damn, women. Knock it off. I can't handle all these tears. I need to get more testosterone over here. Hell, I'd even take your brothers or Chance to even the score," he says to Ashleigh.

Ashleigh throws a dishtowel at him, and he winks at her.

"Matt's not with you, honey?" Mom asks.

I give her a puzzled look. "Why would he be with me?"

"Well, he came with you last time," she says with a shrug.

"Matt came to brunch with you?" Cole looks at me, his face asking a different question.

"Matt's been to brunch hundreds of times. What's the big deal?" I shrug and make my face as neutral as possible.

Cole relaxes and puts his arm around my shoulders, pulling me further into the kitchen. "Yeah, I guess you're right. He spent as much time in this house as I did in his. So where's his sorry ass?"

"Cole, language," Mom gently reprimands.

I shrug. "I don't know. I'm not his keeper. That's your job." I try to keep my tone light but fail. Cole looks back at me and starts to say something.

"Cole, will you grab my sweater from the car?" Ashleigh asks, stopping him from his thought.

He immediately rushes to her side. "Sure, you okay?"

"Yep. Just a little chilled," she replies, rubbing her arms. He kisses her on her forehead and heads outside.

As soon as the door closes, she turns to me, looking like a predator eyeing its prey.

"You've got two minutes to tell me what's going on with you and Matt."

I hear Mom give a slight gasp and then giggle. My mom? With a giggle. I'm doomed.

"Nothing's going on, I swear. Nothing." *Everything.* "I'm just his best friend's little sister."

Ashleigh's look turns lethal. "Yeah, not buying it."

"Suit yourself," I say. "He's been beyond helpful with my project. But nothing's going on. Nothing." *Everything.*

"But you like him?"

There is no sense in lying about this. She's known about my crush since we spent a week together in Nashville.

"She's always crushed on Matt, probably since middle school," Mom chimes in.

"Seriously?" I can't believe my mother just sold me out. I'm with Cole on this one. I think Mom might like Ashleigh best.

"So, what's the problem?" Ashleigh asks.

The front door opens, and I arch my eyebrow. She gives me a knowing nod and a sympathetic smile. With a sigh, she says, "Brothers."

———

Brunch is filled with laughter and great food, just like always. Growing up, we didn't have many family meals around the table. Mom worked full time, and Cole had baseball practices or games several nights a week, which didn't leave us much downtime in the evenings. But Sundays were ours. As Mom would say, Sundays were our day for family, both by blood and by love. Friends were always welcome for Sunday brunch. Most Sundays included Sammie and Matt, Mom's coworkers, neighbors, and old and new friends.

Mom entertains Ashleigh with stories of Cole as a kid under the guise that she needs to know what she's getting into before they get married. The one constant in all the stories? Matt. My heart warms thinking about how ingrained he is in our family.

"You know, Matt asked me out first," Ashleigh shares with us.

Cole rolls his eyes and scoffs at her.

"I didn't know that," Mom says. "My biggest fear was that a girl would come between those two."

"Nah, a girl couldn't wreck what we have. Brothers for life. Besides, it's not like he had a chance with my girl. She only had eyes for me." He gives her a wink and a squeeze and she playfully rolls her eyes. Cole laughs. "But he knows how to push my buttons. Speaking of which, we have just enough time to see this project you're working on and swing by Matt's to say goodbye. Sound good, Darce?"

"Sure. I can't wait to show you the room I'm designing for you two."

"What are you talking about?" she asks. "This is Chance's getaway house."

"Not exactly. It's his family retreat. And you're family. Come on, I'll show you."

———

After a quick tour of the construction zone that's my senior project, Cole and Ashleigh are practically gushing. They loved all the design elements and told me they can't wait to celebrate New Year's here. Thanksgiving will be at Tripp Stevenson's Mexico place with Ashleigh's brothers.

"I can't wait to brag about this place when we're at Tripp's. Chance wanted something comparable, but this place is hand-downs a thousand times more amazing. I've officially felt the Darcy effect," Ashleigh says. She gives me an enormous hug. "Seriously, your future in design is bright. People, houses, doesn't matter. You have a way of giving them the it factor. The Darcy sparkle. I can't wait to help you launch your business after graduation."

"Proud of you," Cole says as he hugs me goodbye with a kiss to the temple.

"Same."

I watch them pull out of the driveway and return to the house. Since I'm here, I might as well get to work.

CHAPTER
NINETEEN

MATT

———

I know there's a standing invitation to the Davidson Sunday brunch, but I can't do it today. I need to step back and clear my head, but even the cold water of the Atlantic doesn't help me this morning. After a surf session that consisted of me floating on my board more than trying to ride the waves, I took a warm shower, which made me think of Darcy. She showered here a few days ago and left the evidence to prove it. I'll admit I used her body wash and enjoyed being surrounded by her scent. Her bag still sits on my dresser. I should get that back to her. Or should I hold it until she needs it again? Wishful thinking? Probably.

I lay on my bed and think about my future. And baseball. And Darcy. Mostly Darcy. I picture scenarios of moving up and getting traded. I think about what happens when I leave Charleston. In every scenario, I want her beside me. *How do you decide between doing the right thing and doing the right thing for you? What if it's both?* My dad's words play on a loop in my brain, along with her words from last night. *I'm nothing to you.* My heart hurts knowing she thinks that she's nothing to me. Surely, she knows better.

I'm startled by a loud knock at the front door.

I open the door and am greeted by a grinning Cole and his blushing fiancé.

"What are you guys doing here?"

"We came to say goodbye," Cole says as he walks in.

"Come on in?" It's more of a courtesy since he's halfway to the couch.

Ashleigh stops and kisses me on the cheek.

"Hey, friend. Sorry about the drop-in. It was my idea." She gives me that look she gets when she's plotting. I've seen it before.

"No problem. You're always welcome." She walks in and takes my hand, pulling me into the den.

"I like this house. It suits you," she says as she looks around.

"Yeah, I guess. It's just a rental. Not all of us can put down roots yet." Their house in Nashville is an actual home. It's a comfortable sanctuary for them to start their lives together.

Cole silently flips me off from the couch as he scrolls through something on his phone.

"Show me around?" she asks.

"Um, sure. The den, kitchen, dining room, and my bedroom are on this first floor. Come on, I'll show you upstairs. I rarely go up there, but it's got a magnificent view."

We go up the staircase off the kitchen to the second floor, that has two more bedrooms and a second sitting area. Ashleigh opens the sliding doors and steps out onto the upper deck.

"It's beautiful. I've always pictured you at the beach." She watches me before turning her attention to the view.

"Yeah, something about the water. I've always loved it."

We both lean against the railing, looking at the waves rolling in. It reminds me of when I saw Darcy and Chance not that long ago.

I absolutely love this time of year when the beach is deserted.

It's like this view is just for me. And Ashleigh. I smile at her. She rubs her arms to ward off the chill, so I grab a blanket off the couch and throw it around her shoulders.

"Thanks, Matt. You're a pretty great guy."

"So I've been told. But you still picked the other one," I tease. There was never anything between us. She was always Cole's.

"Like I had a choice." She chuckles. "I don't think you have a choice either, but you're fighting it. And how's that working out for you?"

"Not sure what you mean." Fuck.

"You know exactly what I mean. We just left a pretty miserable girl. Kinda looks like you do."

My heart twists just thinking about her being unhappy. Those tears last night practically broke me.

"Can't." I barely choke the word out. That's as close to a confession as she'll get.

Her brief look is one of pity, but she quickly shifts to boss mode. It's the same look she gives when she puts her older brothers in their place. I've seen her make them cower when she wants something, and damn if I'm not under her spell too.

"And why can't you? Because of some stupid bro code?" Her attention is wholly on me. The beach no longer a distraction.

"It's not a stupid code. You wouldn't understand," I mumble.

"Oh, because I'm not smart enough? Because I'm a girl?"

I give her my best don't be stupid glare. It doesn't even phase her.

"Let me tell you something, Matt Hartman." She pokes me in the chest with her finger. "That girl is hella awesome and has a bright future ahead of her. And so do you. And the thing about bright futures? They're filled with ups and downs, people who want to help you, use you, and hurt you. The journey is thrilling and terrifying at the same time." She reaches out and touches my arm, getting my full attention.

"Matt, you need someone special to walk beside you to help you navigate the journey. You want someone to celebrate the highs and support you through the lows. But letting some bro code keep you from someone special is idiotic. Do you want her to go through that alone? Do you?"

"He'll never forgive me," I confess.

"Oh, you let me worry about him." My head snaps up, and I'm terrified by her statement. "I won't tell him because that's up to you when the time is right. But you go make that girl happy, you hear me?"

I give her a half-hearted shrug.

She doubles the glare intensity.

"Yes, ma'am. I hear you."

She gives me a wicked smile and a wink. "Good, now finish our tour. We need to head to the airport soon." Her work here is done.

———

Ashleigh added more words to my jumbled thoughts. *What if it's both? I'm nothing to you. Keeping away from someone special is idiotic.* It all plays on a loop that gets louder and more jumbled.

I need to run. Work it out. Figure out the how. The solution.

The steady rhythm of my feet hitting the sand and the pattern of the waves breaking untangles my thoughts. Before I realize it, I'm at the same place I first saw her with Chance. The flash of jealousy subsides as I look up at the house that has brought us closer over the past few weeks. With a shift in perspective, the object of jealousy transforms into a thing of gratitude.

A light turns on in an upstairs bedroom, and I see a shadow pass in front of the window. A smile slowly creeps across my face, thinking about that girl. Who is apparently miserable. I need to fix that.

CHAPTER
TWENTY

DARCY

———

I'm not answering that doorbell. Probably some kids playing ding-dong-ditch. I'm not expecting anyone, and I'm not in the mood to deal with some next-door Karen who is mad about the construction. Again.

I'm hanging the art in Chance's room and second-guessing my selection. What am I doing? I'm not qualified to do this. All this talk from Ashleigh about launching after graduation has my nerves on edge. She means to be encouraging, but she's scaring me to death.

The doorbell rings again. And again. They aren't going away. I stomp down the stairs, unlock the door, and throw it open, prepared to give the interrupter a piece of my mind.

"Hey there, pretty girl." His smile slowly fills his face, making his eyes light up. He scans me from head to toe, and his smile seems to grow. My ridiculous appearance must amuse him.

My hand immediately goes to my hair that is falling out of my messy bun, feeling if it's as bad as I think. It is. I'm not wearing a stitch of makeup, and I'm dressed in the most unflattering outfit I could put together. I realize his nickname of pretty girl has been a joke all along. Sadness creeps up, tears threatening to start again. Why am I crying now? I've never cried this much before, and it's making me mad, which is also a tear trigger for me. Wonderful.

"Hey." Brilliant. Great response.

He stops my hands from fretting and holds them in his. "Mind if I come in?"

"Sure, I guess." I step away from the door and try to pull away. He doesn't let go of my hands as he comes in and gently closes the door. His hands leave mine to slide up my arms to my shoulders and hold me securely in place. The warmth of his touch fills me, and even though I don't know why he's here, that tiny seed of hope grows a little more.

I take a deep breath, and my cheeks heat. I can't bear to look at him. I know my hope will betray the it's no big deal attitude I'm trying to portray. I focus on the floor, his running shoes, and my newer, almost broken in Chucks.

His hand brushes the loose strands of hair away from my face and tucks them behind my ear. His movement startles me, and I look from the floor to him. I'm confused. I mean, what the fuck?

His eyes search my face for the answer to the unspoken question we've been dancing around for weeks. Should we? Can we?

He leans down, and his breath tickles my ear, sending chills down my spine.

"You're all I can think about, Darcy. Day and night. I've dreamed about being able to kiss your perfect lips. Fuck, I'm so tired of fighting it. I don't know that I can anymore." His words are a cross between a confession and an apology.

He lifts my chin, and his lips gently brush against mine. It's sweet and tender. My sadness is erased, and I smile. He must take my response as consent because he deepens the kiss, his tongue seeking entrance, and I'm more than willing to return the favor. His hand goes behind my head, his fingers tugging at my hair, giving him a better angle to deepen our kiss.

This kiss doesn't even compare to my dreams. I am electrified from my toes to my temples. My heart skips a beat and finds a new rhythm. I relax into his body, feeling like he is the other half to making me whole.

My hands reach around his neck, my nails gently brush through the short hair on the back of his head as I pull him closer, and he moans into my mouth. The vibration wakes up my entire body. Our lips meld perfectly, and our tongues dance together, exploring each other with desperate kisses. My body tingles down to my toes, and every nerve ending is like a live wire.

This kiss is everything I've ever wanted. My life has reached its pinnacle. This is the best moment of my life.

He pulls away and places his forehead against mine. We both breathe deeply to catch our breath.

"Wow." I experienced the best kiss of my life, and that's all my brain can register. My ability to communicate left the building.

"Wow is right," he says. He gives me another chaste kiss and tucks my head below his chin as he embraces me.

Not looking at him gives me the courage to speak. "I don't want to overdramatize it, but that kiss was life-changing." My life will never be the same. That's a confession he deserves.

His arms squeeze me against his solid chest, holding me tight. "It was for me, too. But..." Shit. Here comes the part where he tells me it was a mistake. I'm a mistake. I try to pull away, but his hold is solid.

"Darcy, I don't know how to do this. I want to do right by everyone, you know." His tone is soft, the kindness emanating from every word. Still, there's a tinge of sadness. It's like he's about to tell a kid there's no Santa Claus.

He's letting me down easy. That's Matt. The good guy. Always caring about others, the ultimate teammate. He has to tell me I'm not worth the fallout. My insecurity flares. I step back, his hold loosens, and I turn around to walk upstairs and hide. My emotions swirl in my heart and head, sadness taking center stage. That's what happens when you reach the pinnacle. It's all downhill from here.

"That's okay, Matt. I get it." I can't ask him to pursue something that clearly makes him uncomfortable.

"Get what?" His gruff tone surprises me.

"Nothing," I mumble. "You've always been kind to me."

"What the hell are you talking about? I'm gonna need you to tell me what's going on in your pretty little head because we aren't on the same page here. Again."

No truer words were ever spoken. I take a deep breath and summon courage from the depths of my bones as I turn to look at him. "I get it. I pushed you to cross a line you aren't comfortable with. I'm sorry."

I walk past him to open the door so he can leave as he hooks me around the waist, pulling me back into his chest. "Yeah, definitely not on the same page," he mumbles as he kisses the top of my head. "I'm not sorry. Maybe a little guilty, but definitely not sorry. I've wanted to kiss you since I saw you at The Wreck. When I say I don't know how to do this, it's just unfamiliar territory for me." He pulls me in tighter, and I shiver. Could this be true? That seed of hope is growing and taking root.

I reach up, put my hands on his face, and pull him towards me. If he doesn't know how to do this, whatever this means, I will gladly volunteer as tribute. I kiss him again, letting the sweetness and apprehensiveness slip away, putting all my years of longing for him behind my lips. If he decides his guilt wins, I'm not going without a fight.

He returns my kiss, his hands exploring my body, shoulders, and waist. As they travel underneath my shirt, his hand rests on my side, his thumb gently stroking below my bra. Sensual goosebumps cover my body.

Our kiss stops time. I'm lost in our embrace, our tongues seeking pleasure as heat warms my core. I want to spend the rest of the day kissing Matt.

Who am I kidding? I want to spend a lifetime kissing him.

CHAPTER
TWENTY-ONE

MATT

———

I kissed Darcy Davidson. I KISSED Darcy Davidson, and now I'm thinking about her as I stroke one out in the shower this morning. It's not the first time my morning has started with my dick in my hand as I think about her, but this time her kiss has me harder than I've ever been in my life. With my release, I'm hit with a moment of pleasure, followed by panic.

Darcy. My best friend's sister. The girl whose kiss I crave so much I crushed the bro code. Fuck.

I'm not an emotional guy. I'm logical. Loyal. Level-headed. The responsible one. The solid third baseman who keeps the team focused on winning. Now, I feel like all those qualities that define me are stripped away, and I'm floating, not anchored to anything familiar. It's the off-season, and I don't even have baseball right now. I've lost my balance, my footing. I've lost my goddamn head! I stare in the mirror and don't know who this emotional guy is looking back at me.

Sure, I have emotions, but they aren't what drives me. I mean, I enjoy baseball, but mostly, it's because I'm good at it. It's what I know. I understand the angle and force of a ball coming off a bat and its trajectory. I majored in physics, for god's sake. I play ball with my head, not my heart. I don't play with emotion and passion the way Cole does. It's why we complement each other, the yin and yang of baseball.

But now? Emotions assault me from all directions, and I don't know how to combat them. I'm ill-equipped to handle these new feelings, and the one person I want to reach out to, I can't because I kissed his sister. I crossed a line and need to figure out how to fix it.

When you make an error in baseball, you learn from it, try to mitigate the damage, and salvage the inning. But that error still counts in your stats. It doesn't go away. But you move on. Don't let it ruin the next play. Maybe that's what I need to do. Was this an error? I'm not sure.

After getting on the same page with an extensive make-out session, I helped Darcy finish hanging pictures. She's got an eye for what works and her ability to transform her environment is like magic. I'm captivated by her magic and she's transforming me, too.

We focused on her work and tried to get back to a place where we both felt comfortable. Tried to level set. Regroup. It took away the awkwardness and grounded us. Grounded me. Because I admit, kissing Darcy left me untethered. It isn't a bad thing, just an unknown thing. An adventurous thing. A dangerous thing.

Then, it was time to say goodnight. It was as if our first kiss was a warm-up for the main event. I've never been one to put much stock into kissing. It's always been a means to an end. But kissing Darcy? It's different. Kissing her is the most erotic experience I've ever had. Her hands pulled at my hair and made me wonder if she likes things a little rough. Or was it just the excitement of finally connecting? I couldn't get enough of her. I was like a man finding an oasis in the desert.

We finally made it into her car and she drove me home. After the short ten-minute drive, we made out in the car like a couple of horny teenagers. She got out to come in and I kissed her with a newfound passion, pressing her against the car, holding her tight. Her lips are made for mine. Her tongue created for my pleasure. When her teeth nipped at my skin, I wanted more. Damn, that girl is sexy, even in her oversized sweatshirts and leggings.

And as much as I wanted to take her to bed, she deserves better. When Sammie texted her for the fourth time, I knew I had to let her go, even if it was for a few hours. Watching her drive away practically gutted me, but I know it was the right thing to do. She needs rest.

We agreed to go slow because we have time. This isn't something I want to rush, but rather savor. Easier said than done. Darcy is the most incredible, sensual woman I've ever known, and I want to devour her. I need her to know that this is about who she is, not sex. I'm attracted to Darcy — body, mind, and spirit.

I know I need to talk to Cole, but timing will be everything. Ashleigh said she'd lay the groundwork. Not sure what that means, but I have to trust her.

This thing with Darcy feels right, true. *What if it's both?* Both indeed.

———

I've texted a few times with Darcy, but nothing of significance, mostly stuff about the house. I may not know how to do this, but she deserves someone who will figure it out.

> Dinner tonight?

PRETTY GIRL

Sure. We can order a pizza or something.

Nope. I want to take you on a date.

A date?

Yep. I'll pick you up at your place at 7. Wear something nice. But comfortable.

I'll be ready. 😜

I stop to get flowers and a box of Sour Patch Kids, Darcy's favorite candy. I made reservations at a trendy new restaurant that is on the *best of* list. This date may be cliche, but I need to start somewhere. Darcy deserves a guy who tries, gives her the best, and who shows her she's worth it. A guy that lets her know she's everything.

———

"Wow, you're breathtaking." I can't hide my pleasure in seeing Darcy. She's a natural beauty, but this evening, she's dressed in a silk wrap dress that puts all her assets on display. Fucking gorgeous. "Emerald is my new favorite shade of green." The dark color enhances her features and brightens her hazel eyes. The blush fills her face, and it does something to my chest. I reach out and place my palm on her cheek. She leans into my hand, and her eyelashes flutter as she closes her eyes. A smile graces her lips, and I know it's all for me. Her kissable lips greet me, but I remind myself tonight is about letting her know we're more than a physical connection. I want her to know she's everything. But that fucking red lipstick gives me a momentary pause. Damn, she's delicious.

"I thought you might like it," she says coyly.

I kiss her chastely, giving myself kudos for my restraint, and take her hand.

"Pretty girl, you are gorgeous, no matter what you wear. But damn, I just need a second to figure out why you would want to be with me. I'm not worthy."

She swats at my chest, and I snatch her hand and bring it to my lips. I think of these fingers tugging on my hair and consider another make-out session.

"Like we have time for you to fish for compliments," she teases.

"You're right. We have reservations, but I don't know if I want to show you off or keep you to myself." I give her a wink.

"Wow, Matt, when you decide to go all in, you go all in. Are you this charming to all your dates?"

"What? No, Darce, it's all you." I shake my head to settle my emotions. I need to get my level head back in the game. "Come on, let me take you on a proper date."

The dinner was superb, but the company was even better. We made a deal not to talk about school or baseball, nothing that might trigger stress, but all other topics are fair game. The other rule is to answer truthfully, therefore quickly. We can't take time to find the safe or polite words. Tonight is about truth and freedom. We've been going back and forth with questions all evening. The laughter is flowing as freely as the wine. Somehow, our inquisition has become a competition, each trying to make the other think too long before answering.

"The house is burning down. You only have time to grab one thing. What is it?" I ask.

"Easy," she answers. She takes another sip of her wine. "My autographed baseball." She sits back and crosses her arms, and a confident smirk crosses her face.

"You have an autographed baseball? Signed by anyone I've heard of?" This was not the answer I was expecting.

"The one signed by twelve-year-old Matt Hartman and Cole Davidson when they made a pact to both play in the MLB. I'm about to be a millionaire by selling it on eBay in a few years."

I'm stunned. I remember that day. Our travel team won the tournament, and Cole and I were joking around, acting like hotshots. Darcy pretended to be a groupie and asked us to sign her baseball. It was one of those silly things we did as kids.

"You still have that ball?" I can't believe it.

"Of course. My most prized possession."

"But we were just kids." I'm shocked at the sentimentality of it all. Darcy is thoughtful. Supportive. Hopeful. Caring.

"Who made their dreams come true. You and Cole are on your way to the big leagues."

"I can't believe you kept it," I whisper.

"I'm not a hoarder," she confesses. "But I know a good investment piece when I see one." She tips her glass to me in a mock toast and finishes her glass of wine.

The mention of Cole brings the guilt back to the surface. Darcy narrows her eyes at me.

"Don't you dare, Matt Hartman," she hisses. "Get out of your head right now. This is about you and me. Not Cole. So put him away, do you hear me?"

I stare into her eyes that were so happy and bright a minute ago and am now faced with feisty Darcy. The girl who is scrappy and isn't shying away from this new thing we've started. Maybe that's because he's her brother and will always love her unconditionally. I'm not as lucky. But she's right. Tonight is about discovery. Learning more about each other. It's about us.

I roll my head on my shoulders and relax. "I hear you, pretty girl. I hear you."

"Good." She gives a little hmph sound and holds her glass out for more wine. I pour some more and gulp mine.

She puts her adorable smile back on, like her reprimand didn't even happen. Honestly, that transition is frightening. She bats her eyes at me. "So, same question. What are you grabbing if the house is on fire?"

I look at her, and my heart skips a beat. I think I'm falling for her and am equally excited and terrified. But I can't help it. She's everything.

I can't lose our competition, so I respond with the first thing that comes to mind. "You, pretty girl. It's you."

Damn. Here we go.

CHAPTER
TWENTY-TWO

DARCY

————

It's odd not having Cole home for Thanksgiving, but our group has never been one for tradition. Mom, me, the Hartmans, and Sammie's family all serve at the local homeless shelter every year. We serve lunch to our community and love every minute of focusing on others. Our families invite others to join us, and sometimes, we have a large group. Sometimes it's just us. Thanksgiving is like Sunday brunch, but on a bigger scale and with turkey. After everyone is served, we play a highly spirited game of rock-paper-scissors to see who has dish duty for the last serving pieces.

I was taking my instruction from an adorable seven-year-old, and unfortunately, she didn't know the guys usually went with rock. I lost when it was down to Jay and me in the finals. The little girl was sad for me, but I convinced her dishes were my favorite part of the meal because they reminded me of how much good food everyone ate. She accepted my explanation and ran off to join other kids playing games in the back of the room.

As I head back to the kitchen to tackle the dishes, I'm hip-checked by Matt. "You think I'm going to abandon you in your time of need?"

"Well, since you and Cole lost last year, I thought you'd enjoy the victory." Cole and Matt lose almost every year. I'm not sure if they're bad at the game or if they secretly enjoy using the powerful dish machine.

"I didn't want you to learn the real secret," he teases.

"Oh, and what's that?"

"The chef leaves extra desserts back here for the dish crew." He winks and gives me one of his million-watt smiles. "I had fun today."

"Me too. It's one of my favorite days of the year. We've been doing this as long as I can remember."

"Yeah, it was another one of those Darcy Davidson big-hearted ideas. You've been making a difference since elementary school."

"What are you talking about?" He often remembers things I don't about our history. It warms my heart that he knows my past, my family, my successes, and failures.

"Don't you remember? You started talking to a homeless guy one year during the week of Thanksgiving, and you invited him to your house for dinner. He told you he couldn't come because he was having lunch with friends here. So, you invited yourself to lunch with him. You pitched such a fit your mom agreed to have Thanksgiving here. The rest, as they say, is history."

I pinch my face trying to remember. Matt reaches up and brushes his thumb between my eyes, smoothing my wrinkled face. "I don't remember that."

"Yeah, you've always had a heart for those in need. I figure that's why you're hanging out with me these days."

I blush. If he only understood. I've crushed on Matt since I was twelve. He's my Prince Charming. My knight in shining armor. My dream guy. If he knew the level of adoration I have for him, he'd be running faster than a line drive to third base.

"Don't be silly. I'm just hanging out to guarantee you make it to the big leagues, so my baseball is the investment I need."

"Oh, I see how it is. You're just chasing the jersey."

That's totally not true, but is that what he thinks? I like him because he's an athlete. OMG. I'm so embarrassed. What am I thinking? Matt? I'm his charity case. I try to school my face, but I'm unsuccessful. Panic fills his face. "I'm kidding, Darce. You know that."

I nod slightly and turn toward the dishes we need to tackle. Kidding. Right. I start washing dishes and pray this will be over soon. His firm hands grip my shoulders, turning me towards him. "Look at me, pretty girl. Please." Gah. I melt when he calls me that. I've never been one for pet names, but when he calls me that, deep down, I long for it to be sincere from him. That he really sees me that way.

I look into his whiskey-colored eyes and relax. Matt cares for me. It's killed me not to touch him today, but we agreed to keep it between us, so no PDA. He leans down and kisses me. His lips are tender, sweet like he's trying to reassure me what we have is real. Reaching around his neck, I pull him closer, deepening our kiss.

I need him to feel everything I feel. I need him to know I'm not a jersey chaser and what I'm feeling is more than a schoolgirl crush. I love him. Always have. Always will. But I can't tell him that now or he'll freak out and pump the brakes. I need him to catch up. I've been in love with Matt for years. While this is all new for him, I know he's hesitant. Torn. I won't push him. But I will give him my whole heart. Frankly, he's always had it.

"Oh, sorry." We jump apart like we got caught. Which we totally did. Fuck me. Jay is standing in the doorway with a massive grin on his face. "If I had known this was how we washed dishes, I would've volunteered." His laugh fills the dish room. "Just letting you know Sammie and I are headed out. I'll email you the schedule for the next few weeks, Darcy." He gives me a wink, and I return it with a sheepish smile.

"Thanks," I whisper.

I give Jay a pleading look that tells him to forget what he saw. At least, I hope that's what he picks up from it.

"Yeah, well, um, carry on. What happens in the dish room stays in the dish room."

"Well, these dishes won't wash themselves," I say. "Come on, slugger, let's get this done."

After we finish our task, we say goodbye to the people still hanging out in the dining area. I head to my car, and Matt follows. We've been relatively quiet after the interruption, both lost in our thoughts. I worry Matt's gone back to thinking we're a terrible idea. If that's the case, I'll cherish the time we've had. It's more than I could've wished for anyway.

Evening dusk is setting in, and the parking lot has a grey tinge as the daylight fades away.

"Where are you going now?" His voice is deep, husky.

"Home. Mom and I always look through the sale papers and plot our strategy for shopping and grabbing the best bargains for tomorrow. Why?"

The cool air hits my arms, and I rub up and down to warm them. It's always warm in the shelter, and the contrast between that world and this one isn't lost on me.

Matt takes off his hoodie and wraps it around my shoulders. His scent surrounds me, and I pull it tight. I hope he doesn't expect this back. Ever.

The back of his fingers brush against my cheek, and I can feel the warmth as they turn pink. My blush betrays me every time.

"I think my new favorite color is Darcy Blush. Want to Sigmund Freud me on that, Miss Davidson?"

"Sigmund Freud you?" I giggle at his term. I bite my bottom lip, deciding how to answer his question. Any insecurity I felt after his jersey chaser comment vanishes, and I feel bold and brave. "Well, changing a favorite color is quite a big deal. It's more often a slight change on the color wheel. But going from green to pink? That's a pretty drastic change, Mr. Hartman."

He leans down and whispers in my ear, his warm breath caressing my cheek, immediately making my blush deepen. "What can I say? I'm feeling pretty drastic."

I swallow and take a deep breath before answering. "Well, the base of pink is red, and it's the opposite of green on the color wheel. So, that means, well, those colors are complementary."

He gives a subtle nod. "Hmmm, complementary. I like that." His smile spreads across his face, reaching his eyes. He strokes his thumb against my cheek as his gaze warms my body. He leans down, and his lips barely touch mine. the contact curls my toes. "I absolutely like this color," he whispers as he pulls away.

I reach for him when my phone buzzes in my bag, vibrating against the lip gloss tubes and pens, making it sound louder and more urgent. I reach in and see it's a FaceTime request from Cole. Any warmth I feel immediately disappears, and a sense of dread fills my stomach.

I hold the phone up to Matt, and he immediately switches from flirty to friend.

"You'd better answer it," he encourages. "You know he can be persistent."

"Hey, how's Mexico?" It looks like he's outside, surrounded by lush green plants and a water feature.

"Great! How are you? Whoa. Are you okay? You look kinda flushed." I look at Matt, panic hitting full force. He grabs my hand and turns my phone to him.

"She's just warm from having to do the dishes at the shelter. She's not used to it like we are." Cole's laughter carries across the parking lot.

"Damn, now she knows our secret. Did she even appreciate the extra pie?"

"Probably not as much as we do. But she held her own." Matt gives me a wink that I'm sure gets Cole's attention. When Matt rubs his knuckles in my hair like Cole usually does, Cole laughs. Matt is in brother mode now, and I hate it.

Cole laughs again. "I'm sure she did. Where are you guys?"

"Just walking her to the car." Matt puts his arm around my shoulders and pulls me into the video, and I stiffen.

"I'm glad you're there to take care of her," Cole says sincerely.

"Hey, I've been taking care of myself for the last four years," I say indignantly.

"That you have, Darce," Matt says as he pulls me tighter for a side hug. I never thought his touch would make me uncomfortable, but I'm nervous talking to Cole with Matt this close. He'll see how much I crave his touch.

I've also come to realize I don't like this version of Matt anymore. There was I time I was willing to take anything he would give me. That's no longer true. I don't want my brother's best friend version of Matt. It's not enough. Nope. Knowing he can put us back in that box so easily is disappointing and makes me unsettled.

"So, how's Mexico?" Matt asks, switching the focus from me.

"It's gorgeous here, but I'm outnumbered. They had a Decker girl's night and tried to pull me into their shenanigans. I needed my wingman to save me."

I can feel Matt's laughter fill his chest. "So, what color are your nails?"

"Funny, real funny. Tripp and I wandered into town to a bar, did tequila shots, and played dominoes with a few locals."

"Look at you, hotshot. Drinking with your baseball idol," Matt interjects.

"Yeah, he gave me shit for getting you to ask him to sign my baseball card."

"By the way, Decker girl's nights are epic," I say. "Don't knock what you know nothing about."

"All I know is when Leigh came stumbling to bed, she was tipsy and very happy."

I scrunch up my face. "Let's just stop there. So, um, how's the house?" This is Cole's first time at Tripp's Mexico house, the one Chance wants to top.

"Oh, it's nice. But it's missing the Darcy touch. Girl, from what I've seen, you will exceed Chance's expectations. I can't wait for Tripp to see what you've done. I may have been bragging about you after a few shots."

"Oh, I wish you hadn't. I'm nervous enough as it is."

"Why are you nervous?" Matt whispers in my ear.

I turn around, and our faces are so close because of Matt's arm around my shoulder and keeping us both on video. "What if…"

"Hey, hey," Cole interjects. "Knock it off. Darcy, you're fucking awesome." He says it with such force and sincerity. I start to tear up.

"Yeah, you are," a voice interjects from Cole's side. "Hey, Darcy!" Julian's face takes up the screen.

"Hey, can't a guy have a minute here?" Cole says.

Julian laughs and pushes Cole aside. "Hey! Oh wow, it's Matt too. How's my favorite third baseman?"

"I'm good, thanks." Julian is Ashleigh's brother and Cole and Matt's agent. The web is tangled, but I wouldn't have it any other way.

"Hey Darcy, I hear you're killing it at Chance's house. Don't let that lug overwork you. Make him pay," Julian says.

"Is that any way to speak about your best friend?" I ask.

"That's the beauty of best friends," Cole says as he snatches the phone from Julian and pushes him away. "They always have your back."

I can see the walls go up around Matt as soon as Cole's words fill the air. The guilt assaults him from the inside out, it's practically visible. The best friend bro code.

"Yep," Matt answers instinctively.

I grab my phone from Matt and take control of this conversation.

"Hey Cole, good to chat, but I'm getting cold and need to make the shopping strategy with Mom. Talk again soon?"

"Yeah, yeah, sure. Have fun tomorrow, and be safe. Love you, Darce."

"Love you too." I disconnect the call and look at Matt. I watch him put distance between us.

"Looks like Cole is having fun in Mexico." After that conversation, I need to test the waters and figure out where his head is.

"Yeah, seems like it." Matt's voice is hollow. Any flirting or playfulness we had before the call is gone. Both of us go into protection mode, probably for different reasons.

I put my hand on his cheek. He doesn't pull away, so I count that as a win. "Hey, you want to tell me what you're thinking?" I give him a playful wink.

He leans in, and I turn my head up and close my eyes, excited for our inevitable kiss. I wait for his soft lips, and they press against my forehead. Damn. I try to push down my disappointment and give him a weak smile.

"Well, okay then." I step back and reach for my door handle. I will not cry in front of Matt.

Matt reaches for my hand and pulls me back to him. My back is to his chest, and he wraps his arms around my waist, pulling me tight to his body. He kisses me behind my ear sending shivers down my spine. My emotions are on a roller coaster, up and down and loop-de-looping everywhere.

"Have fun with your mom," he whispers. "I'll miss you."

I try to turn around in his arms, but he reaches out and opens my car door. He steps away and walks backward toward his car.

"Text me when you're exhausted, broke, or need encouragement tomorrow. I've got you."

That's the problem, Matt. You've always had me.

CHAPTER
TWENTY-THREE

DARCY

————

The next few weeks rush by in a blur. I fill my days with school, the house, and Matt. We've settled into a routine. Matt spends the mornings at the high school working out and helping his dad while I do a flurry of online shopping for the finishing touches for the house. We grab an early dinner most nights and crash at the beach house with some Netflix and chill time. He usually lets me pick what we watch, and I love finding something we can discuss or even disagree about, like a reality show. I get pleasure from getting him worked up in more ways than one.

Our chill time includes heavy make-out sessions and pushing the boundaries a little each night. Matt wants us to take it slow, and it takes every ounce of patience I have, but I remind myself he's still catching up on us. I've been ready for him for years. Just when I think we're ready to take it to the next level, Cole reaches out, and Matt gets a gut check. It's an infuriating dance of one step forward, two steps back. It's the bro code shuffle.

At this point, I'm still taking what I can get. I mean, any amount of Matt is better than nothing. But I'm becoming increasingly frustrated with my attitude of acceptance too. I want all of him.

I have nothing to complain about. He's all in when it comes to being supportive. He knows when I need encouragement, sustenance, a break, or a push, and kick in the butt.

These last few weeks before Christmas have been extremely busy. I'm lucky I'm only taking one class this semester besides my practicum, so the usual exam pressure is minimal. The practicum? I had no idea these last few weeks would be the hardest part. That's because all the contractor work is complete. Now it's time for the tiny details that make it special, and it's up to me to make it happen. My advisor is letting my grade ride as an incomplete until the new year, giving me time to submit a finished product in my portfolio since it's such an enormous job. I've kept him apprised of my progress and deadlines. He can't believe I'm doing this project myself. Some days, neither can I.

I'm meeting Jay this afternoon for the final walk-thru and sign-off. There are hundreds of boxes that need to be broken down, and I'm becoming an expert with the box cutter. The mess is daunting. I say a silent prayer Chance doesn't freak out when he sees his credit card.

"Darcy?" Sammie calls out.

"In here," I yell.

"Cardboard is an interesting design element," she says teasingly.

"Yeah, it's the new cottage chic. What are you doing here?" I wasn't expecting to see her until tomorrow. I've been staying at the beach house to give Sammie peace and quiet for her exams.

"I told Jay I wanted to tag along. I finished up exams a little early."

I finish breaking down the box in my hand and add it to the pile. I wipe my hands on my jeans and hug her full force.

"I'm proud of you, girl. You must be glad to be done."

"Yeah, one more semester to go. Kinda scary, huh?"

"Just a little." Well, if that isn't the biggest lie I've ever told her. More like terrified. Sammie will no doubt get into medical school, and I'll what? Look for a job? Start my own business? Be a waitress at The Wreck? Depending on where Sammie goes to school, I could live alone for the first time in my life. It's all the hard stuff I don't want to think about, but I've got five months to ignore it all.

"Let me take over cardboard city here," Sammie offers. "Jay's waiting for you downstairs by the pool. Something about starting from the ground up." She shrugs her shoulders and holds out her hand for the box cutter in my hand. "I'm waiting for the final reveal, so I don't want to peek." Her smile fills her face. All the pressure is off her for now, and she looks like a college student on break. I have a little twinge of jealousy. There are exactly twelve days until New Year's Eve. Twelve days left to get this house done.

I hug her again. "Thanks, Sammie," I whisper. "I couldn't have done this without you. I love you."

"Girl, you've got more talent in your little finger than most people have in their entire bodies. Quit doubting yourself and celebrate your awesomeness."

I just hug her tighter. I wish I could make this anxiety and self-doubt go away. There's just so much riding on this. It's not like working at Ashleigh and Cole's house. That was fun. It wasn't for a client. It wasn't for my future.

"I better not keep Jay waiting. Thanks, again."

She smiles, opens the box cutter, and grabs the next box in the pile. "You got this girl. We all believe in you."

I walk toward the back doors to meet Jay at the pool area. I wipe the tear that slips down my cheek. The problem with everyone believing in you? The thought you could let them down weighs a ton.

———

"Hey, Darcy," Jay says from behind the pool bar. "Doesn't this space look great? It's probably my favorite part of the house."

"Yeah, you guys did an amazing job." There's the large screen over the bar, the outdoor kitchen area with a brick oven for pizzas, and the grill big enough to cook a dozen steaks at once. I've learned that athletes eat more food than mere mortals can comprehend. Since many of Chance's friends are professional athletes, food and entertainment are a focal point of this house.

"I love your idea of making the tile around the bar and pool festive. The pops of hot pink and teal look great."

"It turned out well," I muse. "I can't wait to put out the cushions and flamingo pool float." One of my favorite pictures on Chance's Instagram is his large, muscular body floating in a giant flamingo float at Tripp's house in Mexico. It inspired the pool area, and I've blown up that picture and hung it behind the bar with a neon pink sign that says *Outside Chance*. I thought it was a clever name for his bar, but now I'm doubting it.

"Love the bar name. Chance will love it too," Jay says, breaking my insecurity self-talk.

He holds out a roll of blue tape, and I take it, unsure what it's for. "Here's a roll of painter's tape. As we walk around, nitpick everything. If it's not perfect, mark it with the tape. I'll make notes too. We'll take care of it and turn over the symbolic keys to you once it's done to your satisfaction."

"Oh, okay." It's times like this that I realize I don't know what I'm doing. An experienced designer wouldn't have looked at the roll of tape like it was going to bite.

"Come on, Darcy, let's check out your masterpiece."

We start downstairs and make our way to the main living area. Sammie doesn't say a word but keeps breaking down boxes and adding to the stack of cardboard.

"I'll get one of my guys to take all that cardboard to the recycling center for you," Jay says as we finish the main area and head to Chance's bedroom on the next floor.

"Thanks. I didn't realize how much stuff I've ordered." That stack of cardboard is getting taller than me. I'm self-conscious of ordering too much and ruining the environment in the same shot.

"It's a big house. Trust me, you've been extremely conservative."

I know he means it in a good way, but I worry. When we step into the large owner's suite, Jay turns to me and holds me by the shoulders.

"Stop."

His words catch me off guard.

"Stop what?"

"Stop doubting yourself. Conservative is a compliment. Some people think you have to be over the top to get noticed. You don't have to do that. You made a safe space for people to relax and be themselves. It's fun and full of whimsy. Chance will love it, and it's a launching pad for a successful future."

I let his words soak in. Future. "Thanks, I needed to hear that from an impartial party. When Sammie or Matt say it, I feel like they're just being nice."

"First, they both love you too much to lie to you. And second, I'm not impartial. I'm a fan too. But, as a professional, I can give you my expert opinion, which may hold a little more weight." It's hard to explain, but his words give me a booster shot of confidence I need.

We finish our walk-thru and there are very few things to fix. It's almost done. I spin around taking it all in. This house has brought me more than graduation. It's brought me Jay. It's brought me Matt.

"Come on. We're taking you out to dinner to celebrate." Jay puts his arm around my shoulders and leads me to the hall.

Matt's waiting for us in the parking lot when we arrive at the restaurant. He looks so handsome, leaning against the hood of his car, scrolling through his phone. His eyes light up when he sees us pull in, and his smile makes my stomach flip. He walks over to Jay's truck and opens my door, extending his hand to me. The warmth of his touch sends an electric current up my arm, warming my entire body and flooding me with happiness.

He leans down and gives me a chaste kiss on my lips, the feather-like touch of his lips teasing me. I move in, and he pulls away, causing me to scowl at him.

He throws his head back and laughs. "Not sure that's the reaction I was going for, but you're adorable." His finger bops my nose, and I deepen my frown. He leans down and whispers in my ear. "Don't worry, pretty girl. I know how to turn that frown upside down. Later. I promise." He nips at my earlobe, and my resolve to pout melts.

I try my best to hold my glare, but when my eyes meet his, I can see the longing, and I melt into him. "You're such a tease. Ugh... Let's go." I grab his hand and tug him towards the door. I'll enjoy dinner and time with my friends. But after dinner? I know what I want for dessert, and it's not on the menu. I'm tired of Matt setting the boundaries, and tonight I plan on pushing them or, better yet, erasing them.

———

Whenever the four of us get together, we always have fun. We drank a bottle of wine, and when I say we, I mean mostly me and Sammie. The guys laugh as we recount childhood stories, and Matt interjects with his version of the story or detail we'd left out, usually on purpose.

Sammie is telling the story about a prank we pulled in eighth grade, and Matt's smile grows as he remembers. I relax into him and sigh. Matt is part of my entire life story. He knows me and has seen me at my highs and lows. This story Sammie is telling is when my crush on Matt began. I wonder if he knows that? If my younger self knew that I'd be sitting with Matt

Hartman while his hand gently strokes my thigh under the table, I would've died. His lazy strokes move higher up my thigh until he's inches from my center. The shock makes me jump a little.

"You okay," Sammie asks.

"Um, yup. Fine." I look up at Matt, and his expression doesn't change. He's casual as he takes a small sip from his beer.

"I, um, hate to call it a night, but I've got a lot to do tomorrow. Matt, do you mind taking me back to the house?"

"I'm done with exams, so you can come home, you know." I want to smack the smirk off Sammie's face.

"Better commute." I shrug like that's the real reason. I wonder if I fool anyone, but based on the looks I'm getting, I doubt it. My friends are awesome though, because they don't call me on my attempt to justify my decision.

"Come on," Matt says. "I need to get you to bed." He blushes. "I mean, um, since you have a big day tomorrow and all." Is Matt speaking in innuendo? Is he planning on dropping me off so I can rest? The tension between us has me strung tight.

We say our goodbyes, and Matt helps me into his car. He leans over and buckles me in. His cheek brushes against my breasts, sending tingles down my spine and making my nipples come to attention. I let my mind wander and imagine Matt's lips kissing my breasts and exploring my body. Just the thought is making me wet and turned on.

Matt doesn't say a word as we drive toward the beach, his hand not leaving my thigh. As he caresses my leg, he slides his hand higher, his fingers brushing against my center. He can probably feel my wetness through my leggings. His breathing hitches.

"You might want to slow down there, slugger. The last thing you need is a speeding ticket."

Matt looks at me like I spoke to him in a foreign language. He cocks his head to the side like he doesn't understand.

"The speed limit is thirty-five. You're way out of that range."

I smile, letting him know I understand exactly why he's willing to risk a ticket to get us home.

"Don't care," he mumbles, but slows down a little.

We pass the turn to Chance's house and head towards his house. When we pull into his driveway, Matt stills, looking straight ahead.

"Darcy," he whispers.

"Um, hum." Matt is having a moment, and I don't want to spook him. We've been playing by his rules, and something happened tonight that made him decide to change them. It's about damn time. He's caught up with me, and I'm ready. I don't know what prompted this change of heart, but I'm glad he's made his way here.

"If we do this, there's no going back," he whispers.

"I know." I unbuckle my seatbelt and climb over to him. I straddle his lap and kiss him, gently at first, but when I nibble his bottom lip, he opens up, and his kiss devours me.

We fumble out of the car and up to the front porch. My back is pressed against the door as Matt kisses me. It's a wonder he's able to unlock it at all. Once we make our way inside, all semblance of decorum is lost. We frantically tug and pull at each other's clothes until our shirts are on the floor.

Matt slows our kisses and pulls away. Did I do something wrong? Panic creeps in until I look into his eyes and see him staring at my breasts. His hands slowly slide up my sides and gently cup them over my bra. I've never had anyone look at me with such reverence. Goosebumps cover my arms. The pull between us is magnetic.

"Why don't we take this into your room?" My breath hitches as his thumb brushes over my nipple. Who knew a faint touch could be such a turn on?

"Are you sure?" He looks at me, his eyes searching.

"Positive." There's no hesitation on my part.

He scoops me up, carries me to his bedroom, and gently lays

me on the bed. The franticness is gone, replaced with a slow burn and hunger. Indecision crosses his face.

I put my palm on his cheek and pull him to me. I kiss him with everything I have. Everything I am. Everything I feel.

Even though my life is full of questions and uncertainty, there is one thing I'm certain about.

This is no crush. I love Matt Hartman.

CHAPTER
TWENTY-FOUR

MATT

————

How am I so lucky? I lay Darcy out on my bed, and she looks like an absolute vision. I want to fuck her hard, make her cry my name in ecstasy. I also want to go slow and savor every inch of her glorious body.

I'm deciding which approach when she pulls me in for the most desperate kiss I've ever experienced. Her tongue sweeps into my mouth, exploring, tasting, pushing. She's sweet and sexy. Soft and hard.

"Thanks for helping me decide," I say, kissing her jaw. I lick down her neck and across her collarbone. I nip at her skin and her reaction is practically feral.

She writhes at my touch. Oh, baby, I haven't even started. I caress her breast while my mouth sucks her buds through her lacy bra. She's incredibly reactive to my touch, and I'm dedicated to exploring every inch of her luscious body. Every beautiful inch.

"Decide what?" She practically moans her words.

"I couldn't decide between sweet or spicy." I continue my kisses on her other breast, giving both equal treatment.

"Mmmm, which did you decide on?"

I continue kissing between her breasts and reach behind her, releasing them from her bra. Now that they're uncovered, I need to return to the objects of my attention. Each one gets ample time to know how much I appreciate them. Her hands are in my hair, pulling and scratching at my scalp, letting me know when I've hit a sensitive spot. Oh, I'm paying attention, pretty girl. I'm studying her like my life depends on it.

"You tell me." I wet her pert nipple and gently blow, watching it harden further. As I kiss down her stomach, my hands pull at her leggings, and I'm greeted with sexy, pink, lace panties.

I pull her to the edge of the bed and let her legs dangle over the side. I slide to my knees between her legs and spread her further.

"Beautiful."

I kiss my way up the inside of her thighs, alternating between each one until I'm at her core. She's soaked through. I grin because that's all for me. I push her panties to the side and rub at her clit, her juices soaking my fingers. While I rub her with my thumb, I slide one finger in. She rides my finger, and I give her two, stretching her. I bend my fingers to find that magic spot, watching her, learning her. I know I've found it when she throws her head back, losing herself as she chases her orgasm.

"That's it, pretty girl. Let yourself go."

"Oh, Matt, there, don't, don't stop." Darcy's face when she climaxes is the most spectacular thing I've ever seen. She's like a work of art, and I have to see it again. As she comes down, I suck her juices from my fingers.

"Um, delectable. Sweetest taste I've ever put in my mouth. And I need more." I pull her panties down until she is totally bare before me. I kiss her stomach and mound before licking her clit with the flat of my tongue and work my way to her folds before I tongue fuck her. I'm a quick learner and can tell she's chasing orgasm number two. I love the way her body responds to me. I crave it.

"Matt, mmm!" Her thighs hold my head, while her pussy clenches as I fuck her with my tongue.

I can't stop the smile that spreads across my face as I kiss my way up to Darcy's lips. She's sated, and I'm the lucky bastard who sees her like this, making her feel this way.

"I just need a second to catch my breath." Her eyes are half lidded, her satisfied smile my reward.

I chuckle and brush her hair away from her face to gaze at her. The look she gives me is full of contentment and trust. Sated Darcy is exquisite.

She's heaven on earth. Her dark hair spread across my white pillow, the blush on her cheeks, the twinkle in her green eyes, all compete for my favorite color at the moment.

"So, I guess you decided on spicy?" Her hand reaches between my legs and rubs my erection pushing against my zipper.

"As the appetizer? Absolutely."

"That was just the appetizer? Honestly, I'm a little afraid of the main course." She squeezes me, and I take a deep breath.

"We don't have to do anything you don't want to do, Darcy. Ever."

She pulls me in for another passionate kiss.

"Oh no, slugger, you totally misunderstand. I'm ready for the three-course meal." She unbuttons my jeans, sliding the zipper down, letting my cock out to play.

I stand up and pull my jeans and briefs off until I stand in front of her, naked and fully erect. She sits up, rubs her hands over my abs, and fists my shaft.

"Baby, if you keep doing that, we may not have a main course."

A wicked smile graces her face, and naughty Darcy replaces sweet Darcy. I like this side of her too. It's pretty fucking sexy.

She scoots up toward the headboard, and I pull a condom out of my bedside table, quickly sheathing up.

"What's next, slugger?" She nips at my neck as she pulls me down toward her.

I'm too overwhelmed to respond with words. I line my cock up to her entrance and thrust into her in one stroke, sinking to the hilt. Her little gasp makes me pause.

"Are you okay?" I hold still, waiting for her to adjust for me.

Her hands grab my ass, and her nails dig in while her hips move. I'm balls deep in Darcy Davidson, and it's the most amazing feeling I've ever experienced.

"I'm better than okay. Fuck me, Matt. Make me yours."

If those words don't ignite my fire, I don't know what would. I fuck Darcy hard, and she takes it. Her moans the encouragement I need. "Hands up," I growl. She obeys and grabs the spindles on the headboard. I slide a pillow under her giving me a new angle and thrust harder, deeper.

I can tell she has another orgasm building, and I keep going, holding back my own until her walls squeeze around me, and then I lose myself in the most intense orgasm I've ever had. I see stars and then momentary blackness. She's unlocked a sensation I've never had before and fuck me, I want more. It's different. Potent. Special. Fierce. It's all Darcy.

I roll to the side, pulling her with me. I kiss her forehead, eyelids, and nose until I reach her swollen lips. I kiss her gently, tenderly. It's a contrast to the hardness just seconds earlier. That's what Darcy does to me. She makes me wild and tender. She's sweet and spicy, and damn if I can't get enough of her.

I slip out of bed to clean up and take care of the condom. When I return, she's sleeping with the sweetest smile on her face. She's an angel in my bed.

That's my pretty girl. That's the girl I love.

CHAPTER
TWENTY-FIVE

DARCY

———

I just had the most fantastic dream. It's not the first time I've dreamed about Matt and me. No, that's a regular occurrence. But this dream was so vivid and real, I didn't want to wake up. As sleep leaves me, I feel a pull around my stomach while something large and hard pokes me in the back. I open my eyes to the reality that I wasn't dreaming, but remembering the night with Matt.

His gentle breathing buzzes in my ear, and my lips turn up into a wicked grin. I've had sex before, but what I had with Matt? That was more. I've never felt so cherished. Pleasured. Totally fucked. That guy wore me out in all the best ways.

I gently work my way out of his embrace and head to the bathroom, where I notice Matt has a new toothbrush set out for me, and my heart melts a little more. I slip on one of his t-shirts, wondering where my underwear ended up. When I sneak back into the room, Matt is sitting up against the headboard, looking all kinds of sexy. His eyes track me, and I stop, unsure what to do. The morning after is an unfamiliar experience for me. "Damn. You look sexy in my shirt." His smile is sweet, but his bedhead and hooded eyes say the opposite of sweet.

The warmth of my blush rushes to my cheeks. I don't want to ruin this moment. Then he pulls the comforter back and pats the mattress. "Come here, pretty girl."

I snuggle in next to him, and he wraps me in his arms, pulling me into his chest. He places a gentle kiss on my forehead.

"Good morning," I say shyly.

"It is." His smile reaches his eyes. "You feeling okay?"

I'm a little sore. Thinking about why makes me blush. I'm not telling him, or he'd cover me in bubble wrap, and I'm looking forward to an encore of last night. "Yeah, great. You?"

"Never better."

His hand absently rubs up and down my back. I mirror his moves, letting my fingers trace down his chest, admiring his washboard abs. I let my hand drift further south finding him hard. I wrap my hand around his shaft and explore him.

I'm curious. "Is this an every morning occurrence?"

"It is when you're around."

"Well, I should do something about it." I wink, kiss him on his cheek, and move down his chest with my lips. My tongue wants to taste him.

My body is awake, and I can't get enough. I rub the droplet of pre-cum with my thumb licking him from bottom to tip, tasting his wetness. His chest vibrates as he says my name. I've never felt so empowered in my life, and I'm ready to take charge. I take him into my mouth as far as possible without hitting my gag reflex, licking, sucking. His fingers wrap around my hair, tugging, guiding. I've only done this once before, and I can honestly say I didn't enjoy it. But now? I love making Matt feel good. I gently run my teeth along his vein and wrap my tongue around his tip. My hand finds his balls and work them at the same time.

"Darcy," he says, breathless.

"Yes?"

"Darcy, baby, I need you to stop." I worry I'm not doing this right, but he seems to like it.

"Oh, okay." He guides me up his chest and takes my chin in his hands. He kisses me gently, almost chastely.

"What's wrong?" His eyes search mine, seeking an answer to a question.

"Nothing. Was I doing it wrong?" My insecurity washes over me, and I start to move away.

He pulls me into his chest, and his mouth is anything but chaste, his lips pressing into mine, his tongue attacking me, devouring me.

He speaks to me with his lips pressed against mine. "When I come, I want to be deep inside you, pretty girl. You were doing everything right. I can assure you."

His words fill me with euphoria.

He reaches into the nightstand and pulls out a condom, ripping it open with his teeth. He covers himself, reaches between my legs, and rubs against my wetness.

"You're so ready for me, aren't you?"

"Always."

He slides into me slowly, gently rocking his hips. His kisses follow along my jaw and down my neck. His slow movements are driving me crazy.

"I need more," I growl.

His chest vibrates with a low chuckle.

"Are you laughing at me?" I'm feeling a little indignant.

"I love hearing you beg," he whispers in my ear. "I'm gonna make you feel good, baby."

He's slow and methodical, worshiping every part of my body. My need builds, and I chase my release. "I'm so close," I moan.

"Let yourself go, Darce." My release crescendos and washes

over me, turning my body into Jell-O. We come together and exhale. He strokes my face, pushing my hair behind my ear.

"God, you are so beautiful when you come. You're my addiction." He doesn't break eye contact as his finger traces my face.

I giggle. My fingers run through his hair and my nails trail down the nape of his neck. I love how he's let his hair grow out a little during the off-season and goes days between shaves. Relaxed Matt is a whole new level, and I'm here for it.

"Are you going to keep your hair longer or go back to short when the season starts?"

"Depends. I like how it feels when you do this." He closes his eyes and relaxes into the moment. "Which do you prefer?"

I kiss his scruffy cheek. "Honestly, I like the laid-back look. Gives you that surfer vibe."

"Oh, so you like surfers, do you?" He tickles me in my ribs, making me laugh, and I try to move away. He pulls me in tighter and keeps me close.

"I like you." I more than like him, but I know that would freak him out. I'll state the obvious. For now.

"And I." Kiss to the temple. "Like." Kiss to the cheek. "You." Kiss to the lips. "And as much as I would like to keep you in bed and have my way with you all day, I know that isn't what you need."

I snuggle closer. "Oh, it's exactly what I need," I coo.

"No, you need to finish this house. I need you to be relaxed and enjoy the holidays. Especially New Year's. I've never looked forward to the start of a new year before. But this one? Yeah, pretty girl, this will be the start of the best year ever."

New Year? Yeah. It will be everything.

CHAPTER
TWENTY-SIX

MATT

———

This past week has been insane. Darcy and I work side by side to finish the last details of the house. We work, we kiss. When she's unsure of her choices, I inject her with courage and assurances, we kiss, and we work some more until we're exhausted. We still find the energy to make love every night before we fall asleep in each other's arms. It's more than sex. It's a connection unlike anything I've ever experienced.

I never thought I'd be that guy who falls into domestic bliss so quickly, but with Darcy, it feels natural. It's only been a week, but I barely remember what it's like to fall asleep alone. Even at the height of her stress, she relaxes at my touch. I can't get enough of her. How have I ignored this force of nature all of my life? Why have I withheld this level of happiness from myself? It's pretty fucking fantastic.

My phone buzzes. I reflexively smile and accept the FaceTime call.

"Hey, pretty girl."

"Hey." She bats her eyelashes at me. She's such a flirt now that we've crossed the line from friends to more.

"Do I sound like a sap if I say I miss you?"

She giggles. Her laughter is music to my soul. "A little, but you're my sap, so I'm okay with it. Where are you?"

"I'm just leaving the gym. I still have some Christmas shopping to do, and Mom called asking me to swing by. You going to be okay without me today?"

"I'll try." She lets out a long sigh. Darcy's full of drama today. I can't tell if it's real or not. She enjoys teasing me, and it keeps me guessing.

"I'll make it up to you tonight." I try to sound suggestive, and she gives me one of those smiles she saves just for me.

"Really? How do you plan on doing that, exactly?" Her voice is husky, and my dick twitches at the sound.

"Exactly? Hmmmm. Well, I'll start by making you dinner. How does that sound?"

Her bottom lip pokes out in an exaggerated pout. "Meh. That's okay, I guess."

"Oh, but I haven't told you about my special dessert."

"You and your sweet tooth." Her pout quickly turns into a grin, and her eyes sparkle.

"You know how much I love my sweets. You know my favorite sweet?"

"Of course I do." She gives me one of her famous eye rolls. "You love those salted caramel toffee cookies your mom makes."

Oh, I do love those cookies. Mom promised me some if I came over this afternoon to help her with a project in her she-shed. "I do like those, but they aren't my favorite sweet thing." I give her a wink and wonder what happened to my balls. Oh, yeah, I remember. This girl owns them.

She gives me a puzzled look. "You've loved those cookies since we were kids. What's moved into first place now?"

"You," I whisper. "I can't wait to taste your sweetness. You'll come on my tongue, and then I'll fuck you so hard, you'll see stars."

"Stars, huh?" Sammie says in the background. "Tell me more."

"Darcy! You need to let me know when you aren't alone." I blush a little, but can't decide if I'm embarrassed or proud. Maybe both?

Sammie's face appears behind Darcy, her chin resting on her shoulder. "Why, Matt Hartman, are you blushing?"

"Nope. Just jealous of you right now, Sammie. You're with my girl."

"Gah. Ya'll are too much. I'm out of here," she says as Darcy throws a pillow at her.

"Bye," I yell at her retreating figure.

"You owe me some cookies for that," she replies, her shoulders bouncing as she laughs.

"Well, I hope Mom made a double batch."

"Me too," Darcy says. Her giggle makes my heart clench.

———

"Hey, Mom. Oh damn, those smell good." I walk in and drop my keys on the table by the door, just like I've done for years. This is home, even if I don't live here anymore.

The tree is aglow with multi-colored lights, with presents underneath wrapped in colorful paper and bows. Christmas music is playing in the kitchen, and Mom is singing along. It screams holiday festive. I remember back to my school days when Cole and I would come home after practice, and my mom would greet us with a snack and a smile. Today's sounds and smells fill me with nostalgia, and I'm reminded of how unsettled I've felt since graduation. Until now.

I'm finally feeling settled, content. That empty feeling in my chest doesn't feel as gaping anymore. Coming into my childhood home confirms it. What's changed to lessen that feeling? Darcy Davidson. She's home. Belonging. Comfort. Love.

I shake my head to clear my thoughts. Love? Is this what love feels like? Maybe falling for Darcy was inevitable? When did I fall? I've fallen, right? I mean, I wouldn't pursue this thing we have if it was just a fling. Darcy is the kind of girl you love. And I do? I shake my head again to clear that train of thought. Not here. Not now.

Mom's in the kitchen, taking a tray of cookies out of the oven. She's in jeans and an oversized Christmas sweater with the phrase "Santa's Ho" on the front. She's singing and shaking her hips to a song. She hasn't changed a bit, making those memories seem like yesterday.

"Seriously? Santa's Ho? Mom," I groan and roll my eyes, as I kiss her on the top of her head.

"I know you don't like to think about it, but I've still got game," she teases.

"You're right. I don't want to think about it." I give a mock shiver and swipe a cookie off the cooling rack. "Mmmm, this is pure happiness."

"I know all your secrets, don't I?" She gives me a wink.

I cock my head to the side like a golden retriever. "What secrets?" Oh shit. Does she know about Darcy?

"The secret to getting you to come see me. Bake my boy's favorite cookies, and he comes running."

"You know, all you have to do is ask, and I'll always be here for you." Family is everything to me. Darcy was right when she said relationships are what I value most in this world. Family. Friends. People above money, career, things. Those are the values my mother instilled in me my entire life.

"Oh, I didn't mean that as a guilt trip, honey. I know you're busy and have a life of your own. Just when I got used to you being so far away, you're right around the corner, and I want to take advantage while I can." She sighs. "Besides, you're less likely to judge me than your father."

I raise an eyebrow and cock my head. "I'm afraid to ask," I mumble.

"I just need a little help with, um, something in my shed."

I groan and let my mind wander to what it could be. When I was in high school, Mom turned a small shed in the backyard into her private sanctuary. Men have man caves, and Mom has a she-shed. I haven't seen the inside in years. I have no idea what she needs in there, and it must be major if I'm breaching the inner sanctum.

The front porch of the shed has flower boxes and a small table and chairs. It's got a cute cottage feel. The interior space is probably twelve by twelve and is fully climate controlled. It's charming. As we step onto the front porch, my first thought was how Darcy would love it. I wonder how she would elevate the space. Damn, that girl has infiltrated all my thoughts.

"Penny for your thoughts?" Mom gives me her interrogation smile.

"Hmmm, what?"

"You spaced out a bit. Where'd you go?"

I can't lie to my mom. I never did and can't start now. "Was just thinking about Darcy and what she would think of your shed."

"Darcy, huh? What's going on there?"

Deflect. That's the strategy I need to take. I never lie, but that doesn't mean I must respond. "What did you need help with out here?"

I step inside and take in the cozy space, complete with a writing desk, loveseat, and an easel in the corner. Propped up around the walls are various paintings of flowers and Charleston landmarks.

"I didn't know you were painting again." I wander in further and squat down to see the canvases spread along one wall. "Hey, these are good." I pick up one of The Wreck with the shrimp boats coming down Shem Creek. I smile. The people are abstract, without distinct features, but I don't miss the splash of red shoes in the mostly pastel painting. Darcy.

"That's a new smile," Mom says in a sing-song tone. "I know you love the food there, but I didn't think it would make you smile like that."

Her teasing makes me uncomfortable, and I chuckle. I swear this woman is a witch or something. She knows.

"What?" I ask innocently.

"Okay." She shrugs her shoulders, but I know better. It's not dropped. She's just changing tactics. "I need help to find studs."

"Excuse me?!" Now I know why she didn't ask Dad for help.

She reaches into a half-opened box on the loveseat and pulls out a shiny brass pole.

"I need to find the studs in the ceiling for my pole."

I double over, laughing. My mom wants to install a stripper pole in her she-shed. I laugh so hard I start coughing. Mom isn't laughing. She has her hands on her hips, and I'm immediately transported back to when I was a small child, the recipient of my mother's disapproving glare.

"And I thought your father would be more judgmental." She gives me a tsk, turns around and mumbles something about doing it herself.

"I'm sorry." I get my laughter under control and wrap my arms around my mom from behind. "Don't be mad. It was just a bit of a shock. I mean, I didn't know the she-shed was being converted to a red room."

"Red room?" Awareness slowly dawns, and my mom joins in the laughter. "Hardly. I've heard it's a great workout and thought it looked fun."

"Well, let's get it installed properly. I can't have you getting hurt. That would be hard to explain to Dad." I grab the drill and the ladder and figure out the best place for the stripper pole. I consider calling Jay to help, but think better of it. It gives me an idea about possibly having him build Mom a guest house to replace this small space, and she can use it as her studio. That might be a great Mother's Day gift. I smile at my brilliance.

"So, you never answered my question about Darcy," Mom says. She's trying to be casual, but she's failing.

"I should've known better," I mumble.

"What's that?" Her feigned innocence isn't fooling me.

"You missed your calling. You should work for the FBI or something." I go back to drilling the screws into the floor and act like I can't hear her. Unfortunately, pole installation doesn't take very long.

"So? What's going on with Darcy?"

"That's a new tactic, just going straight in."

I look up at Mom, and she has her arms crossed, squeezing Mrs. Claus's face into a strange shape. I know this look. It's the "I can do this all day" look. I've seen it lots of times over the years.

"Just figured the sooner we put it out there, the sooner you can get back to the cookies."

"True." I exhale and think about what to tell Mom.

"I like her."

"Of course you do. She's an angel. But?"

"But what? I like her a lot. She's special, and I'm lucky she even gives me the time of day."

"Why wouldn't she? She's had a crush on you since middle school."

"What? She barely spoke to me."

"That's how unrequited crushes go, honey. But it doesn't sound unrequited anymore, is it?" She quirks her eyebrow at me.

Has Darcy liked me for years? Why did I never notice? The answer is simple. Cole. I wasn't willing to risk it and didn't even think it could be possible. So, what's changed?

"No, but still, we're keeping it private until we figure out what this is. Cole won't be happy, and I don't know if I can handle that. It's hard enough with him in another city, but if we weren't friends anymore," I pause and shake my head, trying to clear that thought. "I don't know."

She reaches out and puts her hand on my shoulder. "I think Cole wants you both to be happy. Don't you? Don't you think he wants you both to find love? And if it's with each other, well then..." She shrugs.

She's just reinforcing the inevitable conversation I need to have with Cole. But what if? Ugh.

"Yeah, maybe." She's much more optimistic than me. Then again, it's not her friendship on the line. "Enough of this. Let's see how this pole works." I take a tug on it to make sure it's secure and climb up it and slide down like a firefighter. If it can hold me, it'll be safe for her.

"Well, if baseball doesn't work out, you can try pole dancing," she teases.

"And those are words I never wanted to hear from my mom." I throw my arm around her shoulder and lead her out of the room. "Come on. I promised to bring cookies to my girl."

Mom grins like the Cheshire cat and leans into me as we walk back into the house.

There. I said it. My girl. Everyone happy? Everyone that knows that is.

CHAPTER
TWENTY-SEVEN

DARCY

———

Cole and Ashleigh are coming down Christmas afternoon after spending Christmas Eve in Charlotte with Ashleigh's family. It's strange not having Cole home for the holidays. I suppose that's what happens when you become part of a pair. You share holidays too.

Mom and I stayed up late watching Hallmark Christmas movies until we fell asleep filled with hot chocolate, peppermint pretzels, and holiday love.

Honestly, I'm not mad about them coming late because it lets me surprise Matt this morning at his beach house. I smile when I see a surfer in the water, knowing Matt is in his happy place. I walk down between the dunes, spread out a towel, plop on the sand, and watch him paddle out over the waves. They aren't huge, but they're bigger than I've seen them lately. I bet he's thrilled with the conditions today.

I tuck my knees up into my sweater dress and rest my chin on them while I enjoy the peace of the ocean. This stretch of the beach is empty except for me and a few seagulls cruising above. Closing my eyes, the sun warms my face and I meditate on the sound of the waves. I understand why Matt finds solace here.

A few drops of water fall on my head, and I'm jerked out of my peaceful space. My frown slowly becomes a smile as my surfer guy squats down in front of me with a goofy grin.

"Merry Christmas, pretty girl." He kisses me on the tip of my nose. "Did Santa leave you on the beach for me? Because if he did, I must've been a very, very good boy this year." His smile reaches his eyes, and there's a twinkle of mischief there.

I wrap my arms around his neck, and my fingers play with the zipper pull of his wet suit. I kiss him on the nose since that seems to be our holiday greeting and give him a wink. "Well, you've been pretty good this year, slugger. I'm not complaining."

"Me either." He puts my face between his palms and gives me a proper kiss.

Water from his hair drips on my face, and I pull away. I stand up and brush the sand off. "You're cold and wet and in need of a shower."

Matt grabs his surfboard and tucks it under one arm while he reaches for my hand with the other. "Care to join me?" He wiggles his eyebrows at me, trying to be suggestive.

"Tempting, but no." I did my hair and makeup today, knowing we'd take pictures when Cole and Ashleigh arrive in a few hours.

He pushes his bottom lip out to pout, and I push him away with a laugh.

"Shower, then I'll give you your present."

"Well, a shower with me sounds like a wonderful gift."

"Nope, not happening. Just pretend to be excited about your actual gift." I struggled with what to get Matt for Christmas. I wasn't sure if we were exchanging gifts, but when I saw the most gorgeous green bedspread, I needed to get it for him.

While Matt takes a shower, I grab his gift and put it on his bed. I know he's just renting, but his house has nothing that says

Matt or home. The bedspread pops against the stark white walls, and the pillow shams bring the room to life. I take the few beachy decor items and put them in the closet. His walk-in is pretty empty compared to mine, but I get inspired when I see his jersey.

Looking at the clock, I calculate how long until we need to head to my house and figure I can give him another present this morning.

When Matt opens the bathroom door, steam escapes, and he comes out with a towel wrapped around his waist, looking like he just stepped out of a *GQ* photo shoot. The water droplets roll down his abs, and I want to lick them all off. Suddenly parched, that water is the nectar of life. He's rubbing a towel over his hair, and when he looks up, his smile lights up the room.

"You like?" I'm lying on his new bedspread, wearing nothing but his unbuttoned jersey. I rub the plush fabric of the bedspread in front of me, inviting him over.

"I like." He swallows, and his lust-filled eyes take me in from head to toe.

"Isn't it gorgeous?"

"Absolutely." He stalks toward me, closing the gap between us.

"Feel it," I encourage.

"Oh, I intend to." He kneels next to the bed and reaches out, letting the back of his fingers trace from my collarbone between my breasts, where the jersey gaps open. The light touch is sensual, sending goose bumps down my arms.

"You're incredible, Darcy Davidson," he whispers. "I'm a lucky bastard that you picked me."

"Oh, Matt, don't you know?" I say breathy. "It's always been you."

"Yeah, I heard a rumor you've had a crush on me for years. Is that true?" His smirk lets me know he's amused.

I roll my eyes and try not to die of embarrassment. "True."

"I didn't know." He sounds sincere and regretful.

"I'm just glad you see me now."

His eyes hood, and he growls, "Oh, pretty girl, I see you."

———

"You like the bedspread?"

He chuckles. I'm not sure he noticed the bedspread, but we christened it with a memory that he can hold on to when he's wrapped in it at night.

"It's perfect. But you in my jersey? I think it should be your uniform from now on." His fingers play with the buttons, a contented smile on his face.

"Yeah, not sure that would be a good idea in public." I love the look he's giving me. Total adoration.

"You may be right," he muses. "I wouldn't be able to keep my hands off you." His lips gently brush mine as he pulls me up.

"Come on, let's get ready. While freshly fucked is my favorite look on you, I don't think Cole or your mom will appreciate it quite as much."

"Always the responsible one, Matt Hartman."

We get dressed, and I notice a painting on the dresser. How did I miss it earlier? Oh, it's because I had sex on the brain and was in a hurry before Matt got out of the shower.

I hold the painting and recognize the building. "It's The Wreck." I smile at the warmth this picture evokes. It's dinner rush at sunset, the shrimp boats coming in, people everywhere, and it's the perfect piece for his room.

"It is. Mom painted it."

"She did? I knew she painted, but this is incredible."

"Yeah, I saw it and asked her if I could buy it from her. I wanted to be her first sale. Her art is amazing, but she hides it in her studio."

"I wonder if she'll let me do something with it?" I'm no art expert, but I like the style and feel.

"You can ask her, I guess. You know what I love about it so much?"

"What?"

"You're in it."

The watercolors blend the features of the people, so I guess he can imagine me there. I spent many of my high school and college years at The Wreck, so it tracks.

"If you say so."

He pulls me back to his chest and reaches to point at a figure. His low voice rumbles in his chest as he whispers in my ear. "Right here, see?"

I look at where he's pointing and laugh. It is me. It's the only spot of red in the entire picture, and it's my shoes.

"Who knew I'd be art?"

"Oh, pretty girl, everything about you is art. Everything."

There's that word again. Everything.

CHAPTER
TWENTY-EIGHT

DARCY

———

I leave Matt's and head back home to help Mom prepare our late lunch. Matt went to his house for family time and will come over with his parents. Sammie's family will also join us, just like every year. Spending Christmas afternoon as a big, blended family has been our tradition since we were kids. We rotate host houses, and this year the Davidsons are hosting.

Cole and Ashleigh roll in right before lunch, and the Christmas greetings go around the room. Everyone is feeling festive, and the love in the room is intoxicating. Jay came with Sammie, and greetings happen again. I love the new faces we have this year. It feels right. Our blended family is growing and changing with the new members.

After eating a huge southern meal full of ham, shrimp and grits, and mac and cheese, that is to die for, we start with a fun game of Dirty Santa. As we've gotten older, the game has become more cutthroat and, honestly, dirtier. It's the highlight of the day.

"Seriously," Jay whines. "Who brought the snuggie?"

"Oh, there it is!" Cole yells. "This is the, what, twelfth appearance of the Reaper snuggie?"

"Is it the same one?" Ashleigh asks.

"Yup," Matt replies. "It's awesome and mint in box. I bought it first and really wanted it, but it went home with who?" He looks around the room.

Sammie's dad raises his hand, looking guilty. "Matt wanted it so bad, I had to throw it back in the mix the next year. Have you ever taken it home, Matt?"

"Nope. But not for lack of trying." His pout is adorable. I'd love to tease him more, but he's across the room. It's difficult to restrain my comments after being so connected in private.

"I'll let Dad's marketing team know they're popular, and maybe we'll get them back to market. Meanwhile, I know what I'm getting Matt for Christmas next year. And since I'm the last pick, I'm stealing the snuggie. Sorry, Jay." Ashleigh gives Matt a wink, and I'm a little jealous she can show him affection, even in a friendly way.

I'm sitting across the room between Mom and Sammie, trying not to look at Matt. It's like Cole, Matt, and Ashleigh are on one team, and I've got Sammie and Jay. Not that I'm complaining, but I wish there weren't any teams here at all.

Jay opens the last gift, and instead of stealing, the game ends.

"And that concludes the end of the family portion of the evening," Matt's mom, Patti, says.

"By the way, Mrs. Hartman, I adore your painting of The Wreck. It's amazing. I'd love to see some of your other works."

"Thank you, Darcy. When did you see it? I just gave it to Matt last night."

Matt glares at his mother as Cole gives me a quizzical look.

"I sent her a picture of it," Matt says quickly. "I needed some advice on where to hang it."

My cheeks heat at the nearly blown cover. I'm also saddened

that we're hiding something so beautiful. But the hiding? That's my decision.

Matt's mom smiles and winks at me. "You're welcome anytime. I'm not sure they're that good, but it's something I enjoy."

"Why don't I get to see them?" Coach Hartman asks.

"And on that note, we'll take our leave. Mandy, anything I can help you with?" Mrs. Hartman asks my mom.

"No, I'm good. I'm ready to crash and leave the kids on their own. I'm glad we could do this again. They're all grown up," Mom says as she looks around the room. "Before we know it, we'll have grand-babies."

Cole and Matt roll their eyes. One step at a time, Mom.

All the parents say goodnight and give us all hugs. A single mom may have raised me, but I have the Chapins and Hartmans as surrogate parents too. Just thinking about all the love in the room warms my heart.

"I get to play Santa," Cole declares.

"Why do you get to do it?" Sammie whines. "You did it last year."

"Yeah, we let him do it because he was all pouty last year," I tease. Ashleigh pokes out her bottom lip, mocking him. He kisses her quickly and semi-tackles Sammie as they both rush to the tree. Jay flinches, and I reach over to hold him back.

"She's got this," I tell him. "Just watch."

In a flash, Sammie has Cole flattened to the ground, face down, his arm twisted behind his back, and is tickling him in the ribs.

"Mercy! Mercy!" Cole calls out as he laughs uncontrollably.

Sammie gets up and brushes her hands together. "And that, ladies and gentlemen, is how it's done." She knows all of Cole's tickle spots. We both do. That's always his weakness with us. Well, tickling and tears.

She makes the rounds for high fives and takes her place by the tree.

Ashleigh looks at Jay and gives him a smile and a shrug. It might take a little explaining for the newbies to figure out our lifetime of inside stories.

"Sweetheart, did you see that?" Cole says to Ashleigh.

"I did, trouble. Come here, and I'll make it better." He makes his way back to his fiancé, and she kisses him and then continues the tickle-fest Sammie started. I like her more every time we're together.

My heart swells with love for them and their bliss. I wonder if Matt and I will ever be that openly affectionate. His eyes meet mine, and he gives me a slight smile and a wink. Is he thinking the same thing?

"Okay," I call out. "Let's get started. Sammie, grab the two boxes wrapped in baseball paper."

She finds the boxes, one in Reapers paper and one in Liberties paper, and hands them to Cole and Matt. We're both excited for the guys to open them.

They rip the paper off and are silent for a second while they realize what they have in their hands.

"No way," Matt whispers.

"How?" Cole asks.

Pride fills my chest that I rendered them both speechless. "I found this website that makes custom bobbleheads. A friend helped with the artwork, but I thought they turned out alright."

"These are amazing," Ashleigh says.

"Someday when you're both kicking ass in the majors, they may make you a bobblehead, but I couldn't wait. I got a pair for you, Mom, and the Hartmans."

Cole comes over to me and hugs me, practically taking the air out of my lungs. "Thank you, Darce. I love it."

Matt gets up to hug me too, and it's awkward. "Thanks, Darce. It's perfect."

I bite my bottom lip to keep myself from reaching out and kissing him. He's so close, his scent invades my space, and I want to snuggle up with him.

Everyone else exchanges gifts, and there's one present left under the tree. Sammie grabs it and looks at the tag. "This one's for you, Darcy. It doesn't say who it's from."

It's beautifully wrapped in white paper with a big orange ribbon holding it together. "I hate to open it. It's so beautiful." Shaking the box tells me there's something of substance inside. I pull off the ribbon and open the box to find an orange bound portfolio with the words "Darcy Davidson Designs" embossed in forest green on the cover.

I open the book and find incredible, professional photos of Chance's house. The lighting and angles are perfect and the spaces look amazing. The pictures are gorgeous and totally magazine worthy. Every room is documented with before and after pictures. The before pictures are from the first walkthrough and are part of the project management spreadsheet. It highlights every little detail, from the up-cycled items to the locally sourced artwork. It's all in there. There's even a narrative that includes Chance's vision and his client testimonial about my professional work ethic and personal touch.

Tears fill my eyes, and the pictures blur as I'm overwhelmed by the gift. It's lavish and extremely generous. I note the photographer's watermark and remember seeing her pictures in a design magazine. Holy shit. These are very professional pictures. This had to cost a fortune.

"How?" I whisper, looking at Matt. He gives me a slight smile and doesn't break eye contact.

Jay is sitting next to me and lets out a low whistle. "Damn, girl, that's nice."

"What is it, Darce?" Cole asks, getting up to come closer.

"It's a portfolio of her project," Jay says. "A very professional portfolio, by the looks of it."

Everyone crowds around to look at the pictures. Everyone except Matt. He sits across the room after giving me the most thoughtful and extravagant gift I've ever received. As everyone clambers to flip through the pictures, he quietly gets up and moves into the kitchen.

"Girl, this place is amazing," Ashleigh says. "OMG, the pool area is incredible. Is that a pizza oven?"

"Sure is," Jay says proudly. "She thought of everything."

"Everything," I whisper to myself.

CHAPTER
TWENTY-NINE

DARCY

———

Waking up, I stretch my body like a cat in the sun. I'm sore in places that have never been sore before. I'd like to say it's from the fabulous sex I had last night, but that's a different kind of workout.

Now that Chance's house is complete, and the party is in two days, Matt decided I needed a mini staycation. We've been staying at his place, and he's been spoiling me rotten. Sleeping in. Rom-coms. Spa day with a facial and mani-pedi. He gave me the massage himself, something about not wanting someone else's hands on me. Jealous much? But deep down, I loved the feeling of protectiveness from him.

This gift of pampering means more to me than he'll ever know. I'm not used to being the girl that's cared for by someone else, and, honestly, I could get used to it. Especially when it's Matt.

Yesterday, like most days, he started his morning surfing. So instead of watching him from the comfort of the deck with a hot coffee in my hands, I stupidly asked to go with him. I would like to blame my colossal failure on the wetsuit that didn't fit, but I can't. Matt had the patience of a saint and seemed to enjoy being the teacher, but unfortunately, I didn't get a passing grade. The only time I could stand on the board for over six seconds was when he showed me how to stand while we were still on the beach. If there was a song to my surfing soundtrack, "Wipeout" would have the most plays.

Failure aside, it was fun. I loved the twinkle in Matt's eyes as I panicked because I thought I saw a shark when a dolphin popped up beside me. His genuine laugh warmed my heart so much that I barely noticed the cold water. Unfortunately, my muscles remind me of that fun this morning. Now I know the secret to his incredible abs.

I groan and rub at my side, working out the ache there. My arm reaches over to snuggle with Matt, and his side is empty, his spot cold. I throw myself back on the pillow and close my eyes. He's probably out surfing, making it look easy. I know the truth now. It's not easy.

I start to get up when Taylor Swift's song about turning twenty-two blares through the house, and it hits me. Matt enters the bedroom with a silly party hat on his head, a tray full of my favorite sugary breakfast foods, and a mug that probably has more caramel than coffee in it. An orange Gerber Daisy decorates the tray, and I smile at the sight of my favorite flower. He remembered.

"Happy Birthday, pretty girl!" He sits the tray on the nightstand and leans down to give me a quick kiss. "How does it feel to be twenty-two?"

"I'm sore. I'm old and don't recover easily." He laughs, and I grab a fistful of his shirt and pull him down for a more substantial kiss, my favorite way to start the day. He pulls back with a grin and a twinkle in his eye.

"Nope, breakfast first, while it's still warm." He turns down the music, but T. Swift still plays in the background. He sets the tray across my lap and crawls into bed to snuggle beside me. Wrapping his arm around my shoulder and absently playing with my hair, I contently sip the gourmet coffee. Yum!

I moan with approval, and his smile grows. "I swear, that sound is going to be the death of me," he mumbles.

"This is so delish and thoughtful. You didn't have to go to all this trouble, but I'm glad you did." I feed him a perfect bite of waffle, whipped cream, and strawberry dipped in syrup.

"I enjoy doing things for you. You give so much of yourself to others. It's my job to give to you." He caresses my face, and I lean into his warm palm. He gives me a light peck and leans back against the headboard.

"You don't have to do that. I'm pretty self-sufficient, you know." The song switches to "Everything Has Changed," and as it plays, I think this song is perfect for this moment. His eyes feel like coming home.

He turns back toward me, his hand cradling my face. "I know you are. But you don't have to be." His callused finger absently rubs the faint scar above my eyebrow.

He kisses me, and he tastes like sugary goodness. I try to roll on top of him but am pinned under the breakfast tray. I roll back to my spot and groan.

He laughs. "Eat up, pretty girl. You're gonna need your strength." He gives me another quick kiss and settles back with his arm around my shoulders, content to let me enjoy my breakfast.

I finish, feeding Matt every other bite. He reaches for my coffee, and I smack his hand. "No, sir. I'll share my food, but never my coffee. Got it?" I give him my best attempt at a menacing scowl.

He laughs. "Got it. My apologies." He reaches over and hands me the card under the flower. "I wasn't sure what to get you for your birthday, and I almost got you shoes, but I haven't really inspected the shoe inventory, and that was intimidating. So, I went with something I hope is as good as shoes."

"You didn't have to get me anything, but thank you."

"You haven't even opened it yet. Why are you saying thank you?"

"Because you've given me so much already. And if your first thought was shoes, then, well, that tells me this is a thoughtful gift. So, thank you."

He gets up, puts the tray on the nightstand, and I open his card. This is the first card he's ever gotten me. Will it be sappy? Generic? I mean, do guys pay attention to cards? The fact he got me one at all is surprising. I open the card, read it, and double over, laughing. He went with a spot-on funny card. It's perfect! My muscles remind me of their workout yesterday, and I grimace.

"You okay?"

"Yeah, I know how you get those washboard abs. Just a little sore from yesterday."

"Well, let me give you your present, and maybe we can do a little stretching this morning to work out the kinks."

"Kinks, huh?" I arch one eyebrow at him. "You have any?"

"Just making you happy, pretty girl. Your smile is my kink."

"I swear, you're so swoony, I can barely stand it."

"Swoony, huh?" He laughs. "In that case, let me give you my gift." He hands me two envelopes, each with a big red number one and two.

I open the first envelope, and there are plane tickets for Miami in January. I'm curious. "Miami?"

"Yeah, it's just for a weekend, but it's before school starts back for you, and I thought we could have a little getaway."

"It's perfect." I move to thank him properly and pull him towards me. We fall back, and I quickly get him out of his clothes so I can stretch out my sore muscles. I like that euphemism.

When we break our kiss, both gasping for air, he covers my face with kisses, starting above my eye and working down my jaw, down my neck, to my breasts, where he stops and gives them his focused attention. He licks and nips, and I barely notice his hands massaging my sore side. Everything feels so good. Matt's mouth on my skin heats me, and I rub my legs together, aching for some attention there.

Matt reads the signs and works his way down. His finger sweeps across my folds, teasing me.

"You're so wet, pretty girl. I love that your body does that for me." His sexy voice is deep, seductive. I melt from the inside when he talks like this. I'd do anything he asks when he uses his bedroom voice. It's such a turn on.

He slips one finger in, stretching me, then slips in a second, filling me and curving it, and then, yes.

"There, yes. Oh, that feels so good," I whisper.

He kisses down my stomach, and his tongue laps at that bundle of nerves, sending me over the edge. My walls pulse, and I come on his hand. His hands are magical.

I can feel his hardness against my leg, and I want to make him feel good, too.

I reach for him, wanting him to fill me. He gently takes my hand and pulls it away from my objective.

"Nope, not yet, pretty girl. That was for the first envelope." He gives me a wicked grin, like he enjoys withholding what I want.

I attempt to pout, but I'm too sated to do it properly. He reaches over and pulls the other envelope off the floor where it fell.

"Open it," he orders.

"Wow, you sure are bossy, and on my birthday, too." I smile and tease him.

I open the second envelope and look at the tickets. Everything stops. I squeal, wrap my arms around him, and squeeze him with all my might.

"Happy birthday, pretty girl," he chokes out because I'm probably cutting off his air from squeezing his neck so tight.

"OMG, Matt! How?" I'm bouncing up and down on my knees.

"Well, I might know a guy who knows a guy."

"But how?" I look at the tickets again, reading the details. "Are these really backstage passes?" I can't contain my excitement.

"Yep, and front-row tickets for Taylor Swift's biggest fan. She's kicking off her tour in Miami, and the date was perfect."

"Thank you, thank you, thank you," I say between kisses. "Let me say thank you properly," I say against his lips. I kiss up his jaw, nibble on his ear, and whisper everything I'm going to do to him. I lightly run my nails down his chest, admiring those abs, running my tongue along the ridges. He squirms, and I'm thrilled at what my touch can do to him. Two can play at this game.

My hand grazes along his shaft as I lap at the pre cum at his tip.

"Baby, you don't have to," he starts. I take him in as much as possible and work him with my hand and tongue. He groans, and I smile.

"Is this okay?" I ask innocently.

His hand gently fists in my hair, guiding me.

"Pretty girl, you have a perfect mouth. So perfect, but I need to be inside you when I come."

He pulls me up, and I straddle his lap. "Well, this is still my birthday, and my thank you, so settle down, slugger, and let me work." I impale myself with his cock, riding him.

After the initial shock wears off, he tries to stop me. "Condom," he growls out.

"I'm on birth control," I say. "Relax, and let me say thank you, please."

Matt doesn't let me do all the work, but I enjoy trying. He gives me two more orgasms before he comes. We both collapse into the pillows, and he pulls me into him, so I rest my head on his chest.

We're quiet, resting in the contentment we find in each other.

His hand plays with my hair, and his finger lazily brushes back and forth over my scar.

"Why do you do that?"

"Do what?"

"Rub my scar, kiss my scar. Is it that noticeable?" I'm suddenly self-conscious about it. Maybe it's more prominent than I thought.

"I'm sorry." He says this with force and conviction. I'm taken aback by his shift in tone. His pained eyes look into mine. "It was one of the scariest days of my life."

"It was?"

"Yeah, when I hit that line drive, and it went foul and hit you, I don't think I've ever run so fast in all my life. It knocked you out cold. I was hysterically yelling for someone to call 911. When the ambulance came, I was going with you, consequences be damned. Cole, Dad, and your mom insisted I stay at the game, but they couldn't get me out of the ambulance. Dad was so mad, but I didn't care. I don't think I breathed until you opened your eyes at the hospital."

"I was fine, just a few stitches." I shrug, reaching up to touch the spot.

"And a concussion. Terrifying." He shudders.

"I'm fine."

"Yeah, I know. But you were still in middle school, and I was trying so hard to show the others why I made the varsity baseball team as a freshman." He lets out a breath like he's reliving the memory. "I was more focused on the force of the hit, not the angle. It went straight at you. And you were doing something on your phone. You didn't even see it coming."

"It wasn't your fault. Foul balls happen." I didn't know he remembered that day, especially in such detail.

"Dad benched me three games for leaving. Cole kept telling me you were fine. Your mom was with you, but I just couldn't keep playing a game without being able to say sorry. You probably don't even remember that day, do you?"

"I do." I give him a smile that conveys all of my feelings. "I woke up with a headache, and you were right beside me in your uniform, holding my hand."

Of course, I remember that day. How could I not remember the most monumental day in my life? It was the day I fell in love with Matt Hartman.

CHAPTER
THIRTY

MATT

———

Darcy, Jay, Sammie, and I are ready to greet Chance when he gets to his house before the big New Year's Eve party. The caterers and bartenders will be here after lunch to set up, and he expects his guests to arrive later this evening.

But this moment is all about Darcy and Jay showcasing their hard work for their client, Chance Fuller. I tamp down my jealousy as Chance wraps her in a hug that lifts her feet off the ground when he greets her in the driveway.

"Darcy, just from the street view, it looks like a different house," Chance says. "You did good, beautiful."

"You haven't even seen the best part," she says as she swats at him.

He puts her down, and my heart beats steady again. I know Chance sees my girl as a little sister, but I thought of her that way not too long ago too.

After Chance greets all of us, Darcy takes charge of the tour.

"I'm glad you like the color change. I can't take credit for the landscaping, but Jay's friend did a great job finding the right plants to complement the feel we're going for. Remember what you asked for?"

"I think I wanted a house that would put Tripp's Mexico house to shame," Chance says.

"You did," Darcy confirms. "You also wanted a place that felt comfortable and fun. Dare I say hygge with a touch of whimsical? You wanted the feel to be luxurious, but not so posh people can't relax. You wanted a retreat for your family. It needed to be livable and still have a resort feel."

"And is that what I have? Did I get hygge?" Chance asks. He cocks his head and challenges her for an answer.

"You tell me when we're done. And we'll save the best part for last, which is outside." Chance quirks an eyebrow at her. "Let's start inside."

"After you, beautiful," he says, following my girl. Sammie and I are like the proud parents, ready to trail behind, taking videos and pictures to document the reveal.

In every room, Chance notices and comments on the details and feel of the space. He correctly identifies the rooms inspired by each of his friends and loves the names she gave each suite. As they go room to room, Jay interjects with budget information and gives Chance information on how Darcy used a lot of recycled products and up-cycled items, saving money and the planet.

When she shows him the outdoor space, he's blown away. His laughter fills the air as he jumps up and down like a kid at Christmas. Darcy did it. She listened, connected, and exceeded her client's expectations. Chance isn't faking his reaction. It's honest, and he loves the house. I'm so fucking proud of my girl. Her talent is off the charts. As her radiant smile beams at Chance, I think she might finally believe me.

"Outside Chance? I absolutely love it!" He grabs Darcy into his fifth hug since the tour began. Not like I'm counting. He laughs at the large picture of him in the flamingo float from Mexico and looks tempted to jump in the same float now, despite the December temperatures. Jay takes a few minutes to show him the tech setup with the video doorbell, sound system, and all the features of the enormous outdoor TV.

I pull Darcy into the outdoor shower stall and kiss her while Jay shows off the tech setup.

"What's that for?" she asks.

"I'm so damn proud of you, pretty girl."

"Thanks. I'm glad he likes it. I can exhale now and enjoy the party tonight." Her shoulders visibly relax, an enormous weight lifted off her shoulders.

"You deserve every bit of joy tonight. You. Are. Amazing." I kiss her forehead, the tip of her nose, and her luscious lips.

"Stop, you're going to make me blush." She playfully pushes at my chest, and I capture her hands and hold them to my heart.

"And the blush of your cheeks is my second favorite color, remember? Wonder what that says about me now?" The color of her face, flushed with pleasure and satisfaction after an orgasm, is my favorite color now.

I give her another quick kiss and let her get back to Chance.

When the tour is over, we crash upstairs to get out of the way of the caterers. Jay and Sammie go for a walk on the beach, leaving Chance, Darcy, and me to relax before the party.

"Well, Darcy, you checked all the boxes and then some. The creativity and details are extraordinary. You've made this house cozy and inviting, exactly what I wanted. And I may greet all my guests from this massage chair. It's incredible," Chance says.

"You can thank Matt for the chair. He helped pick out a lot of the furniture," she says. "He liked these so much we got them for both levels. I hope it wasn't too much?" We're sitting on the couch, cuddling under a blanket. She squeezes my hand.

"Not too much at all. I think I want one for my place in Raleigh. Matt, thanks for stepping up and being there for Darcy. I know it may have been more work than a ballplayer like you is used to, but you did it." Chance likes to bust my balls for playing baseball, but I know better to engage him when I've gotten more from this project than he can imagine.

"I should thank you for the assist," I tell him sincerely. I give Darcy a little kiss on the temple.

"So, are you two…"

I look at Darcy, and we both smile at each other.

"It's complicated," she says.

"How so?" Chance asks.

"Well?" She bites her lip and plays with the fringe on the blanket. "We haven't really gone public."

"Why not?" Chance sure asks a lot of questions. A look of understanding finally hits him. "Cole doesn't know, does he?"

We both shake our heads no.

"I'm going to head down and check on the setup," Darcy says. "Can I get you guys anything?"

"All good," we both say.

When Darcy leaves, Chance turns off his massage chair and looks at me. "Well, tonight's a party. And fair warning, I'll be keeping Darcy by my side because I need to share her talents with the world. I'm doing it for her. And you. I'm fond of that girl in all the non-romantic kinds of ways and want to help her soar. Just so you know, we're both team Darcy."

"Why are you telling me this?"

"Because you young baseball boys seem to jump to the wrong conclusions when it comes to your girls. I think of Darcy like Ash. Incredible, beautiful, talented, smart, and fucking adorable. But like in a kid sister kind of protective way. So, I'm not making a move, and I won't allow anyone else to either. I've got her. But if you hurt her, just know I get most of my minutes in the penalty box for fighting. I'm team Darcy all the way. Got it?"

When he puts it that way, it's hard to be jealous of Chance. He's a protector like me. He cares for his people, and I'm strangely comforted that Darcy is one of his people now. He's also helping me tonight by keeping her close in case anyone else has the wrong idea and wants to hit on her.

"I'm catching what you're throwing. Doesn't mean I won't be watching out for her, too, just so you know."

"I wouldn't doubt it. Listen, I'm not going to tell you what to do, but if you want to tell him, Jules and I have your back. We'll keep you safe, Matty boy."

I'm a little surprised after the Team Darcy talk. "I thought you'd be team Cole, since he's practically a Decker now."

"Nah, we're Team True Love, all the way." I can't miss how Chance talks in the collective 'we' regarding him and Julian.

Team True Love? I scoff at this label. I love her, but I haven't told her because we're complicated, as she so eloquently put it. Does Chance think this is me and Darcy?

"I'm not sure what to do. I want to tell him, but I'm not sure how he's going to react. He's got a bit of a temper."

"Yeah, he's got a bit of a protective streak. I like that about him, especially with Ash. But listen, this isn't our first rodeo. Team True Love is just that. We're all about a happily ever after. Sometimes, you need someone to believe in your love, even when you can't see it yourself. You need someone to walk beside you during the process. Just know we've got you. Cole may have a temper, but deep down, he's a softie."

I don't know what the hell he's talking about. Team True Love? Who's ever heard of a hockey player being a matchmaker? But even with their support, can they save a friendship? Because that's what's at risk. I've known him longer than anyone and I'm pretty confident how he'll react. But maybe they see something I don't. Like not seeing the forest through the trees kind of thing. I can only hope.

"I can't believe that sap writes love songs now."

"You talking about me, brother?" Cole says as he steps into the room.

I freeze, wondering how much he heard of our conversation.

Chance and I both greet him with a half hug.

"Where's Ash?" Chance asks.

"Downstairs with Darcy. This place is amazing," Cole says, eyeing the massage chairs.

"That's one talented sister you've got there," I say.

"Damn straight. She's amazing. Thanks for being by her side through this. She was really stressed and doubting herself. I'm glad you could be there for her during this vulnerable time." Cole is thanking me for being a surrogate brother.

"I'm glad I was there for her," I say quietly.

Chance is behind Cole, giving me a WTF look and making enormous eyes and arm gestures. I should tell him. But he just described her as being vulnerable. Will he think I took advantage of her? Did I? I give a slight shake of my head to Chance.

"Drink?" Chance offers. We all congregate around the bar in the corner while Chance pulls beers out of the cooler. I wonder if this will be a manned bar tonight?

"How many bars did she put in this place?" Cole asks.

"Three, I think," Chance replies. "She didn't want anyone too far from supplies. And the outdoor kitchen is brilliant. It's like she knows how we like to eat or something."

"She's grown up around baseball players her whole life. She gets it," Cole says. "I'm sure someday she'll be glad to settle down with a regular guy who eats normal meals and doesn't live like a nomad."

"You think that's what she wants?" I ask. Yes, that life would be better for her. The reality is, I'm not sure how much longer I'll be in Charleston. I could get traded at any time, and we play over 160 games a year. That isn't the foundation for a new relationship. Sure, Leigh and Cole are doing it, but she's been raised around Major League Baseball all her life. She's used to it. I think about the picture of The Wreck and Darce being at home there. Home is important to her. She didn't even leave town to go to college. I turn that thought over in my mind, and a seed of doubt grows. Am I what's best for Darcy?

"Probably," Cole says, taking a long pull of his beer. "It's gotta be why she stayed with Ryan for so long. He represented that stability she's seeking."

"Playing Dr. Phil again," Julian says as he enters the room. "You and that damn psychology degree." He laughs as he embraces Chance and gives me and Cole a smile and a head nod. "Who are we talking about?"

"Darcy," Chance says, quirking an eyebrow at Julian.

"Ohhhh," Julian says. "What do YOU think she wants, Matt?" Shit. Team True Love is ganging up on me.

I clear my throat and wish I had something stronger than this beer in my hand. I finish it while I think about how I want to respond. "I think, I, um, think, she wants to be happy and have the freedom to be uniquely Darcy. She's so special. She deserves to be loved fiercely because that's the way she loves. I wouldn't think logistics would matter to her, do you?"

Cole looks at me with his mouth hanging open. "Damn, bro. That's insightful for a physics major." He likes to tease me about my logical brain. He's the emotional one, and I'm the practical thinker.

"I agree," says Julian, throwing his arms around our shoulders. "Come on, let's go downstairs, and I'll introduce you to some of the guys while the ladies get ready."

———

Chance's exclusive guests are here, and the party is in full swing. His intimate gathering of one hundred or so include MLB, NHL, NBA, and NFL athletes at the top of their game. New Year's Eve falling on a Sunday gave most everyone a day off. An A-list actress is on Julian Decker's arm, and a few *Sports Illustrated* models are sprinkled in for good measure. Even though the dress code is casual, all the girls elevate it a bit. While the guys mostly wear henleys or high-end hoodies, the girls make casual look sexy, especially my girl.

Despite all the celebrities here, Darcy is the belle of the ball.

Chance keeps his word, introducing her to everyone and bragging about her talent. He's kept her by his side most of the night, and if it weren't for the earlier conversation, I'd be worried. Occasionally, his arm drapes casually over her shoulder, mostly when someone's eyes linger a little too long on her. I start to approach when he gives me a quirk of his eyebrow. Is he challenging me? Nah. He's Team True Love, right?

Darcy looks absolutely gorgeous in her tight, ripped jeans that hug her perfect ass. The same ass I spanked this morning. The red sequined sweater and her red kitten heels give her a pop of color and contrast. It's a mix of dressy and casual, and I'm not sure anyone but Darce could pull off that look the same way. On her, it looks fun, carefree, and runway ready. That sparkly red sweater clings in all the right places like a beacon calling me to put my hands and mouth on those parts. Her hair is in a high ponytail, and I want to wrap it around my hand and pull her in for a deep kiss. The girl is killing me tonight, and I'm working hard to keep my distance. The best way to do that is to stick with my guy Cole, a constant reminder of why I'm avoiding my girl tonight.

I need to talk to him, but the timing doesn't feel right. And how do I approach the topic? Yeah, you told me to get laid, but guess what? You know your sister? Nah. She's more than that. But how do I convey that to Cole? Would he believe me? Or would he see me as someone who took advantage when he thinks she's vulnerable? His words, not mine.

I'm not sure Darcy has ever been vulnerable. She was confident and self-reliant until this extensive project. Was she a little overwhelmed? Sure. But vulnerable? Never. That girl has the world by the nuts and is squeezing hard.

The partygoers flock to her like moths to a flame gushing over the house. They're getting her socials, and I'm watching her followers multiply by the thousands tonight. Everyone takes selfies with her and posts them with hashtags like #DesignsbyDarcy, #DesignGoddess, and even #Ifoundherfirst. I think

Ashleigh posted that to Chance's account, and I wonder if I should thank or kill her.

Even Tripp Stevenson invited her to Mexico to work on his house there. He conceded that Chance's house is better and now wants a rematch. That's my superstar. She's laughing with a group of girls, and my heart swells watching her live her best life. It's killing me being across the room from her, but every time our eyes meet, she gives me a smile and wink, and my heart calms a little.

Cole is getting handsy with Ashleigh, and I figure I should mix and mingle a little. After all, I never know when this surreal "this can't be my life" bubble will burst.

I go downstairs to Outside Chance, which Julian Decker has dubbed the No Chance Bar. There I find Julian, his brother Alexander, the GM for the Reapers and my boss, Tripp Stevenson, star pitcher for the Reapers, and Trevor Lewis, owner of the Savannah Pajamas.

I wouldn't have believed it if anyone had told me last year that I would be part of the circle with these people at a party.

"There's my money maker," Julian says as I approach the group. Since he's the sports agent to most of the superstars at this party tonight, I seriously doubt I'm the money maker he's referring to, so I look around to see if someone is behind me.

"Not quite," I laugh.

"Not YET," he emphasizes. "I can't wait to make my brother pay you handsomely when you go to the show." He puts his arm around Alexander, who gives him a scowl.

"In due time," Alexander says. "I don't want you wishing ill on my current third baseman, Jules."

"It's good to see you again, Hartman," Trevor says.

"Yeah, man, looking forward to you joining us at spring training this year," Tripp says. "I remember my rookie camp. It scared me shitless."

"Um, thanks, I think." Julian said they might invite me to spring training, but nothing is official yet.

Everyone laughs, and the conversation flows around baseball, prank wars, and the other party guests.

"As much as I hate to admit it, I love this house," Tripp says. "I hear you had a hand in it, Hartman?"

"I guess. I was Darcy's lackey and errand boy, but she did all the heavy lifting on this project. It kept me busy these past few months. It's the first downtime I've ever had, and I didn't know what to do with myself."

"Haven't you been working out with your teammates?" Alexander asks.

I don't want him to think I'm not a team player, so I answer carefully. "No, not really. I've been volunteering with my dad at the high school and working out with them. I'm not gonna lie. Jumping into an established team mid-season was tough. It's also the first time I've played without Cole, and, well, I had some adjustments to make."

Trevor joins us with a tray full of shot glasses. "We're on the countdown to midnight, so shots are in order!" It goes down smoothly and doesn't give me the usual shiver that accompanies a tequila shot. So this is what expensive liquor tastes like? I'm living in the reality of the big leagues.

"I get it," Tripp says. "It's hard coming in and taking over someone's spot who had it before you. But remember, someone else is gunning for your spot too. Keep working hard and stay focused, and you'll earn their respect."

Trevor throws his arm around me. "This kid here is one of the hardest working guys I know. You've got what it takes. You'll be moving on before you know it."

And there it is again. Moving on.

Chance joins us with another tray of shots.

"Where's Darcy?" I ask. I look around to see if she followed him downstairs.

"She said she needed a minute, and I told her to use my bedroom to catch her breath." He gives me a wink, clinks his glass against mine, and takes the shot. I down the second shot with everyone and shift side to side, indecision written on my face.

"Hey, let's all get upstairs for the countdown," Chance says. "I'm sure those of you with dates would like a midnight kiss."

We all make our way upstairs, and I go to find Darcy. I lightly knock on Chance's bedroom door and hearing nothing, I crack open the door. She's alone on the balcony, her ponytail blowing in the breeze. I'm not sure she heard me, so I go out to meet her at the rail.

"Hey, pretty girl." I wrap her in my arms and pull her in tight. The edginess I've felt all night slips away, and I can breathe normally for the first time since this party started. "You okay?"

"Yeah, just needed a break. It's been a crazy night."

"You're the star of the party, baby. I'm so proud of you."

She looks up, and her eyes meet mine. Her tongue darts out, and that's all it takes to break my willpower to stay away tonight. I wrap my hand in her ponytail and pull her face to mine as I kiss her hard, my tongue demanding entry. I'm tired of sharing this girl tonight. I want her. All of her.

I kiss her jaw and nibble on her ear. I kiss down her neck and find that sensitive place where her neck joins her shoulders. She leans her head back, giving me better access. My tongue trails up her neck, and I find her lips again.

"I want more," she says. She's pressing her thighs together, and I know her need is building.

I don't have time to give her the proper attention she deserves, not to mention the party of people downstairs, but I can give her an orgasm to ring in the new year.

I unbutton her jeans and slide my hand in, my calloused finger finding her sensitive spot and circling it.

"You're so wet for me," I growl in her ear.

As I finger her slit and work her clit, her breathing hitches.

"Oh Matt, yes, right there," she moans.

Even though the music is loud, I don't need anyone to hear her moans. They're mine and mine alone. I kiss her, swallowing her sounds. I'm so hard I could hammer nails, but this isn't about me. I need to make my girl feel good. She comes around my fingers, and I kiss her hard and deep.

I lick her taste off my fingers as I give her a smirk.

"Feel better?" I ask.

"WHAT THE FUCK IS GOING ON?"

Darcy flinches, and I stand protectively in front of her to keep her from exposure and embarrassment.

Cole storms into the room and comes at me with a look of rage I've never seen before.

I step away from Darcy because I know what's coming next, and I can't let her get hurt. Cole swings and lands a punch square against my jaw. He pulls back to land another one on my face, and I don't fight back. I deserve this. I broke the code.

The countdown starts from the partygoers downstairs. *Ten, nine, eight.* Darcy is crying, and I reach for her hand as I get my balance, only to find air where I thought she was. I shake my head to get my thoughts to form. *Seven, six, five.* Where's Darcy? *Four, three, two, one. Happy New Year!* I see red sparkles in my blurred vision. My eye is swelling shut, but I think Darcy is wrapped in Ashleigh's arms. As long as she's okay.

"I can't believe you." Cole takes another swing at my gut, and I double over. Man, this guy can punch.

"It's not what you think," I say, trying to catch my breath.

"Oh, it's exactly what I think," he snarls. "You took advantage of her crush when she was vulnerable and moved in on her because you were lonely."

"No." My hands are on my knees as I pull air into my lungs to speak. "I…." I what? I love her.

Ashleigh comes back into the room and puts herself between us.

"Sweetheart, go back to Darcy," he growls.

"She's with Sammie. She's fine. That's enough, Cole. Come on. You owe me a New Year's kiss." She puts her hand on his chest, and he moves back.

"I trusted you, man. How could you? You were supposed to watch out for her." He turns his back to me. "You were my friend." Were. Yep. There it is.

His voice drips with disdain as Ashleigh leads him out of the room. She looks back at me and mouths, "Sorry."

I guess no amount of talking to him prepared him for what he saw. I admit it wasn't how I wanted him to find out about us. But is he right? Does she need someone better than me?

Jay finds me cleaning the blood off my face in the bathroom.

"Oh man, let me get you some ice," he says.

"No, it's okay. I'm going to head home."

He pulls out his phone, and seconds later, Darcy and Sammie come flying into the room.

"Oh my god, oh my god, Matt," Darcy cries. She reaches for my face, and I flinch at her gentle touch. "I can't believe he did this." Tears run down her cheeks, and I only want to comfort her.

I lean down and kiss the top of her head. "It's okay, pretty girl. It's okay." I hug her and wince at the pain in my side. I hope I didn't crack a rib.

"No, it's not," she cries.

I look down and wipe the tears from her cheeks. I'm grateful for the tequila shots because I'm sure they're killing some of the pain.

"Listen, I'm gonna head home and let him cool down. It's going to be alright."

"Okay, I'll go with you."

I peel her arms away from me. "No, not tonight. Stay with your friends. This is your night, pretty girl. Celebrate, okay?" The pain in my chest is worse than any physical pain I've endured tonight. Walking away from her is tearing my heart in two, but I know it's the right thing to do. It's best for her.

"I can't. Not without you." Her plea damn near breaks me.

"You can. You've taken on today all by your fierce self. Keep it up. I'll see you later. Okay?"

"No. Don't go." She's begging me, her eyes full of unshed tears.

Sammie steps in and puts her arms around her, giving me a nod. She's got her. I kiss Darcy on the temple. "Happy New Year, pretty girl," I whisper. "This is your year." I walk out and head for the front door. Chance looks up and tries to stop me, but I'm out the door faster than stealing home plate.

Happy New Year, indeed.

CHAPTER
THIRTY-ONE

MATT

———

"You look like shit." Julian slips onto the bar stool beside me and waves to the bartender, pointing to my beer.

"Good to see you too," I mumble.

"You know, they should rename this bar the Corazon Roto." I don't know what he's spouting off, but I figured someone would track me down eventually.

"What the fuck does that mean?"

"The broken heart? Yeah, it seems every time I'm in this bar, I'm with some poor, broken-hearted bastard."

"I'm not brokenhearted. It's called self-preservation." I had to get out of there. I couldn't be anywhere that reminded me of her. My house, my parent's house, the entire city. She consumed those spaces. Memories of her were everywhere I looked. Leaving the country might've been a little extreme, but as the bruises fade from my face, I'm not sure I went far enough.

"OK, slugger. If that's what lets you sleep at night." I wince at his nickname. The bartender places two beers in front of us.

Julian takes a long pull from his bottle. "But it looks like you aren't sleeping either. You really look like shit, Hartman."

"You already said that. I thought we paid agents to give pep talks and blow sunshine up our ass? Because if that's the case, you suck."

Julian laughs at me. "No, the terrible agents do that. The great ones like me? We tell you straight, so remember that. I'm in your corner. But I'm not here as your agent. I'm here as your friend. It seems like you might need one right about now."

The concept of friendship seems foreign and bitter on my tongue. I've given up on friendships. I had one that was the foundation for all friendships, and I fucked it up. It blew up like one of those implosions you watch on TV. The detonator goes off, and in less than a minute, the entire thing is nothing but rubble. It's all my fault too. I set the charges one by one and lit the fuse. I knew what would happen. It crumbled, obliterated into dust. Then I left because there weren't enough pieces to put it back together.

"Yeah, I'm not a very good friend, so don't waste your time."

"It's my time, so let me decide how to spend it. Besides, I love this place. I spend more time here than Tripp these days."

When I ran out of Chance's party, Tripp was outside, alone, scrolling through some girl's socials, looking all moony-eyed. He took me home, I packed a bag, headed to the airport, and we flew to Mexico. He didn't ask many questions, just said something about how we both needed to get away, and he knew just the place. After a few days, Tripp made sure I wouldn't do anything stupid, and left. He told me to stay as long as I wanted, but he had to get back to his cat.

I didn't have a better plan, so here I am.

The house is on the beach, which should soothe my soul. But it doesn't. I've tried to surf, but I'm just going through the motions. I've worked out more than I should, but only when I push myself well past the point of exhaustion, sleep finally sets in for a few hours.

I'm spending too much time in my head, and it's not a pleasant place. Maybe having Julian as a distraction isn't such a bad idea.

"This place is pretty nice. How long are you staying?" I ask.

"The better question is, how long are you staying, Hartman?"

"I've got nothing to go back to except baseball. Figured I'd stay here until spring training."

"Nothing, huh? Want to fill me in on what nothing entails, exactly? I mean, Ash gave me a brief rundown, but if we're going to be roomies and all, I figure I might as well know all the deets. Do I need to be hiding the weapons and locking my door at night or buying a lot more booze?"

"You buying the booze?" I turn to him with a smirk. He gives a shrug that I take as a yes. "Hey, amigo," I call to the bartender. "Bring us your best bottle of tequila."

Julian claps his hand on my shoulder. "I gotcha, roomie."

We clink our glasses together and take a shot. No chaser. No salt. No lime. This isn't the kind of story that gets garnishes.

"It all started when I was eight, I met a smart-ass kid named Cole, and I didn't wait for three Mississippis."

CHAPTER
THIRTY-TWO

DARCY

———

"No, really, I have shifts at The Wreck this weekend." Even if it's the slow season and I purposely signed up, no one needs to know that.

"You're getting your ass on that plane and coming to Vail. We'll ski, drink, get pampered, and enjoy the hell out of each other's company. You hear me?" Ashleigh is practically yelling at me through the phone.

"But," I start.

"No buts. Sammie is looking forward to it, and you don't want to deny her this all-expenses-paid weekend getaway, do you? You know she won't come if you don't. We've had this book club trip planned for months. Now head to the airport, or I'll send Chance down there to drag your ass on that plane."

"Fine, but guilting me with Sammie is a low blow. And I told you I don't know how to ski. I'm a Southern girl. We don't get snow." I mumble the last part. It's true. I'm not in the mood to get out of bed most days, let alone fly across the country. I don't have the energy to act like I'm okay for three days. Truth is, I don't want to ruin everyone's good time. I'm heartbroken.

Matt left, and I haven't heard a word from him since the party. I didn't even warrant a breakup text. He must hate me for causing him to lose his best friend. The thought brings another wave of overwhelming sadness. It's been five weeks, and I've just become functional. Barely.

"Duh, we're all Southern girls. I already have lessons lined up for us with an adorable ski instructor named Katie. I've got you, Darcy. Come on, work with me here." Ashleigh's begging is raising my guilt meter.

"Fine. We'll be out of here in the next twenty minutes. I promise."

I hear a cheer in the background and a champagne cork popping.

"Great! See you soon."

I look at the bags Sammie packed. They mean well. I put on my best fake smile and call out. "Looks like we're going skiing this weekend. You ready?"

Sammie pops her head in my room, trying to hide her grin. "Yep. Come on. This'll be fun. And I've never flown first class before. Let's go see how the other half lives." She grabs my bag and tosses me my coat. I guess I'm going on a girl's weekend. Yay.

———

Even though this is technically our book club getaway, no one intends to read or discuss a book this weekend. Ashleigh has our days filled with ski lessons, wine tastings, massages, and drinking in the hot tub surrounded by snow. Emma, Ashleigh's best friend, who lives in Savannah, joins us to round out our foursome. I'm sure the Instagram pictures look like four girls living their best lives on a girls' getaway. Just another example of the lies that are sold on social media.

If I weren't so sad, I'd enjoy this. Unfortunately, my sadness is rooted deep in my bones. The harbinger of ruined relationships reporting for duty.

Everyone tiptoes around me. I thought they'd want to hash it out. Ask me how I am. Talk about Matt. Strangely, his name never comes up. Neither does Cole's. It's like the male gender is non-existent. So color me surprised when we return to the house after dinner to find Julian and Chance in the living room.

"I thought this was a girl's weekend," I comment.

"Darcy, you wound me," Julian says dramatically. He clutches his heart and falls over on the couch.

"I'm playing the Mountaineers tomorrow." Chance mimics a hockey shot that looks more like a golf swing. "Thought you guys might want to come to my game?"

"Absolutely," Sammie quickly responds. She bounces with excitement.

"Like we would miss it," Emma says enthusiastically.

Chance's million-dollar smile lights up the room. "It's a girls' weekend, so I assume you have glitter and stuff. Are you going to make signs?" Chance says to Emma.

"They'll be so great, we're guaranteed to make the Jumbotron," Emma says. "Hey, I'm playing bartender. Who wants what?"

Everyone shouts out drink orders, and Emma heads into the kitchen.

"I'm going to lie down for a little bit," I say quietly and try to leave the room unnoticed.

I pass by Chance. He reaches out for my arm and stops me. "You okay?"

I give him a half-shrug. "Just tired. All this fresh air, you know?"

He gets up, and before I know it, he wraps his arms around me, enveloping me in an all-consuming hug. I don't mean to, but I sob. I've been holding it together. Why am I losing it now? And why with Chance? My tears drench his shirt.

He kisses the top of my head and pulls me in tighter. "I got you, beautiful. I got you." Everyone keeps saying that. Everyone except. Well, I can't think about him.

When I finally catch my breath, I step away and notice my outburst cleared the room.

He pulls me toward the couch he and Julian recently occupied and sits me on his lap, his arms still around me. It's intimate, but not romantic. Comforting.

"Want to tell me what I can do to help?"

"I don't think there's anything anyone can do. It'll just take time to heal my broken heart." I look at Chance, and his eyes are sorrowful. His hand gently rubs circles on my back.

"I know it hurts. It's painful when you experience loss. But Darcy, I'm worried about you. It's okay to be sad, but this? This is something else. You've lost your spark. And I'm not gonna lie, I'm concerned." Chance looks me in the eye, searching for some kind of reassurance.

"I'm not going to do anything drastic. I promise." Wow. My attempt at acting like I'm okay was for naught.

He gives me a slight nod. "What do you need?" Throughout the house project, that's what he always asked me. What do you need?

I shrug. If I knew, I'd do it. "It's the not knowing. Where is he? Is he okay? It was so abrupt. There wasn't any closure, you know. Too many questions."

"Well, I can answer some of those questions if you really want to know."

"You can?" I sniffle, and a box of tissues comes flying across the room. Apparently, clearing the room doesn't mean vacating the premises or the conversation. Chance grabs the box and hands it to me. I grab a tissue and blow. If that doesn't send Chance running, nothing will.

I would think Chance Fuller would be the last person Matt would reach out to, so the fact he's in the know has my curiosity piqued. Do I want to know? What if I find out he's fine? Moved on. At least I'll know.

"Yeah." He looks over his shoulder. "Come on, get in here."

A few seconds later, Julian, the tissue box thrower, comes into the room and sits next to us on the couch. "How can I help?"

Julian can help me? We sit silently while I pause, thinking about what I want to know. "I just want to know that he's okay."

Julian looks at Chance, and they have some unspoken conversation. "He's about as good as you are, I'd say."

"Have you talked to him?" Is he talking to Julian? I'm relieved he has someone to lean on since I took Cole away from him.

Another look passes between Julian and Chance. "Yeah, we've been amigos and roommates for the past few weeks. He doesn't talk much, but I've been keeping an eye on him. He's functional and headed to Florida with the Reapers soon."

Amigos? He's at Tripp's in Mexico. Not sure how that happened, but I'm glad Julian, Tripp, and Chance are there for him. Florida? He was invited to spring training? That's huge. I'm excited for him. The mixture of emotions washes over me, and I hiccup another sob. Chance pulls me in tighter.

"I'm glad he has you guys," I mumble. I take a deep breath and try to fill my lungs for the first time in weeks. He's not hurt. He's okay. He has friends. Now I can breathe a little easier, knowing he's not alone.

Part of my guilt and sadness stems from the fact that my best friend is still by my side. Hell, I'm on a girls' weekend, surrounded by people who care about me. I've worried he had no one. A tiny spark flickers in my soul. He's going to be okay. That's all I want for him. I need him to be okay, then eventually better than okay. I want him to live his dream and have it all. Everything.

"Is that a hint of a smile?" Chance teases.

"Knowing he's okay and has you guys, well, it makes me feel better." I'm still heartbroken, but I feel a little better. I still have questions. "And he's going to be playing with the Reapers in Florida. That's great news." I know my voice is flat, but really, I'm excited for him. That's a big deal for his career.

Sam, Ashleigh, and Emma join us in the room. They approach us apprehensively.

"You better?" Sammie asks.

I nod. "A little."

"Good. Decker girl's night book club meeting is in session," Emma declares. She hands us our drink orders. Since I didn't ask for anything, she brings me a bottle of vodka and a shot glass. Everyone lifts their glasses, even me.

"Here's to believing in happily ever afters, even in the darkest chapters," Julian says.

Do I believe in HEAs? Or do they only occur in romance novels? I'm not sure, but I'm willing to keep moving through the story to find out.

CHAPTER
THIRTY-THREE

DARCY

———

"Order up for table twelve," Jeff calls from the kitchen.

"Got it." Table twelve isn't in my section, but anything to keep moving, stay busy. I grab the food, balance the plates with my arm, and walk across the room.

"Who had the shrimp platter?" I ask as I approach the table, looking at the plates in my hand.

"Hey, Darce." I'm startled by the voice and almost drop the food.

"Of course," I say as I place the plate in front of Cole. "Mom always gets the flounder, and that leaves the scallops for you, Ash. Can I get you guys anything else?"

I can't believe they're here. It's been six weeks since I've seen Cole. I've texted with Ashleigh once since Vail, and I wonder what she shared with him. I've gone to Sunday brunch a few times. What do they want from me? I'm doing my best, going to class, working more hours than usual, but I need to save money for life after graduation. I'm just busy.

"Can we talk?" Cole asks.

"Sorry, I'm working. Enjoy your dinner." My voice is flat, no emotion.

I turn to walk away, and Ashleigh's hand reaches out to grab mine. "Please," she says.

I look around the restaurant. It's a Tuesday night in February, and it's not busy. I don't really have a good excuse.

"Give me a minute, and I'll take my break. Go ahead and eat up while it's warm." I give Ashleigh's hand a little squeeze and step away.

I tell Jeff I'm taking my break, pour myself a large sweet tea, and grab a plate of hushpuppies. I'm not hungry, but I'm thinking ahead. It's hard to talk with a mouth full of food.

I take the empty chair at their table and put on the fake smile I've perfected. Or at least I think I have. Sammie says it's scary, but I'm working on it.

"I didn't know ya'll were going to be in town." I look at Ashleigh, pleading with my eyes. Please tell me it's okay. From the look on her face, it's not. I sigh.

"On our way to Florida for spring training," Cole says, his voice sounding timid. That's a tone my normally cocky, fun-loving brother doesn't use often, if ever.

"Yeah, I guess it's that time, isn't it? Congratulations on getting invited." Under other circumstances, I'd be elated for him. Of course I'm happy for him. It's just hard because our relationship is in this uncomfortable, unfamiliar place. Strangely, he doesn't look all that happy either.

"Thanks," he mumbles. I barely hear him. Why are we making small talk? Awkward small talk at that. This isn't us. I mean, the first words he says to me in weeks are about baseball. Honestly, it tracks. He probably thinks it's a safe topic. Unfortunately, it's not.

I eat my hushpuppy, practically putting the entire thing in my mouth. I look around the table when I feel three sets of eyes watching me.

"What?" I ask with a mouthful of food.

"How are you?" Ashleigh asks. Her face is full of concern. Not much better than the last time she saw me. But she knows. She's been there. What do I say? Heartbroken. Gutted. Lost. No. I won't admit that. Not to my family.

"Good," I choke out. I take a big gulp of tea to wash down the lump in my throat. "Working. School. A few consultations. You know, busy." I shrug like it's just another Tuesday. Which it is. Just making it through another day. My new normal.

"Yeah, I know," Ashleigh says. Her look damn near breaks me. It's what isn't being said that guts me. "Been there. Senior year, right?" She knows exactly what I'm talking about.

"Yeah, senior year." I want to ask about Matt. Has Cole talked to him? Are they still friends? Can I fix this mess? How is he? I can't seem to muster the words. I'm not sure I can handle the truth. Living in the what if and maybe world is safer for me at the moment.

"Are you working too much?" Mom asks.

"No, it's good. I'm saving some money so I can, I don't know, try doing my thing on my own after graduation." That's what they all want me to do, so I tell them what they want to hear. But really? I'm not sure I have it in me. The only place I feel comfortable is The Wreck, which is one reason I'm working so many days. It keeps me busy. No one asks about how I'm doing. They let me be. Until now.

"You know I can help you, right?" Ashleigh says. I assume she's talking about after graduation, but I'm not sure if her words have a double meaning. Doesn't matter.

"I know. I'm just not ready yet. But when I am, you'll be my first call." Because my first call won't answer anymore, so I quit trying.

Cole remains quiet, pushing food around on his plate but not eating. I glance his way, but just that small look brings a swirl of emotions. Anger. Love. Hurt. Frustration. Guilt. Embarrassment. Shame. Heartbreak. Mostly shame. I destroyed a brotherhood.

That constant pain I've had in my chest roars back full force. I thought I had it somewhat contained, but seeing him like this brings it to the surface. I'm a monster. Just weeks ago, Cole's happiness was visible, oozing from every pore. Now, he can barely look at me. His typical smile, gone. I hurt him too. I'm a danger to those around me.

This is too much. Apparently, running away is the solution, so I go with it. I mean, it must be working for Matt. He's been radio silent for weeks.

"I need to get back to work." I push my chair back and start to stand.

Faster than a line drive, Cole is out of his chair. His arms wrap around me, pulling me into his chest. His chin rests on my shoulder. He whispers, "I'm so sorry. So fucking sorry. I love you." His hug is so tight I can barely breathe.

I feel tears well in my eyes and will them not to fall. "I know. Me too." I try to pull away, but he's holding on to me for dear life.

"We going to be okay?" He says it so quietly, I wonder if he really said it at all. "Tell me you forgive me."

"Of course," I mumble. With those words, his grip on me loosens. Without turning around or looking at them, I say, "I've gotta go. Enjoy your dinner." I'm not sure why he's asking forgiveness. I'm the one who broke his friendship.

I go to the kitchen and tell Jeff I need to leave, that I'm not feeling well. He hugs me and tells me to get some rest. Jeff's such a great boss and friend. I've no doubt he witnessed the intervention. He quit asking me if I was okay a few weeks ago, because he knew when to give up on me. I guess that's why I like him so much. He's a lot like me. He knows when to move on.

That's what I'm trying to do. Move on. It's time to give up on fantasies and dreams. The best I can hope for is being okay. It's time to focus on my life without Matt, my future and myself. Starting now.

CHAPTER
THIRTY-FOUR

MATT

————

"Are you ready to play with the big boys?" Julian asks.

I'm headed to Florida in a few days. From a career perspective, it's a dream come true. I'll be playing with the MLB greats, even if they're preseason games. It's my chance to show them what I've got, why they signed me, and why they should promote me to the show. It's rare guys my age move up so quickly. I'm fortunate and need to take full advantage of this opportunity. It's time to step up and show them why I'm the guy for the job.

From a personal perspective, I'm scared shitless. It means I leave this sanctuary where I've hidden from everyone and everything for the past six weeks. Reentering the world - not something I'm ready to do.

Julian has been in Mexico with me, occasionally leaving for a day or two, but popping back in like he never left. I told him I don't need a babysitter, and he says, "I know," and stays anyway.

He's the poster child for working remotely. I admire how he conducts business with his clients and team, always listening and keeping everyone happy. Watching him work is like a master class in peopling. It's a gift. He's one hell of a protector and caretaker. I used to relate to those traits. Not so much anymore. Caretakers don't betray people.

Julian also spends a lot of time typing away on his laptop. I assume he's answering emails, but every once in a while, he asks me a random question about love and grand gestures. Then he looks at me, mumbles never mind, and goes back to typing. I don't know what's going on in his head, but I've enjoyed his company more than I thought. He's the most laid-back Decker sibling but also the most complex - his layers seem infinite. Even though he's my agent and my once-best friend's future brother-in-law, I consider him a friend too. And at this stage in the game, I need a friend.

"Yeah, I head out on Thursday. Nervous, though." I'm going straight to Florida for spring training from Mexico.

I've asked Mom to pack up my rental house and send a few things to me in Florida, like my baseball glove and cleats. She didn't ask many questions, giving me the space I asked for. She knows the highlights of my situation and is optimistic things will work out for the best. I text every few days to assure her I'm fine. A few pictures of the beach now and then keep her at bay. For now.

I'm not sure what my future holds, but when I return to Charleston, I'll need a fresh start. I'll miss Isle of Palms, but I can't stay in that house and not think of Darcy. Hell, I don't know that I'll be able to be on the island at this rate.

Tripp and Chance arrived yesterday, telling me something about a last hurrah before we all get back to work. Chance has the week off because it's the All-Star break. I feel bad for intruding on their traditions, but they blow me off and act like I've been part of the group all along. They throw out comments about mentoring the next generation, making me feel more out of place. I don't belong.

"Nothing to be nervous about, just be on the lookout for rookie pranks, but I think after your Pajamas experiences, you'll be fine," Tripp says. Spending three summers with the fun-loving Savannah Pajamas exposes a player to every prank in the book, so he's probably right. I'm prepared for that part of the team culture. Tripp dives into a gigantic platter of nachos, his advice dispensed.

That's something I've thought about a lot. Where do I belong? Who do I belong with? I used to answer those questions with unwavering certainty. Now, I just don't know.

I don't feel like I belong with the Ghost Peppers yet. I know that team relationship and bonding takes time to build. Last year, I came into the team fast and during mid-season. It made for awkwardness. I've discovered that individual competition is even more cutthroat at this level. Unlike college, where we know the odds of getting the call and all have degrees as a backup plan, minor league ball is MLB or bust. These guys have given up a lot for this game, and there is no plan B. Hell, I get it. I want it too.

I don't belong with the Davidsons anymore. Honestly, that one hurts the most. They've been my family for as long as I can remember. They're part of my core identity. Cole was the foundation of where and who I belong with, and that's gone. I've called him a few times, and it goes straight to voicemail. My texts go unanswered. After two weeks, I stopped trying. Ashleigh said to give him time but to trust the process, whatever that means. The uncertainty of my friendship is unsettling.

Darcy Davidson? That's a certainty of not belonging. I don't belong with her to start. She deserves better than me, and I've always known that. I'm not good enough for her, and the fact she even gave me a chance doesn't go unappreciated. She deserves someone stable who can provide her with a home. That's a fact. My career is unstable. I can be traded or moved at any time. Or I can be injured or let go, unemployed. It's a massive amount of travel during the season, and it's long, March to September, maybe October if we're lucky to be in the playoffs. She deserves more than that. And she damn sure deserves a man who doesn't betray his friends. She deserves a man that will love her with everything he has. Of course, I'll always be that man, but she deserves the entire package, and that's not me. She's meant to soar. Her future's so bright I can't be the guy who keeps her from reaching her maximum potential. No, she is not where I belong.

I admit I've been stalking her socials, but she's been pretty quiet. Her followers exploded after New Year's, and I bet Ashleigh is encouraging her to build on the boost. The few posts have included people she's styled or a room she's brought to life, but nothing of her. Nothing that shows the world how special it is because she's in it. It's unfortunate because she's everything.

At night, I scroll through my phone and look at the pictures I'd taken of her. My favorites are of her in those oversized sweatshirts, hair a mess, and her smile lighting up the room as she works or dreams. She's so damn gorgeous. Just thinking about her makes my chest tighten.

Chance drops down on the couch next to me and throws me the Xbox controller. "Yeah, Matty boy, you're gonna blow them all away."

"Did you just quote Hamilton at me?" I ask. He made us watch the musical last night. I won't lie. I liked it. Who knew these guys were musical theater fans? Layers. Serious layers.

He grins, wiggles his eyebrows, and unpauses the game. Chance is an enigma if I've ever met one. A brute of a hockey player on the ice, a musical-watching, romance-reading, stray dog-loving, kindest guy you've ever met, off the ice guy. I was skeptical of him, but he's honestly one of the nicest human beings on the planet. It takes a lot of effort not to like him.

"I can't believe you passed up the All-Star game," Tripp says to Chance.

He shrugs. "Yeah, knee's been acting up a bit. Don't want to risk injury for something fun like the All-Star game. I'm in my golden years."

"I hear that," Tripp says. Both are at the peak of their careers, but realistically, they're probably in the last few years of playing before their bodies say enough. The extreme wear and tear professional athletes put on their bodies for the sake of the game is extensive.

"Besides, I'd rather be here with you goofballs. Damn Hartman, how did you see that one?" Chance says. We're playing Call of Duty, and I took out the sniper that was about to kill him.

"That's what I do. I look out for people." I realize what I said. "Or at least I used to," I mumble.

Chance hits pause and grabs me by the shoulders. He tightens his grip, making me feel slightly uncomfortable under his scrutiny. "Damn, boy, you've been working out. I swear you've gained twenty pounds of muscle since New Year's. You practically look like a hockey player."

I chuckle. I've been working out for hours every day, not because I'm trying to build muscle, but because it's a way to channel all the excess energy. The muscles? The outcome of my fucked-up life.

"Tripp has a helluva gym here, and I've had nothing but time, so..." I shrug my shoulders.

"All these beautiful girls around here, and you've spent all your time in the gym?" Chance asks.

"Yeah, not interested in the girls." Admittedly, girls have talked to me on the beach or when I've been in town, but the thought of another girl makes me want to throw up.

"Told ya," Julian says to Chance.

"Yup, just checking," Chance says.

I swear, sometimes these guys speak their own language.

"So, what's your plan?" Chance asks.

I'm so lost in this conversation. I think he's talking to Tripp until I notice three sets of eyes staring at me, waiting for an answer.

"Plan for what?" I ask, confused.

"Dude, this is a meeting of Team True Love. What are you going to do to get the girl?" Julian says.

Oh, I get it. They take this Team True Love thing seriously. They're delusional. Fucking romance-loving busybodies. "Um, nothing. She's better off without me. I'm gonna focus on baseball. It's what I have left."

"Seriously?" Chance asks, his face is full of disbelief. "You're going to let her go? Without a fight."

"She's already gone," I say, reaching for the nachos, hoping to end this discussion.

"I like Decker girls' time better," Chance says under his breath.

"Me too, buddy," Julian says. "Me too."

CHAPTER
THIRTY-FIVE

MATT

———

I look around the spring training stadium, the Carolina Reapers logo looming over the outfield. I take a deep breath, the thick humidity of the Florida air making it difficult to breathe easily.

"Is it what you thought it would be?" Alexander Decker, General Manager for the Carolina Reapers, pulls me from my thoughts.

I haven't seen him since New Year's, and seeing him today brings back memories of that night. Most of the partygoers were totally unaware of what happened. I'm not sure how much Alexander knows. Knowing that gossipy group, he probably knows more than I do.

I was on top of the world. My girl was the belle of the ball, and I was going to tell her I loved her that night. The feel of her in my arms on the balcony. Then, the look on her face when Cole found us. That look of devastation. Sadness. I did that to her. Her night was ruined because I couldn't find the courage to talk to her brother. I wasn't disciplined enough to keep my hands off her for one night. The shame has eaten away at me throughout my time in Mexico, but I need to put that away for now.

I can't dwell on my past. Forward. That's where I need to focus my energies. Looking ahead. At what I can control. I can't control the past, can't change it. God knows I've wanted to.

"Thanks for the opportunity."

"You earned it." We stand shoulder to shoulder, looking out over the stadium. "This is just a little taste of your future, Matt."

"Thanks. I hope so. I'm looking forward to a long career as a Reaper." It's what I've wanted since I was a kid. Me and Cole, Reapers. Now he's a New York Liberty. Not part of my future on the field or off. Because I crossed a line. The one line I knew better than to cross. My action. My own consequences.

"How was Mexico?" He arches an eyebrow, giving me a knowing look. Yep. Gossipy group. But I can't picture the serious, broody Alexander Decker part of Team True Love. It's laughable just thinking about it.

"Um, it was nice. A good break, I guess. I worked out a lot. I'm ready for the season." Yep. His look is a dead giveaway. He knows.

"You know, this game isn't just physical. It's mental too. Maybe even more so. You got your head sorted out?"

The question reminds me he's my boss, not my friend. The lines can get blurred with the Deckers. "I'm ready to give you one hundred fifty percent."

"I like your work ethic. You talking to Cole yet?" I shrug.

He grins at me, something I haven't seen before in my encounters with him. It's practically unsettling. Alexander is a grumpy guy. His smiles are reserved for his sister, and only when he doesn't think she's looking.

His hand clasps my shoulder. "So you know, we'll be playing the Liberties in a few days. I hear Cole's at camp with them, just like you. That going to be a problem?"

"No, sir. No problem at all." I swallow hard. "I'm here to play ball."

I'm excited for Cole. Getting invited to spring training is a big deal, especially with the Liberties. They have a solid, mature team with serious World Series contention this year. My excitement wanes. He didn't tell me. He didn't share one of the highlights of his life so far.

"Well, glad to hear it. But take it from me, ball won't last forever." He squeezes my shoulder and walks away. "And people aren't around forever either."

Alexander Decker is a man of few words, and damn if those few words don't hit home. I remember Ashleigh told me he had a promising baseball career until injury ended it around the same time their mother died of cancer. Two significant losses at the same time when he was my age. No wonder he's a surly bastard. Unfortunately, he's right. People and relationships don't last. Trust me, I'm living proof.

———

"Check your pockets," Tripp mumbles as we head out of the clubhouse. He gives me a wink, and I reach into my pocket and find a few pieces of bubble gum. I'm on heightened alert. Is this gum safe? Is Tripp saving me from some prank? Or is this the prank? Either way, it's a total mind-fuck. Bastard. I cock my head at him as he walks to the bullpen, laughing.

It's our first game of spring training. These games don't count in the season, but it's a time to evaluate young talent like me. Several of my Ghost Peppers teammates are here too.

Jake Yelle is one of my Ghost Pepper teammates who's had four years in the minors and this is his first time at Reaper's spring training. It's nice to see a familiar face here. Last night, I asked him to dinner, conscious I hadn't attempted to bond with him or my other teammates much last season. At dinner, Jake let me know my lone-wolf attitude got me a reputation as a player who thinks he's better than the rest of the team. He recommended I work on building relationships with them. Well, yeah, that's what I learned last night. Peachy. Unfortunately, he's right.

He also told me I'm going to have to deal with several jealous teammates. I stepped in and got a starting spot and made it to Florida my first year, when most had to work their way here after several years in the minors. It's not that I didn't work, but I've been on a fast track. On the positive side, he said they also admire my talent and work ethic. Contrary to their belief, I'm not a lone wolf and I want to be a leader in the clubhouse. I vow to be a good teammate, effective immediately. Jake offered to help me build the connections and I'm taking him up on it.

I opened up a bit with him, not sharing all the drama, or specifics. I appreciate his candor and willingness to speak the truth to me. It was the first step to making a new friend. Honest communication. The irony isn't lost on me.

My other potential landmine is appearing close to Tripp or the Deckers because that doesn't need to add to my reputation too. Now this thing with the gum. If I'm not pranked with the other guys, is it another example of me not being one of them? Or am I the one getting pranked? I want to skip the gum, but superstitions and baseball go hand in hand. I've never played a game without my bubblegum. Fuck.

The weather is warm, and the sun hits my face as I stand behind the first baseline for the national anthem. I'm starting on third base today, and our team is a mixture of Reapers and Ghost Peppers, like me. Paul Jackson, their starting third baseman, confidently sits out, knowing his spot with the Reapers is safe. Many starters don't mind sitting out, avoiding the possibility of injury in games that don't count and giving them more energy for the golf course. Spring training is a warmup to the season for them. For guys like me, it's a time to prove to the team why we should get called up to the show.

My nerves keep me on edge as I grasp for something to steady me. As I take the field, I hear cheers from the crowd. Even at a spring training game, Reaper fans show up and stand out. I see my parents cheering me on above the visitor's dugout. I'm shaken to find they have an entire cheering section with them. The McIntyres, the family I lived with during my Savannah Pajamas days, are sitting there too. Behind them are Julian and Trevor, both enjoying a cold beer and a laugh. When I see Ashleigh and Emma, I freeze. Ashleigh is here. I swallow the lump in my throat. They're all here for me, and I had no idea. Of course, I haven't been great at communicating, so another thing that's my fault. I'm rattled.

"Let's go, boys!" Jake yells from behind home plate. He's sliding his mask on, getting us focused. My attention shifts from the stands to the job at hand. My focus is winning this game against the Philadelphia Patriots and showing Alexander Decker he made a good decision when he drafted me.

I smile at my cheering section and concentrate on the field. This game may not count in our statistics, but it definitely counts for me. It's the start of a new chapter. One of heartache and loss. One of new beginnings and searching for a place to belong.

We leave the field after an easy inning and are in the dugout preparing to bat. Jake reaches into the tub of bubblegum and tosses a piece into his mouth.

"Awww, fuck!" he yells. The Reapers keep their eyes on the field, but I can see their shoulders shake with silent laughter.

"What's wrong?" I ask. He spits out his gum and reaches for his water. His eyes are tearing, and he's coughing.

"Hot." That's all he's able to get out. He's still rinsing his mouth and spitting. After a minute, he's able to talk. "Tastes like a fucking hot pepper."

Tripp turns around and finally acknowledges him, a smile taking up his entire face. "It's Reaper gum. Welcome to the hottest team in the MLB." With a tip of his cap, he turns around to cheer on our batter.

The entire game, Ashleigh and Emma are relentless with their chirping, harassing the players from Philadelphia. The crowd is chill, so when they yell, both dugouts can hear them and laugh. The Philly guys try to be more low-key with their laughter. It's the top of the sixth inning, and Sanders is up to bat for the Patriots. He was a Reaper until he went to Philly two years ago, when he became a free agent and signed a huge contract. I think the Reapers are still a little bitter about him leaving for money.

"Hey, Sanders! You've been to more Taylor Swift concerts than you've hit a baseball." Ashleigh is cracking everyone up. She knows the players and just the right thing to say.

"It's true," his third base coach says to me. "He's a Swiftie."

"Who isn't?" I respond. I let my mind wander for a moment and wonder if Darcy went to the concert in Miami.

The music starts overhead with a little "Bad Blood," and the crowd goes wild. It must be the motivation Sanders needs because he hits a line drive straight to me. I catch it for the last out. I jog back to the dugout but not before glancing at the stands and winking to Ashleigh. Maybe all hope isn't lost.

The clubhouse is loose after the win. Alexander joins the coach to offer his congratulations. "Great plays on the bag, Hartman," Alexander says. "Solid hitting."

I nod my acknowledgment.

He goes around the room with praise and a few pointers when necessary. It's interesting to see the GM this involved with the daily operations and performance of the team. Alexander Decker's leadership is impressive and I respect him for it. His actions show the Reapers are more than a job or business for him. It's his family.

I exit the locker room and am greeted by my cheering section. "Nice fan club," Jake says as he walks past.

"Yeah, it is," I say. Seeing them all reminds me how much I missed everyone when I fled to Mexico. My mom wraps her arms around my waist and hugs me tight. Mrs. Mac, Emma, and Ashleigh follow her.

Dad shakes my hand and puts his other hand on my shoulder. "Good game, son. Damn, good game. I'm proud of you."

"Thanks, Dad." I scan the group. "Thanks for being here. It means a lot."

Trevor and Julian walk up, slapping me on the back.

"I love to see a Pajama all grown up," Trevor says. "I'm like a proud papa." He winks at Dad.

"You're drunk," Emma says, slapping him on the arm.

"Not yet, but working on it," he says, giving her a smirk.

"Hey, our Uber's here," Julian says to Trevor. He turns to me. "Good game. We'll catch up soon. Stay focused, amigo."

"Sounds good."

My parents and the McIntyres say their goodbyes, and we agree to meet later tonight. Emma leaves with Julian and Trevor, leaving me and Ashleigh.

"Can I meet you back at the hotel?" she asks. "Grab a drink?"

"Well, I never took you for a cleat chaser, but that line sure did come out smooth." I test the water with our usual banter.

"Once a jersey chaser, always a jersey chaser." Her genuine smile reaches her eyes. She takes my hand, her diamond engagement ring catching my eye.

"You're done chasing, remember." I hold her hand up and kiss it. I chuckle and wiggle my eyebrows.

"Yep. Just locking down the best man."

My smile disappears. "I'm sure that offer has been rescinded."

"Nah. Meet me for a drink. Please."

"You know where we're staying?"

Her looks say "Duh" without a word. Her family owns the team. This may be my first spring training, but it isn't hers.

"Yeah, of course, you do. Sure, I'll meet you in the bar."

The ride back to the hotel on the team bus is chaotic. Everyone makes dinner plans, talks to loved ones on their phones, and the pitching coach blasts music through the speakers.

"Who was that hottie? I heard you're meeting her at the hotel. She sure knew the players enough that her chirps were on point. I bet she's fire if you know what I mean," Jake says from across the aisle. He wiggles his eyebrows suggestively.

"What?! No." I shake my head, ensuring my no is loud and clear. I debate telling him who she is, but I don't want my connections to add to my "I think I'm better than everyone" reputation that needs to change. No doubt if I say her brother owns your contract and her daddy signs your paycheck, that would shut him up, but I let it slide. I go with the less controversial response. "She's a friend from school."

"Well, maybe I'll hang around and get her number."

"I wouldn't recommend it," I mumble.

When we arrive at the hotel, several of us head to the bar. Ashleigh is curled up in a chair looking over the drink menu. Tripp walks past and squeezes her shoulder, but keeps going to a table in the back with the other guys. No doubt he knows why she's here, and it's not to catch up with him.

"Hey." Now I'm nervous. My mouth is dry, and I don't know the proper protocol here. She's not here for friendly chit-chat. It's time to face the music, and I've no idea what to say or how to fix this. Hopefully, she'll take the lead.

"Hey, I just ordered some appetizers and you a beer. That okay?" She's relaxed, not nervous at all.

"Yeah, sure. Thanks." I sit in the chair across from her and lean forward, my elbows on my knees, head down, looking at the flower vase on the cocktail table between us. I'd like to blame my emotional crash on the adrenaline dying down, but I can't. Not if I'm being honest. Which is something I've had difficulty with lately.

"So?" she asks.

I look up to find her blue eyes looking me over. I'm not sure what she wants me to say, so I just shrug.

"Okay, fine. If you want me to do the talking, I will. First, you look great. Did you just eat protein and pump iron in Mexico because, damn." She gives me a once-over and smiles. I cock my eyebrow and give her a smirk. She knows better than that.

With a deep breath, I begin my confession. "I didn't know what else to do. I figured everyone needed space. And then, I didn't want to leave once I was there. Figured it was best for everyone. Out of sight, out of mind, you know?"

She listens and nods. "Well, you weren't out of mind, and I think you gave everyone more than enough time."

"Cole didn't answer my calls." Let's talk about him instead. I can't even crack the door to ask about Darcy. I didn't even give her the courtesy of a breakup text.

"No, he didn't. But after we left Charleston last week..." Her sentence trails off. They were in Charleston?

"What? What happened?"

"You guys need to talk." She makes it sound so easy.

The waitress brings our food and drinks. I take a hard pull of my beer, drinking half the bottle down.

Ashleigh picks at the appetizer platter and sips her drink, watching me. We eat and drink in uncomfortable silence. She's letting me stew in my indecisiveness. I slam the rest of my beer.

"Thirsty? Or am I making you nervous?" She quirks her eyebrow at me.

"Honestly, a little of both. So, is she?" I fumble with what I want to ask, what I want to know. "How is she?"

Ashleigh is not here to kiss my ass. She squares her shoulders, looks me right in the eyes, and is about to lay it on me. "Matt Hartman. For a smart guy, you sure are dumb. How do you think she is? She won't talk to Cole, barely communicates with me, and drives Sammie crazy because she's like a zombie. Our full-of-life, fun girl, Darcy, is a fucking zombie, Matt. She's lost her spark."

The thought of Darcy without her spark guts me. She brings so much love and beauty into the world, and now she doesn't sparkle?

I'm drowning in guilt. I did this to her. My shoulders droop under the weight of my actions. "She's always had a crush on me. When she meets someone new, she'll realize it was just a crush."

She looks at me in disbelief. "Matt, she's heartbroken. Believe me. I know the signs." She winces at the memory. "She loves you. It's more than a silly schoolgirl crush. So, the question is, do you love her back?"

Of course, I love her. I love her so much that it physically hurts. I can't even think about her without my chest tightening, my heart trying to hold itself together. But none of this changes the fact that she needs a stable foundation, and a baseball player is not stable. And she's Cole's little sister. Off-limits.

I stare at the table. I can't look Ashleigh in the eye when I lie to her. "It was just a fling. She'll get over it."

I wait for Ashleigh's response, but I'm met with silence. When I garner the courage to look up, she's halfway out of the bar.

My phone buzzes with a text. It just says one word.
LIAR.

CHAPTER
THIRTY-SIX

DARCY

———

"I can't believe I let you talk me into this," I mumble to Sammie.

"Look, it means a lot to Cole. It's his first MLB spring training. Things aren't great now, but you'll hate yourself years from now if you miss it." She spins around, arms wide open, as we walk toward the gates. "Besides, it's spring break. We're in Florida, and it's warm and sunny. Charleston is nice, but not this nice."

She's got me there. It's hard to believe it's February here. The sun does its best to warm me, but I've been cold since, well, for a while. Today the Liberties have a late afternoon game, and the weather is perfect.

We find our seats behind the home team dugout and are in the middle of a Cole Davidson fan section spanning three rows. Ashleigh and Emma have their heads together, conspiring about something, I'm sure. They're like me and Sammie, soul sisters. Ashleigh sits next to Mom, who is absorbed with something on her phone. I'm surprised to find Matt's parents here and the

McIntyres, whom I met on draft day. I say hi to everyone as we take our seats in the front row. Matt's mom, Patti, gives me a sympathy smile. I return her greeting and put my shields up. I can do this for one game. These past seven weeks have given me lots of practice.

Trevor and Julian laugh and lean down to add to Ashleigh's and Emma's whispered conversations. I may be paranoid, but I feel like everyone is looking and talking about me. I pick at the string from my worn jeans, making the distressed hole larger, taking my look from fashionable to homeless. I tug on my Liberties baseball jersey sleeves and attempt to hide.

After the intervention at The Wreck, Mom convinced me to talk to Cole. She guilted me into easing the tension between us because it could impact his performance with the team. The last thing I want to do is mess up his career, his dream. We've texted. Nothing major. Just keeping it surface, but at least I'm not ignoring him anymore. Because when I think about it, it sucks being ignored. He asked me to come to Florida, and Sammie wouldn't let me say no. So here I am.

Is Matt in Florida? I don't ask. The pity looks are hard to handle now as it is.

The game gets underway, and Cole's starting on first base. Everyone is having a good time, and the heckling is strong from our group. Matt's dad mumbles an occasional "good one" but pretends he disapproves of it. As a coach, he acts like it's about the performance, but sometimes, it slips that he's a fan of the game too.

Trevor and Julian are laughing and being obnoxious.

I turn back to Ashleigh and whisper. "Are they drunk? It's only the second inning."

She looks back at them and snickers. "Yeah, it's technically the eleventh inning for them. They've been at it a while."

Emma turns around and glares at them. "Behave," she hisses. "I don't want to get thrown out again."

"Again?"

Ashleigh gives me a genuine smile. "Yeah, they come down here every year and just cut loose. It's their annual boys-who-can't-grow-up spring break. They get rowdy, pull pranks on different teams, and sometimes get caught." She laughs. "It's a bit of a Decker tradition." Decker traditions. This family of friends who love each other fiercely. Cole is blessed to be in this circle, and I'm lucky they include me, too.

She looks down at her phone and answers the FaceTime request.

"Hey Ash, how's our guy doing?"

"Chancey," Julian yells at Ashleigh's phone.

"He's good," Ashleigh says. She pans her phone around at us, where everyone says hi, and at the field where Cole is on first base, watching the runner as he creeps closer to second.

"Sorry I can't be there," Chance says. "Business trip."

"Yeah, how's Vancouver?" she asks.

"A lot different than Florida, that's for damn sure." Chance's laugh is so warm, reminding me of his easygoing demeanor and big heart.

"I bet," she says.

"Hey, did I see Darcy there? Take me off FaceTime and let me talk to her a sec."

I feel the phone tap my shoulder, and Ashleigh hands me her phone. "Your friend wants to talk to you," she says with a wink.

Chance has texted and called a few times over the past few weeks under the guise of giving me feedback that he's still hearing about my work, but I know he's checking up on me. They all are. So I try — for them. I don't want any of them to worry about me. He broke me when we were in Vail, with the concern I might hurt myself. I never want anyone to worry about me like that.

"Hey, how are you?" I greet him, putting as much fun in my voice as I can muster. Sammie gives me a fake golf clap, acknowledging my performance.

"I'm good, beautiful. Although snowy Canada doesn't compare with fresh air and Florida sunshine. How are you?"

"Okay." When I realize that doesn't sound convincing enough, I add, "Good."

"Yeah, right. Broken hearts are a bitch." His sincerity seeps through the phone.

"Yep." No truer words were spoken.

"Well, just remember, I'm Team True Love, so I believe it'll all work out."

"Team what?" What is Chance talking about?

"Never mind. Just hang in there, okay? Have faith."

"Hey Chance, I never really got to thank you for having faith in me. Your house blew my professor away. I wouldn't be graduating if it weren't for you. I won't ever be able to repay you."

"You did all the work. I've told you before, you did an amazing job. Just promise you'll always have space on your calendar for me when you're a famous designer."

"Always."

"That's what I needed to hear. Hey, tell Cole I said hi and good luck. Big things happening for the Davidsons this year. Big things."

"Thanks, Chance. Play safe and win."

"Stay strong, beautiful. You got this."

He hangs up, and I go to pass the phone back to Ashleigh. I see she has a text preview she hasn't read yet. It was sent an hour ago.

MATT

It was a mistake.

With a trembling hand, I give Ashleigh her phone.

"Darcy, are you okay? You don't look good? Did Chance say something?"

"No, I, um, don't feel very well. I'm going to head out. You guys enjoy the game." I grab my purse and head to the concourse.

Sammie follows me up the stairs.

"Hey, what's going on?"

"Nothing. I really don't feel well. Stay with everyone. Cheer for Cole. I'll see you later, okay?"

I've got to get out of here now.

"Are you sure? I'll come with you." Concern fills her face, searching for the truth.

"I'm sure. I promise." I hug Sammie. My ride or die. My girl who has my back through everything. I love her, but the thought of anyone seeing me like this adds to my pain.

It was a mistake. An error. Like an "oops, my bad" kind of mistake.

"Love you, Sammie," I say as I pull away and head to the exit.

I order an Uber, swing by the hotel to grab my things and go to the airport before Cole's game ends. My phone is blowing up with texts checking on me. Everyone gets the same answer. I'm fine. But I'm not.

I'm a mistake.

CHAPTER
THIRTY-SEVEN

DARCY

———

Some things make sense at the time, but in hindsight, they probably weren't the best decisions. I've been making more and more of those bad choices lately. Let's start with flying home without telling anyone my plans. I left the ballpark, packed my stuff, and was on the first plane out. I didn't even bother with a direct flight, so that's how I ended up in Atlanta. Then the weather came in, and they canceled my flight to Charleston.

So now I'm stranded in an unfamiliar city. I have no place to stay, no plans, and a heart that's moved from broken to shattered. I turn my phone off airplane mode to find a slew of text messages.

ASHLEIGH

Where are you? Are you okay?

SAMMIE

Seriously, why didn't you take me with you?
Ride or die, remember?

MOM

Honey, I'm worried. Are you ok?

SAMMIE

Thelma, it's Louise. Where are you?

ASHLEIGH

It's not what you think. Call me.

COLE

You ok? Where are you?

SAMMIE

Getting seriously worried now.

CHANCE

Hey Beautiful! I hear you're out in the wild somewhere. You and that baseball boy are so alike. Let me know how to help or what you need.

COLE

I know you're an adult, but I need to know where you are! Call me.

SAMMIE

I know you aren't home - I watched the camera. Girl, just let me know U R alive, K?

My gut twists with guilt. I have everyone worried. I text Sammie quickly and tell her I'm fine and I'll be in touch.

Scanning through the texts, one catches my eye. I call Chance.

"Hey, beautiful." His voice is full of kindness and compassion, with a touch of hesitancy in his tone.

"Hey." Now that I've called him, I'm not sure what to say. I feel tears fill my eyes and I wipe them away with the back of my sleeve.

"Want to tell me where you are?" He's talking to me like I'm a spooked animal. It's endearing and makes me love this guy even more. Not romantic love, of course, but brotherly love.

"Atlanta." I sigh. "I just took the first flight out, and now my connecting flight is canceled, and I shouldn't have left, and now I'm stuck and don't know what to do." I sniffle, and I'm full-blown crying. My strong facade crumbles down around me.

"Okay, just breathe with me." I can hear him take a deep breath in and then let it out. He does that three times, and by the second time, I'm breathing with him. "Better?"

I sniffle again. "A little." My voice is quiet and timid. I'm talking to this big NHL guy while crying in an airport. How did I get here?

"First things first. Let's get you out of the airport and fed. I have a buddy in Atlanta, Lawsy, who lives with his sister, Harper. She's a few years older than you and a great girl. Let me reach out to them, and they can take you back to their place. They're cool, and they may be exactly what you need. Give me a minute. Is that okay?"

"I don't want to be a burden." Or a mistake, I think. "I can just get a hotel or something."

"I promise they won't mind. I was there last week and told him about you and the great job with the house. He would love to meet you, and Harper is the best. She reminds me of Emma. Oh, hang on, he's already texted back and said he's coming to pick you up."

"What? No, really, I can't."

"If you're uncomfortable," he starts.

"No, no, if he's a friend of yours, I'm sure he's great. I'm just a hot mess."

"Girl, I'm familiar with hot messes, and I can assure you, it doesn't scare me. And it won't scare Lawsy either. He's raised Harper since their parents died when she was in high school. He's like a big brother and dad rolled up into one."

"He sounds great. If you're sure, they won't mind." Honestly, the thought of a hotel room makes me uneasy, so even though I'm crashing, I feel a little better being around others.

"Nope. I sent him your number. He'll pick you up at the valet area. Think you can find your way there?"

"I'll find it."

"He'll be there in twenty minutes. And beautiful, I'm glad you called me. I'll always be there for you."

The tears start back up. His kindness means everything. "Thanks. I'm lucky to have you. I appreciate everything. But can you do me a favor and not tell everyone where I am? I can't take the interrogation right now."

"You have my word. I'll let them know you're safe. They care about you. Just take your time, beautiful. But a little piece of advice? Breathe. And listen to your heart. It knows more than your head when it comes to Matt. He may be a baseball player, but I like him anyway. I'm cheering for you two."

"But Chance, I can't cost him his friendship with Cole. Besides, he said I was," my breath hitches. "Never mind."

"What did he say?" His voice takes on a slight edge, his kind tone gone.

"A mistake," I whisper.

"Nope. I don't believe it." There's a pause while he thinks of what to say next. "Take care of yourself, but stay open. Focus on Darcy right now, and let time heal your heart from the hurt. You're amazing."

"Thanks. I don't deserve you."

"You deserve everything, Darcy. But let Lawsy and Harper take care of you, and you decide when you want to return to the world. Let me know if you need anything. I'm back home tomorrow."

"Thanks, Chance. You're going to make a girl very lucky someday."

He laughs. "Yeah, someday. I'd check in after my game, but I'm on the west coast tonight, so that might be late for you. But text me if you need me, okay? Take care, beautiful."

"Thanks again. Play safe." I hang up and shake my head. I can't believe Chance Fuller, an NHL superstar and total sweetheart, is my friend and knight in shining armor.

I make my way to the valet area to meet Lawsy, knight number two.

———

Lawsy picks me up in a tricked-out Jeep. The extraordinarily tall, buff hockey player is like a living teddy bear. His shaggy brown hair, amber eyes, and smile make him look kind and gentle. He wraps me in a hug and welcomes me to Atlanta. He's acting like everything is normal, like he usually picks up strangers at the airport during a thunderstorm.

He throws my bag in the back, and we drive through Atlanta traffic, the storm coming down around us. He's chatting away like this was a planned visit, and we're old friends. I'm not sure how much Chance shared with him, but he's taking it all in stride.

"I'm sorry to meet you under these circumstances." I try to tuck myself into the smallest space possible.

"Nonsense. Chance told me so much about you. Any friend of his is always welcome, circumstances be damned. He thinks the world of you." He gives me a million-dollar smile. That's when it hits me. Lawsy is Lawson Cartwright, star Atlanta hockey player and spokesman for Jeep, a cell phone company, and several other products. His eyes quickly appraise me, and his focus returns to the road. He's Mr. *come on an adventure with me* Jeep guy. Every time his commercial comes on, I hear Sammie sigh. She'd die if she knew where I am. Guilt hits me in the gut. Again.

"Chance talks too much," I mumble.

Lawsy's laugh fills the car. "That he does. He's like a middle school girl, but damn if I don't love that guy. We grew up in Minnesota and were high school rivals. But then we played together our rookie year in the AHL, and we've been friends ever since. You met him through the Decker Connection?"

"I've never heard it put that way, but that's a perfect way to describe it. The Decker Connection. My brother, Cole, is engaged to Ashleigh Decker."

"Yeah, the Decker Connection is like six degrees of Kevin Bacon, but with Deckers. Sometimes we make a drinking game of it." We both laugh at the comparison. "Ashleigh is Julian and Alexander's sister, the social media genius, right?. I've just contracted with her to help with my online presence. She's great."

"She is. She and Cole are perfect together."

"Cole plays baseball, right?"

"Yep, for the New York Liberties triple-A team in Nashville. I was at his spring training game when I sort of bolted. I took the first flight out, and here I am. My flight to Charleston was canceled because of the storm." Like I need it to validate my story, thunder booms around us. The wipers keep a steady beat against the windshield.

"What made you bolt?" He glances my way and gives a slight smile.

A call comes through his speakers. Saved by the bell, so to speak.

"Hey, Harps, I'm on my way home with Darcy. Should be there in twenty or so."

"Hi, Darcy." Her upbeat tone reminds me of Sammie, and the guilt slams into me. I left her with no explanation. Some friend I am. "Any food allergies or preferences? I'm cooking dinner, and it should be close to ready when you guys get home."

I drop in unexpectedly, and I get a personal chauffeur and chef. These people are incredible. "No, anything is great. But don't go to any trouble on my part."

"It's no trouble at all. I'm making chicken parm if that's okay. It's one of my favorite comfort foods."

"Sounds great," I say. Their kindness makes my eyes water.

"Okay, now you've made her cry," Lawsy says with a chuckle.

"I'll have the wine ready when you get here. Drive safe. See you soon."

The car fills with silence, except for the rain and the rhythm of the wipers.

"So, what made you bolt? Baseball is boring compared to hockey, but no need to run away from it." He gives me a quick wink, letting me know he's teasing.

"Yeah, it's complicated."

He nods, like he gets it. "Complicated. Understood. You're welcome at Casa Cartwright as long as you need. Harper's on spring break and will love the company."

"She's in school?"

"Yeah, she's working on her Master's in English Literature. She loves books and stories. So be warned, complicated will be like catnip to her. If she pushes, tell her no and squirt her with the spray bottle. She's used to it." The sound of his laughter lifts my spirits a little and I can't help but smile. A real one this time.

And then I laugh. It's the first time I've laughed in weeks. It's a foreign feeling, but I embrace it. I shake my head in disbelief. Chance did it again. He knew exactly what I needed. Their names are Lawson and Harper Cartwright.

———

Harper welcomes me with an enormous hug and an extra-large glass of wine. Lawson takes my bag to my room somewhere in the back of the house and joins us at the kitchen counter. The house is not what I was expecting from this superstar. It's homey and ordinary with high-end finishes. This suburban house looks like it should be the home of a married couple with two-point-five kids and a golden retriever, not a bachelor pad of a famous NHL player.

"Smells great, Harps," Lawson says. "What can I help with?"

"Finish the salad?" She pulls the chicken out of the oven, and my stomach growls loudly.

"When was the last time you ate?" she asks. The question makes me take pause. When was the last time I ate? My appetite disappeared around New Year's, but the last time I ate a full meal? I had a granola bar this morning, I think.

I give her a shrug. "It's been a while, but this smells delicious. I appreciate ya'll taking me in. Today has been a little unplanned."

"So, give me the deets. Spare nothing," Harper says.

"My flight was canceled because of the weather."

"Nah, I know that. How about the why behind you getting on a last-minute flight?"

"How do you know this wasn't planned?"

She looks at her brother, and I sigh.

"Well, okay." I blow out a breath. "My brother, Cole, plays for the Liberties triple-A team and was invited to spring training. My best friend and I went to Florida to watch him play. Everyone was there. He had a huge cheering section." A small smile escapes, thinking about how many people support Cole's baseball career.

"That's cool," Harper says.

"His fiancé is Ashleigh Decker," Lawson says for clarification.

"Oh, the Decker Connection. I get it now." She nods in understanding. "Continue."

"Yeah, the Decker Connection. Anyway, Chance FaceTimed Ashleigh at the game, and then I talked to him for a minute. When I gave Ashleigh her phone back, I saw a text. It upset me, so I took off. Got the first flight out to Charleston, with a stop in Atlanta. Bad weather, and here I am."

"So, the text?" she asks.

"It was from Matt, Cole's best friend."

"Oh, the plot thickens," she says, eyes full of curiosity.

Lawson serves the food and puts a full plate in front of me at the bar. The chicken parmesan smells delicious, and my mouth waters.

"Want to eat here or take it into the dining room? Where would you be more comfortable?" he asks.

"Whatever's normal for ya'll. Please don't make a fuss around me."

"We both have hectic schedules, so normal is nonexistent. But let's eat at the bar and keep the wine close," she says with a wink.

They both take a seat, and we all dig into dinner.

"Fantastic as always, Harps."

"Yeah, this is great," I say between bites.

She laughs, pours some more wine, and tilts the bottle to me. Why not? I nod yes, and she tops me off.

"Lawsy doesn't drink during the season," she says as she points to his lemonade. "I can't believe you're even eating the pasta on a non-game day." She may mock his diet, but her eyes are filled with love and affection.

"When you cook like this, I enjoy the treat. I'll burn it off at morning skate." Their banter reminds me of Cole and me before the mistake.

"So, back to Matt," Harper says, not letting the conversation lag. "Brother's best friend and…"

"Yeah, it's complicated."

"Ohh, I love complicated. Spill!" She rubs her hands together like an evil villain.

"Told ya," Lawson mumbles. "Spray bottle's by the sink." I look over and see an actual spray bottle and laugh.

She slaps his arm. "Hush! The girl has a story to tell." She props her chin on her hand and bats her eyes, waiting for me to continue.

I exhale loudly and smile. After a large gulp of wine, I tell the story. All of it. Well, most of it. I start with my childhood crush, the house project, Matt, the assistant, the secret relationship, New Year's party, ghosting, and the text. They both listen intently. When I'm finished, Lawson looks skeptical, and Harper looks downright giddy. Did they both hear the same story?

"Clarifying questions?" Harper asks.

"Sure. Shoot." I mean, I just spilled my guts to them after knowing them for an hour. Why not answer their questions?

Lawson surprises me by going first. "So, your brother punches him, he leaves, and ghosts everyone?"

I nod. "Yep, as far as I know, he hasn't talked to anyone. I found out weeks later he went to Mexico. Julian was keeping an eye on him."

"Except Ashleigh," Lawson points out. Why hadn't I thought about that? And maybe his parents? So maybe even Cole? So that means I'm the only one he's actually ghosted. Me. The mistake.

"Oh, I see the wheels turning," Harper says. "Stop them now." Her look is stern. She's already invested. Whether it's me or the story, I'm not sure. "Now, what did the text to Ashleigh say? Exactly. Word for word."

"It said, 'It was a mistake.'"

Harper jumps in her seat, clapping her hands together. "Exactly! Not you were a mistake. It. It could be anything. It could be the fact that he left. It could be what he ate for dinner or a poor fashion choice. Maybe that he walked away from you. Don't you see? He didn't say you were the mistake. Just that he made one."

"Maybe," I say with hesitation. "But either way, he hasn't reached out to me. It's over."

"He broke the code," Lawson says. He casually shrugs his shoulders, communicating it is what it is. Breaking the code is taboo. "That's a lot to work through. Not impossible, but like you said, it's complicated. The only way it's an unforgivable sin is if it was careless, a fling. If it was real, and it sounds like it from your side, then it just takes a little untangling. Don't give up." Lawson returns to his dinner, scooping another bite of pasta into his mouth.

Is a spark of hope trying to find its way back into my heart? I don't know. It's pretty dark and cold there these days. Not very hospitable for growth.

CHAPTER
THIRTY-EIGHT

MATT

———

"Hartman, get in here!" Alexander Decker calls from the coach's office.

"Oh man, good luck," Jake says.

We're dressing after warm-ups, preparing for our game with the Liberties. I feel like I'm about to lose the contents of my stomach, but I'm not sure how much of that is from the game or the blanket of guilt I'm wrapped up in after my conversation with Ashleigh three days ago. I lied to her twice. Fling? Mistake? Two words that damn near killed me to say about Darcy. I'm an idiot.

Several sets of concerned eyes watch me as I scan the locker room. I've performed well, so I doubt this is about my gameplay, but who knows?

I knock on the open door to the office, where a grim-faced Alexander greets me.

"What's up?" I ask, pushing the nerves down.

"Close the door, Hartman," Alexander grumbles. "Take a seat." He motions to the chair in front of the desk next to Julian.

"I'd rather stand, if you don't mind." I can't feel closed in. Not now. Not when I might hurl all over the desk.

I look at Julian for some sort of lifeline. He smirks and shrugs. That's not helpful, Julian. I thought we were friends.

"Suit yourself," Alexander says. He looks me over, head to toe. "That Reaper logo looks good on you."

I look down at my chest, reminding myself what we're discussing. "I like it."

"You talk to Cole yet?"

"No." I shake my head. I meant to, but after what I said to Ashleigh, I didn't know how to approach him. I never should have told her Darcy was a fling. I'm trying to do what's best for Darcy, but it feels like my house of cards is tumbling down around me.

"Is it going to be a problem?"

"No, sir. I'll take care of it."

Alexander looks at me and sighs. His tough manager tone gone. "Look, Matt, I like you. You're a great defenseman and not bad on the bat. But more than that, I think you have heart. You care about people, relationships. I know this thing with Cole is eating you up, and I need you to resolve it. Not only for the team, but for you." His words are wrapped in kindness and compassion.

"Why are you telling me this?"

"Because my sister cares about you. She's an excellent judge of character, even if she is marrying a Liberty." He gives me a sly grin. "I don't know the details, and frankly don't care to, but you need to value friendships. Work your shit out with Cole."

He's right. I need to work it out after the game.

"Is that all?" I need to leave this office and get out on the field.

"Yeah, that's it. Have a good game."

I turn to leave and hear him say, "And the right girl is everything."

"Don't I know it," I mumble to myself.

———

We go through the pre-game ritual, but I can't keep that word from bouncing around in my head. Everything. Darcy is everything. She means more to me than baseball, than my friendship with Cole, than my happiness. That's why I let her go, right?

As some local beauty queen sings the National Anthem, I look over at Cole. He's wound tight, all his energy looking for a release. I've seen him like this before, and it rarely ends well. He won't look at me, his eyes focused on the outfield. I wonder if he's nervous about playing today or if it's more. As his friend and teammate, it was my job to talk him down and get him game ready. Who does that for him now? No one, it seems, because he looks like he's about to explode. Even though he doesn't look my way, I'm sure he knows I'm here. Ashleigh would've told him.

The acid swirls in my stomach. She must've told him I said it was a fling. I couldn't have told a bigger lie if I tried. It probably added fuel to his hatred.

The Liberties take the field while I prepare to bat. Despite it all, I smile. Cole looks good in his pinstriped uniform. He's kept his preference for high socks with this new uniform, and I like it. We're both traditionalists that way. I'll always be proud of my friend, even for the small things like how he wears his uniform.

I'm second in the batting order, and I take a few swings with the donut and watch their pitcher, trying to get a feel for his style. There wasn't much film to watch since he was a late substitution. I'll figure it out. Franklin strikes out on a high pitch he should never have swung at. My turn.

With a deep breath, I take my place at the plate. I block out the noise, the chatter, the cheers. The pitcher throws a wicked curveball, but I don't swing. Ball one. The second pitch is a fast-ball in my sweet spot. I swing, and the bat's crack tells me it's probably a solid base hit past the shortstop. I take off running for first, and my foot hits the bag a split second before I hear the ball hit his glove. The umpire calls me safe.

It all happens quickly. Cole swings around and shoves me off the base, knocking me to the ground. Over my shoulder, I see my team ready to come to my defense, but Alexander Decker tells them to stand down.

"What the hell?!" I yell as I get back up.

Cole gets in my face, nose to nose. "Fuck you!" He yells so hard spittle hits my face.

"Cole, calm down, man. Stop. This isn't you." I push him back, putting some space between us. We need to talk, but this isn't how I thought it would happen. Is this about me or the game? My mind is racing a mile a minute.

"Me? That's rich coming from you?" His tone is full of disdain.

"Coming from me?! What's YOUR problem, Davidson?" His eyes are wild, just like our New Year's encounter. He's still pissed. Time did not heal this, not one bit. He's shaking with anger.

He shoves me again, only this time I stay on my feet. The umpire approaches to break us up, but Alexander is on the field and asks him to step back to let it play out.

My focus is only on Cole. He's not the only one who's angry. My frustration, loss, and anger sit right below the surface, and Cole's reaction is giving me permission to let it out.

He steps closer, and now we're chest to chest. This time, I hold my ground. Last time, I didn't fight back, but now? Nope, I'm not taking it from him this time. I've paid for my sins with the highest price possible. I let her go. What more does he want from me? I've given everything. Everything.

"How could you toss her aside like she's some common cleat chaser?" His voice is full of rage.

"Seriously? Do you really believe that?" My hands go to the top of my batting helmet. Does he not know me? Does he think I'm capable of that?

"You said it was a fling!" He throws his arms out to his side, ensuring I see him standing in front of me.

"Fling? Are you that clueless? I fucking love her!" I yell at the top of my lungs. My words echo in the silence.

"You love her?" His tone is normal, practically hushed. He cocks his head to the side like a confused puppy. He flipped a switch and now I'm looking at my best friend, eye to eye. All his anger is instantly gone.

I nod. "I love her so much it hurts." My hand is on my heart, hoping it will ease the constant pain.

Cole gives me one of his signature cocky grins. "Okay."

"Okay?" What the hell does that mean?

"Yup. Okay." My best friend is back, that familiar mischievous twinkle in his eyes. I know that look, and it usually results in some kind of trouble.

"You two wanna play ball?" The umpire asks.

We laugh and embrace while both benches let out an audible sigh of relief. The stadium breaks out in cheers and applause.

"Yeah," Cole says. "My best friend is about to get his ass kicked on the field."

"Good luck with that," I tease. "Loser buys dinner."

"Bet," we both say. It's time to get back to the game. And then, we'll talk.

CHAPTER
THIRTY-NINE

MATT

———

Reapers won six to three, with Cole hitting a home run in the fifth inning. I didn't have a bad day with a single, double, and two RBIs. Now that the game is over, Cole texts me an address and time to meet.

Cole and Ashleigh are staying at her family's house and invited me for dinner. Even though we won, I'm bringing dessert as a peace offering.

"Sure beats my hotel room," I say to Ashleigh as she greets me at the door. It's a large home close to the Reaper's facility. Do the Decker's do anything on a small scale?

"Yeah, Jules and Trevor stay here every year, so we're crashing," she offers.

Great. Julian and Trevor too. Fuck.

She senses my apprehension. "Look, I know you two need to talk. We're all headed out for a bit while you guys catch up and grill the steaks. Everything else is ready. We'll be back in time for dinner." She hugs me. "Love you. And I knew you were a liar." She kisses me on the cheek and makes her way out the door. Julian and Trevor are in the car waiting for her.

"Hey man, come on in," Cole says. "What's this?" He eyes the bakery box in my hands.

"Cannoli from this great little place I found near the strip."

"With pistachios?"

"Your favorite."

"Damn, I missed you." He wraps me in a hug, crushing the cannoli box.

"Same. Look, I'm sorry," I start.

"Nope. We're going to do this properly. Come on in, throw that in the fridge, and grab a beer. Let's go sit by the pool and start from the beginning."

I do as he says, and we sit by the pool, watching the sunset. I've missed him.

"Good game today," he starts. "You look good. And buff. What's up with that?" He laughs at me as he gestures his beer bottle at my chest.

"It's called the Mexican workout plan. A great gym and nothing but time." I shrug. My attempt at a joke isn't really funny.

Cole chuckles anyway. "Yeah, if you're gonna lay low, that's a good place, I suppose. So, what's up with that?"

"Well, you see." Where to start? "There's this girl. But it's complicated. She's my best friend's sister. I know I broke the code, but damn, she's so fucking amazing. She's funny, kind, beautiful, talented, and so many things. I couldn't help it. I tried to resist it, but I couldn't." I look at Cole for a reaction, and he has a faint smile on his lips.

"I wanted to tell you, but we wanted to see where it went first. I didn't want to keep it a secret. She's not the kind of girl you want to hide, you know? Then I was going to talk to you after the party, because I was planning on, well, things didn't quite go as planned."

"What were you planning?" Do I tell him? Does it matter now?

"I hadn't told her yet. I was going to tell her I was in love with her."

"Was?"

"Am."

He lets that hang between us. I've known Cole my whole life, and I can see the wheels turning in his head. He's thinking, planning, plotting.

"Yeah, I know my reaction wasn't the best. Trust me, Leigh has let me know her displeasure on more than one occasion. I'm sorry for the shiner. And for not answering your calls. I should've listened."

"I didn't mean to cause issues with you two." And there's another consequence of my poor decisions.

"Oh, we're fine. She tells me I'm an idiot and I finally listen. We're good. But you aren't."

"What does that mean?"

"I reacted without thinking. Matt, I know you. You would never hurt her. At least not deliberately."

"Never."

"But you have."

I flinch. Of course, I've hurt her. I ghosted her. I ran away. I hate myself even more.

"How is she?"

"Not great. She barely talks to me. She was here, and everyone was watching her, but then she bolted."

"Bolted? Where is she?" My heart stops. Is she okay? She's run away from her family?

He shrugs. His relaxed expression turns tense. "We don't know." He runs his hand down his face. "Chance texted and let us know she's safe but wants to be left alone."

"She's with Chance?" Of course, things get rough, and she goes to Chance, who takes better care of her than I do.

"Down, boy." Cole pats me on the shoulder. "She's not with

him. He just knows where she is because she reached out to him. He assures us she's okay. Chance is a protective fucker, like all these Decker bros. If he says she's safe, she is."

"What made her take off? Why would she do that?" I'm worried. My stomach is in knots. Where is she? Should she be alone? What does she need?

"I'm not sure. But I think she saw your text to Leigh. My guess is it upset her." He shrugs.

I finish my beer and look at his. He gets up to grab us another one. I bury my head in my hands and tug at my hair. What have I done?

Cole comes back and hands me a fresh beer. "Look, I'm worried too. We all are. She's miserable and heartbroken. And by the looks of you, I'd guess you are too." I nod in agreement.

"I fucked up."

"Yep." He agrees way too fast. "So, how you gonna fix it?"

"I'm not sure I am."

He turns in his chair to look at me. "What the fuck does that mean? Don't you want to?"

We sit in silence for minutes. Seems like hours.

Finally, I break the tension. "I'm not sure that's what's best for Darcy."

Cole gives me an appraising look. "Okay." His tone says he doesn't care, but I don't think that's the case. He said that earlier, too. What's up with saying okay? Is it his version of a female fine? Like when girls say fine, but it's really not.

He gets up to go back inside. He returns with a platter of steaks and puts them on the grill. He sits back on the lounger, letting the steaks' sizzle fill the silence. After a few minutes, he gets up to flip them. When he turns back around to sit down, I can't stand the okay comment.

"What do you mean by okay?" That is not the expected reaction, and I'm a bit thrown.

"We both want what's best for her, right?" He shrugs.

"Of course."

"And if you think there's another man out there better suited for her, then...okay. She'll hurt for a while, sure. But she'll get over it. I mean, we'll try to keep things from getting awkward at the wedding, but... okay. If she's not worth fighting for..."

I jump up from my chair and grab him by the shirt. We are nose to nose again.

"Of course she's worth fighting for." I practically growl at him. "She's fucking everything." The blood courses through my body like I'm stealing home. I'm pissed. How dare he say she's not worth it? Her own brother.

A smile spreads across his face, and he puts his hands on my shoulders. "You bet your ass she is."

Julian, Trevor, and Ashleigh come out on the patio and find us about to go to blows. I hear Ashleigh, "Tsk, tsk." Julian practically giggles.

"Looks like the official Team True Love meeting is about to begin," Julian says.

Trevor sighs. "Great, another Decker family meeting. I'll start the margaritas." He turns and goes back into the house.

I step back from Cole, and for the first time in weeks, I can finally breathe.

CHAPTER
FORTY

MATT

———

Spring training wasn't what I expected. If I'm honest with myself, it was overwhelming. I played decent ball and got better as the games went on. The extra muscle didn't hurt. I'm surprised I played as well as I did, all things considered.

Cole and I are finding our way back. We talk several times a week, text, and compete. That part's a little different, but it brings a new dynamic to our relationship. The wagers are fun and involve a good bit of humiliation for the loser. Yeah, we'll be fine.

We both make the Forty Man Roster, which means this season could be a lot of extra travel for us. Travel to the show, that is. We could be pulled up and down, depending on the needs of the team. It's the next step to making it to the big leagues. I never thought I'd get there so quickly.

It also reminds me how unstable my life is right now. I'll be traveling a lot this season, but adding the possibility of being in

Charlotte instead of Charleston gives me pause when thinking about her.

Team True Love, which has apparently expanded to include Cole and Ashleigh, agrees Darcy and I need to focus on ourselves for the next few weeks. We're both unbalanced and need to make decisions when we're on more sure footing.

One decision I'm sure about? I love Darcy Davidson. Of this, there is no doubt.

I log into the scheduled Team True Love video call. They're routinely checking in on my progress and these calls are both helpful and a pain in my ass. They've given me assignments and these sessions are supposed to keep me in check. This group isn't messing around when it comes to holding me accountable. We agree I need to go slow with Darcy. But it's time to open the lines of communication. That's the subject of tonight's meeting.

"There you are," Julian says when I log in. "Good game tonight."

"Thanks. I can't believe you follow my games." I'm a small fish in the Julian Decker Agency pond.

"Gotta protect my investment. I'm expecting big things from you, Matty boy. Big things." Julian's laughter cuts off when Ashleigh chimes in.

"Hey Matt. Cole's game ran late tonight, but he said to tell you, hold on." She looks at her phone and reads from her text. "It's time to reach out. He said to send texts, but nothing pushy. Friendly. Oh, and not to fuck it up." She rolls her eyes as she reads it out loud.

"That boy's a fucking wordsmith," Julian adds. "How he writes heartfelt love songs, I'll never know."

"Me either," I mutter.

"But I agree, it's time," Julian says.

"Yep, it is," Ashleigh says. "You've got some homework tonight. You ready?"

"I'm ready. Nervous, but ready."

We all think I need to focus on myself and my career while

Darcy focuses on graduation and Darcy Davidson Designs. While we focus on ourselves, we'll work on building a relationship as two individuals. Friends. Because with the baseball lifestyle, Darcy needs to have her own thing. Besides, she's fiercely independent and needs to know I support her and her career. I'd never want her to come second to baseball. Never.

"How's it going with your new roommates?" Ashleigh asks.

I told Julian about my conversation with Jake, and he told me to focus on my team. I didn't do a good job as a team player last season and got a reputation I need to repair. Unfortunately, I lost part of myself, my identity, so I need to fix that. As Darcy said, I value team, family, and relationships. Working on reconnecting to my values this season is a priority.

I rented a house with Jake and Hunter, two guys also on the Ghost Peppers' Forty Man Roster. We'll all be in the same situation this year, and since each of them has been with the Ghost Peppers for a few years, they offered to help me break into the team culture. I have mentors in every segment of my life now, and I vow to carry on the tradition as my career grows.

My one housing stipulation? I wanted to live on the beach. That wasn't a hard sell for them, so we found a house at Folly Beach. It's the perfect place for us to unwind and get away from baseball when we need it. The chill beach vibe is perfect for all of us, and the commute to the ballpark is half the time it was when I lived on the Isle of Palms.

"Good. It's good. Jake and Hunter are solid, and it's been positive for me. Jake and I are teaching Hunter how to surf." Jake's a California surfer, so while our waves aren't the same, it's a connection he appreciates. Hunter's from Texas, so he's adjusting to the beach life.

"I'm glad to hear they're good guys," Julian says. "The Reapers like to maintain that all-American image, you know."

We all laugh. I was sure my dust-up with Cole would get me reprimanded for blowing that image. No one has mentioned it. I still don't know what that means, but I'm grateful.

"Hey, before I reach out, can I ask? How is she?" They've kept me on a need-to-know basis when it comes to Darcy, which apparently, I don't need-to-know much. She's back in Charleston, safe and sound. They support her, but Team True Love is working with me, not her. I'm the one that needs the assistance. I'm the fuck-up.

Darcy's healing from the Matt induced wound. She needs to graduate and get her future mapped out. Then, maybe I can see how I fit into that. I don't need her to plan her life around me. Around us. I need her to be the main character in her story. She was born to shine. She needs to heal, recover. Sparkle. My pretty girl.

"She's good. Moving forward. I don't hear "All Too Well" as often, so that's a positive sign," Sammie chimes in. Oh yeah, she's joined the team too.

I wince. "Not the ten-minute version?"

Her look is sympathetic, but for me or her, I'm not sure. "Yeah. But it's not even every day now, so that's better. I miss her when she's in Atlanta, though."

"What? Atlanta? What's she doing in Atlanta?" My anxiety rises.

"Good job, Sammie," Julian chides. A beautiful woman walks behind him, drawing his attention away. Wasn't she in that last Marvel movie? "Sorry guys, I've gotta bounce. I've got reservations at Nobu. Never said this would be easy, Hartman. Do the work. Hang in there." He disconnects and leaves the meeting.

"Not your fault, Sammie," Cole says, joining the meeting. This video chat is like a fucking revolving door. He's on his phone in the locker room, chatter going on around him. "He might need to know about Lawson, so he has time to process."

"Lawson? Who the fuck is Lawson?" Add jealousy and a touch of anger to my anxiety mix.

"Do you think he'll still be able to go slow and do this right?" Ashleigh asks.

"Hello! Guys! I'm right here. Who the fuck is Lawson?" I toss the computer on my bed and pace. Is she seeing someone else? Maybe this is futile?

"Um, Lawson Cartwright," Sammie says, meekly.

"The hockey player? How did she get with him?" I'm yelling at the screen. I can take a guess how they met.

There's a knock on my door and Jake sticks his head in. "Hey, you okay?" My yelling got the attention of my housemates. Great.

I drop to my knees so I can see the laptop screen again, pull at my hair, and take a cleansing breath. "Yeah, Jake, just reevaluating my friends at the moment."

"Understood." He shakes his head and closes my door.

"Remember when we told you she was MIA during spring training? Well, she was in Atlanta with Lawson," Cole says matter-of-factly. "Chance hooked them up."

I grind my teeth so hard I practically break a molar. Hooked her up? He may be a founding member of Team True Love, but Chance Fuller is dead the next time I see him. "What do you mean, hooked them up?" I say each word slowly, breathing through my nose to stay calm.

"It's not like that," Ashleigh interjects. "Lawsy and his sister, Harper, rescued her when she got stranded in Atlanta. Darcy's been working on their house. They've been super-supportive friends to her. It helps that they don't know you, so she doesn't feel like they're taking sides."

"How supportive has Lawsy been, exactly?" My jaw ticks.

"Dial it down," Cole says. "I don't think it's like that." He doesn't think it's like that? Are they trying to kill me here? So much for me thinking they could help.

"Oh, it's not," Sammie interjects. "Not at all. He's like an extension of Chance. Lawsy is giving her a job, and it's building up her confidence. It's helping, I promise. And if anything, Harper is rooting for you because she's a hopeless romantic."

"So, stick with the plan," Ashleigh says. "Send a text. Don't mention Lawsy. You've got this."

"Don't fuck it up," Cole says. "Love you, sweetheart," he says to Ashleigh in a totally different tone. His ability to switch it up like that is terrifying.

"You can do this," Sammie says. "We believe in you."

I let out an audible sigh. "Fine. I hope you're right about this because I've never been so nervous about sending a text in my life."

We disconnect, and I stare at my phone.

"Okay, homework time," I say to myself. Their need-to-know rule makes sense as I attempt to put Lawson Cartwright out of my mind. Fucking Lawsy. Ugh. Nope. This is about Darcy and me. I let him go. Or try to. I'll never buy a Jeep, that's for sure.

I've started and erased dozens of texts. What do I say? We can't jump back to where we were. That's not the best way to start. We're both in different places. I want to grow our relationship if that's what she wants. I probably need to grovel and beg forgiveness for ghosting her, but Cole says to keep it light. We need to rekindle our friendship first. And apparently, that starts with a text.

I stare at the message and hover my thumb over the send button. I hold my breath and push it. And now I wait.

> Hey pretty girl! Graduation is just around the corner. Congrats! I'm proud of you. Are you excited?

I watch as bubbles begin and stop. She's responding. I watch the bubbles like they're a lifeline. Then they stop. They start again and disappear. This goes on for a few minutes. An hour later, no message. I get it. She's hurt and needs time.

Yeah, I fucked up.

CHAPTER
FORTY-ONE

DARCY

———

My phone pings for the millionth time today. Another text congratulating me on my big day. They should make me feel happy and excited as I prepare for our graduation ceremony. But they don't.

COLE

I wish I could be there, but know I love you, and we'll be watching the live stream. So proud of you Darce. 🎓🤍👰

MOM

Don't get mad at me if I take too many pictures today. I want to capture the moment my beautiful daughter begins her new chapter. See you after. I'll be the proud mom trying not to cry.

HARPER

> Congrats on your big graduation day, girl.
> Sending you hugs. I want to see pics of your
> dress. You respond to him yet?

No. I haven't responded to the texts that Matt sends. Sometimes they're an attempt to start a conversation, and others are updates on his day. They started six weeks ago, and I get at least one daily. I almost blocked him, but I can't. The thought of cutting him out hurts too much.

Each text sends me through a flurry of emotions. I get excited when his name pops up, and a sense of longing hits deep in my soul. Then I fill with anger at the thought we were a mistake, then switch to regret and loss. It's a whole emotional workout with each text.

I open his text thread and a slight smile escapes, and my stomach flutters as I scroll through the last few texts this week.

MATT

> Graduation is this weekend. I'm so proud of
> you, pretty girl. Did you make your dress or buy
> one off the rack? I'll be there in spirit.

> I'm in a little batting slump, so I need to change
> my walk-up song. Any suggestions?

> I should be used to striking out, but you know
> what I've learned? Keep swinging for the fence.
> Don't give up. I'm not giving up, Darcy.

> It's late, but I wanted to say sweet dreams,
> pretty girl.

> I saw you today when I got carryout from The
> Wreck. I was going to say hi but you were busy.
> Your sparkle was a little dim. You taking care of
> yourself?

Road trips are the worst part of this job, but I'm making friends. My teammates aren't so bad after all. I just wanted you to know new things aren't so bad once you jump in.

Good luck today. You'll be the most gorgeous girl getting a diploma. Beauty and brains. A wicked combination. You're the whole package, pretty girl.

———

"Wow." Sammie stands in my doorway, slowly shaking her head. "You look amazing."

I turn to look at her and give her the signal to spin. "Stunning," I say. Sammie wears her hair in natural curls, and her dark skin under the sheer white lace sleeves of her dress is gorgeous.

Sammie giggles. "I told Jay we wear white dresses for graduation. It will look like a bridal convention but don't knock the tradition. Our graduations are special." She walks towards me, puts her hands on my shoulders, and I turn to look at her in the mirror. "Want me to do your hair? A partial updo would look great with your dress."

"Thanks." I don't have the energy to think about my hair or make myself presentable today.

Sammie brushes out my hair, and then her nimble fingers create braids that look like a work of art. "So, have you decided which med school you want to attend? I know you want to stay in Charleston, but getting into Colombia is incredible, too. When's the deadline?"

"I have to let them know next week. I wasn't sure I'd get into any school, and getting multiple acceptances is wild. I'm still leaning toward staying here. I mean, it's an elite school. I'd be close to family and friends." Her hands still, and I look at her in the mirror. "You. I'd be here with you," she smiles.

I move my head back to get her to keep working. "We'll always be besties. I mean, in theory, I could go to New York with you. That's the beauty of being my own boss. I can go anywhere." I empathize with Cole and Matt when I think about this next step. Sammie being somewhere else will be like losing a limb.

She's quiet and finishes my hair, taking a step back. "I love it." My hair is in loose braids that knot in the back. She left the back down, giving it a soft look. It's perfect with my simple tea-length tulle dress. I bought the old wedding dress at a thrift store, made a few modifications, giving it a more modern princess and less wedding vibe, and plan to pair it with my red Chucks. Unconventional, I know. But that's what everyone expects from me. The shoes will complement the red roses we carry. The perfect statement piece.

The reality of graduation is upon us. No more soon, or in a few weeks, or before we know it. It's here. Now. We could go our separate ways. I'll always be there for Sammie, and I know she'll do the same for me. Long distance can work in any kind of relationship, or so they say.

"What about you? You hanging your design shingle here?" She wiggles her eyebrows at me and makes me laugh.

"Kinda. I told you about the two jobs I have lined up in Atlanta. I can do a lot of the planning here, but I need to be onsite when it's install time. So when I take jobs in other cities, I'll be on the road some. Ash and Cole invited me to Nashville, and Chance offered me a room in Raleigh. I don't know where I should go." I release my tense shoulders and lean into her. "I'm staying here and finishing our lease through August, so there's still time to decide. I'll pick up shifts at The Wreck for rent money."

"Sure you do. But let's both enjoy today. We'll worry about this tomorrow. Today, we celebrate!" She wraps her arms around me, giving me a tight hug. "I love you, girl."

"Love you too, Sammie. No matter what." I cry, and she pulls away, wiping a tear from my face. My crying is practically a regular thing these days. I'm doing my best keeping my emotions in check, but they still leak out.

"No more tears. Let's go get ready and let the world know we're ready to kick ass."

"Yep, totally kicking ass." I put on a smile, mostly genuine, and finish my makeup. We're ready for the future. I'm happy to start this new chapter. Really. I am. But if I'm ready, why do I feel so hollow?

———

The graduation ceremony was a blur. A typical May morning in Charleston, under the grand Live Oaks - it was everything I imagined. The girls in white dresses, the guys in white dinner jackets, and red roses bring a splash of color against the old Charleston buildings. Everyone was smiling and laughing despite the humidity and the no-see-ums biting bugs in attendance. Sammie and I weren't seated near one another, which allowed me a little alone time among the crowd.

What am I going to do now? I no longer have the protection and excuse of school to hide behind. I need to face my future, but honestly, I'm scared. Everyone wants me to launch my design company, or as Ashleigh calls it, my brand. While I like the idea, there's a lot of pressure to succeed. What if no one likes my brand? What if I don't have steady work? How do I know what to charge? I've mostly done things for my friends, for free, because it's my love language. I want people to be happy. I want them to be comfortable and enjoy the freedom to be themselves in their space. So far, everyone seems to love what I do for them, but is it because they're friends and don't want to hurt my feelings? Or do they like it because it's free? How do I make money from my hobby? And how do I do this by myself? My insecurity overwhelms me, and by the time graduation ends, I'm practically having a panic attack.

After we make our way out of the ceremony, everyone is connecting with their families. I escape, find my favorite bench behind the English Department house, and attempt to get my breathing under control.

I miss Matt, and my heart constricts at the thought of a future without him. He was my number one cheerleader when I was doing Chance's house. How do I do this without him?

Like magic, just thinking about him conjures another text.

MATT

> Wow. So damn proud of you! You looked gorgeous this morning. You made Cole cry. He mumbled something about your wedding day would kill him when he tried to wipe the tear away. I'm not making fun of him. I openly cried. Just wanted you to know we were there, even if not physically. Can't wait to hear what's next for you. You're going to do great things, Darcy Davidson. I'm your #1 fan.

I reread the text. He's with Cole? That's surprising. I pull up Cole's schedule and see they're playing against Matt's team in Nashville this week. Okay. That makes me hopeful. They're friends again. I'm glad. It's the best graduation present I could ask for.

Matt and Cole need each other. I should respond, knowing we'll both be around Cole and Ashleigh. I should hit the reset button and put us back in the friend zone. Well, maybe not friends, but more like we can be in the same room zone.

I start to respond with a simple "thanks" when Sammie finds me and sits next to me on the bench.

"Hey girl, you okay?" She puts her arm around my shoulders and pulls me into a half hug.

"Yeah, just taking a minute." I put my phone away, and she doesn't let it go unnoticed.

"Anything interesting?" She nods at my phone.

"Not really. Well, maybe. Did you know Cole and Matt were hanging out again?"

She looks away like she's trying to decide how to answer. With a loud sigh, she takes her arm from around my shoulders and clasps her hands together. She picks at her manicured nails. Why is she nervous?

"Yeah. At spring training, after you ran away to Atlanta, they kinda had an incident."

"What kind of incident?" My heart races again. My mind relives my anxiety when Matt called me a mistake.

She blows out a breath. This must be bad. "With your social media hiatus, you missed it. Anyway, they almost went to blows on the field. It would've cleared the benches if the coaches hadn't stopped them."

"Ohmygod, why? That can't be good for either one of their careers. Shit." Yep. That's me. Darcy Davidson, the harbinger of failed futures.

"Oh, it was fine. They had words, but they kissed and made up, so to speak. When Matt texted me congratulations, he said he was going to Cole's to watch the live stream."

"Matt……. Matt told you that?" I shouldn't be surprised he texted her. They're friends, and just because I screwed up, their friendship shouldn't end.

"Yeah. Their relationship is special. Like ours. Nothing can change that." She bumps shoulders with me to emphasize her point. "You two had a special relationship too. Any reason you don't want to fix that?"

"You know why." I close my eyes, the sunlight too bright for my dark thoughts.

"No, I really don't. You didn't want to ruin their friendship, but look, they're fine. Can't you try with Matt again?"

"No, they're fine because we aren't together. If we were…."

"Then Cole would be supportive."

I shake my head. She doesn't understand. I can't bear that

responsibility again. And besides, I was a mistake. My heart can't take another blow. I'm barely holding on as it is.

"Look, you know I love you. It kills me to watch you being fake happy. I haven't said anything because you thought you were doing a good job convincing everyone you're fine, but girl, you were not a theater major. Your acting isn't that good. I can tell you're heartbroken. Maybe talking to Matt can help you move on?"

"Maybe." I square my shoulders and stand up, reaching my hand out to Sammie. "But today is about celebrating our gradua-tion. Let's go have fun with our family and friends." She takes my hand and stands next to me.

"Let's go." She gives me a wink and doesn't let go of my hand as we walk back to the graduation crowd.

"And my acting isn't that bad," I mumble.

"Girl, it's Razzy Award-level bad."

FML.

CHAPTER
FORTY-TWO

DARCY

―――――

"Girl, this place looks amazing," Harper squeals. "I love everything you did."

"Yeah, this place looks great, Darcy. Thank you." Lawsy pulls me into a half hug.

"Thanks. Do you really like it? Does it feel like you? You can tell me the truth. I need to know to improve."

"It's perfect," Lawsy says. "It doesn't feel girly at all." He gives me another little squeeze and lets me go. "I'll admit, I was afraid there would be an explosion of throw pillows, but this is great. And my office is functional and cozy. The bar cart with my bourbon collection is brilliant."

"Yeah, now he'll never leave that room," Harper teases.

"Well, you guys already had a great start. I just bumped it up a bit." This really wasn't difficult. Lawson hired a decorator a few years ago, and while it was a little impersonal, it was easy to build on the foundation.

"I may never want to leave," Harper coos, winking at me.

Lawson moves to Harper and wraps her in a brotherly hug, kissing her on the head. "This will always be your home. But you should find your own place too, so you can date, and I won't have to know about it." He gives an exaggerated shudder.

"Well, that's not in my future. Between you and your teammates scaring anyone who dares to come around me, I'm practically a nun."

"Aw, Harps, you know we want you to be with a guy worthy of you. And trust me, none of the last few dates measured up."

"How do you know? You never gave them a chance?" she whines. She pokes him between his ribs, and he winces and steps back. "If you guys let us figure it out for ourselves, we'd be fine, right, Darcy?"

"Hm, what?" Their sibling argument has me daydreaming about my relationship with Cole. I wonder if all big brothers are overbearing or just big brothers who are professional athletes.

"I mean," Harper continues, "if it weren't for Cole, you'd be living your happily ever after with Matt."

"Oh, I don't know. I'm not sure we were meant to be. I mean, it was a forced proximity kind of thing mixed with a childhood crush. A lethal combination. Just not sustainable." It wasn't real. It was a mistake.

"He still texting you every day?" Harper asks.

I nod and half-shrug. Matt sends me a text every day. Sometimes it's a gif. Sometimes it's a joke. If I don't hear from him all day, there's a sweet dreams text sent late at night I see in the morning. I'm not sure what to make of it. There's no sense in responding. We were a mistake. And I'm doing better. Why pick at that wound? It's healing. I'll tell him to stop. Eventually.

When I talk to Cole, he never mentions Matt. It's like he purposely avoids his name. I know they talk now, even hang out, it seems. My conversations with Cole focus on my projects, his wedding, or begging me to come to a game.

I've lost my taste for baseball. Totally. I don't watch it anymore. What if I see something about Matt? And, well, I can't.

Not yet. Taylor Swift said it right in "All You Had to Do Was Stay." Seriously, why did he ghost me? Any why the texts now? He's confusing.

"Well, it's a long weekend. You aren't due back in Charleston for a few days. I have to go to New York to meet with a literary agent, and…."

"You sold your book?!" Harper is a talented writer and wasn't ready to put her work out there until I challenged her. We agreed if she sent her book out to agents, I'd work on putting my design company out there.

"Well, not yet, but an agent wants to meet me. Come with me to New York. We'll make a girl's trip out of it. Invite Sammie too. I can't wait to spend quality time with her."

"I don't know," I hedge.

"Consider it my graduation present to all of you," Lawson chimes in. "It's on me. Call your friend and see if she can go. I'll take care of everything."

And just like that, I'm off to New York City for a girl's weekend. Is this my new world?

———

Sammie and I roll into our apartment, which is smaller than the New York City suite Lawsy put us in. Harper and Sammie hit it off immediately. I knew they would. After our first day of shopping and sightseeing and a Broadway show, we crashed. Over breakfast, they ganged up on me about Darcy Davidson Designs. Oh, as if I had any doubts about it being a planned attack, Ashleigh showed up that afternoon to complete the foursome. When she pulled out a laptop to create an entire social media identity and plan, I knew. It wasn't a girl's weekend. It was an intervention.

"I still can't believe you conspired behind my back." I plop on the couch and put my feet on our secondhand coffee table.

After the luxury weekend in New York, the poor student look feels less homey and more shabby.

"Conspired is such a harsh word. It implies a negative intent. Which none of us had." She crashes on the comfy reading chair and shifts to avoid the spring that punctures you in all the wrong places. "I know you weren't thrilled at first, but you're pleased with the final product, aren't you?" She looks at me with unsure eyes.

"No, you guys came up with an amazing business plan." They really did. Ashleigh and Harper have a good sense of business and how to set up the structure. Ashleigh set up separate Instagram, TikTok, Facebook, website, and email accounts and posted a few pictures to tease the launch that's coming soon. She crossed it to my personal accounts plus the Decker Connection accounts. I already have over twenty thousand followers without any actual content. That girl is a wiz. Even so, it still terrifies me.

The launch is coming soon. I don't even know what that means. They set the business plan up to lessen overhead by keeping many of my services virtual. I can do video consultations from anywhere. The client pays travel expenses. They even helped me come up with hourly and project rates. I about choked when they calculated what the cost for Chance's house was using the proposed rates. Now I understand why he insisted on paying my rent and meals.

"I already heard from Mr. McIntyre with the numbers I'd need and the promise to be my silent partner. He'll wire the money once the business account is open." Mr. Mac is thrilled to be an investor in my company. He's a retired Silicon Valley executive and part of Cole and Matt's surrogate family from Savannah and I'm humbled by their support system extending to me. I'm nervous about being able to pay him back, but he seems confident he's making an excellent investment.

"That's amazing!" Sammie joins me on the couch and playfully throws a pillow at me. "So quit moping. This is the start of something great, Darcy. I just know it."

"Yeah, it's great." My voice lacks the enthusiasm it should.

"This launch party will be lit. And Cole can come, too, since he'll be down here for a series. It's perfect." They picked a date for a launch party and my only responsibility is to show up.

"Yeah, I guess. I just don't want to use my start-up money for it. It seems, I don't know, premature?" And irresponsible.

"Girl, it's fine. Besides, the bill is being picked up by an anonymous donor."

"Oh, who?"

"Dunno. Guess that's why they call it anonymous?" She gives me a wink and a look that tells me she knows more than she's sharing.

"It was sweet that Chance offered his house, but it just feels off somehow."

"It's because you've been off. You need to hit that reset button and move forward. It's time to face your future."

The thought of a big party at Chance's house makes my stomach sour. It's been six months since I was there, yet it seems like yesterday. So much has changed. I graduated. Matt and Cole fought and made up. I'm launching my company with no safety net. I've learned to live with a mended heart. Yeah, she's right. I'm moving forward, even if I'm dragging my feet.

CHAPTER
FORTY-THREE

DARCY

———

I leave all the details of the launch party to Ashleigh and Sammie. Sammie has never had a summer off and is going stir-crazy. This is her project, and being an overachiever, I shouldn't be shocked when a hair and makeup expert shows up at the apartment.

"I want you to be pampered today. It's a monumental moment for you, and I want you to feel special. Besides, I don't trust you since you're still in a funk."

"I'm not in a funk," I snap back. I'm not. This is just my new normal.

"Yeah, whatever. I want to see the Darcy sparkle today, you hear me? Everyone who loves you will be there, and since we've already determined you're a sucky actress and your internal sparkle seems to be broken, we'll dazzle them from the outside. You are your company, and it's all about style. You need to personify it today. Hear me?" She's in Sammie boss mode.

"Yes ma'am. I hear you." I turn to Julia, the stylist. "Sorry, I promise to be nice."

She laughs. "Oh, don't worry about it. I've been following your IG all year. I'm honored to be here. Now, show me what you were thinking about wearing."

Sammie comes into the room with a garment bag. "She's wearing this today." She shows the contents to Julia, who oohs and breaks out into a huge grin.

"Where did that come from?" I snap.

"That donor of yours wants you to shine. It's just a small part of the little surprises for the day. Don't worry. You'll love it." Sammie zips up the bag and hangs it on the back of my door. "We have exactly ninety minutes until a car picks us up. Let's go!" she shouts.

"Since when have you kept secrets from me?" I snark at my best friend.

"Since you let me do this for you. I take my duties seriously. Lots of moving parts today, so don't mess them up." She claps her hands at me. Sammie is a force.

I give her a harsh look, but her excitement wears me down. I smile slightly, saying, "I promise not to mess up your day."

She's busy typing something into her phone.

"Today will be amazing, Darcy. Just wait and see. And it's not my day. Today is all about you. I have to get ready too. Have fun!" She gives me a wink and leaves me with Julia.

"Shall we?" She points to my vanity bench, and the stylist becomes the stylee. What an interesting turn of events.

———

"Wow, Julia, this looks incredible. Thank you." My makeup is clean and natural, and her contouring and colors make my eyes pop. My hair is down around my face with loose tendrils, the perfect amount of curl, and a chignon at the nape of my neck. It's very adult and put together, with a touch of young, fun, and flirty. Perfect for the event today. Even if I don't feel very flirty. It's exactly the look I would've styled for someone.

She hands me a pair of gold dangle earrings that complete the look.

"Now, do I get to see what I'm wearing?" I've wondered about it since Sammie hung it on the door. Who picked it out? Who is this anonymous donor?

"Now is the moment of truth," she smiles. Julia unzips the bag, and a gorgeous chiffon skirt falls out of the opening. It's a viridian green. The color is so peaceful, the dress whispers calm. The halter style is modest in the front, but the wide satin ribbon that ties at the neck and hangs loosely down my bare back gives it a little sex appeal. The pleated skirt manifests a sense of whimsy and playfulness. This dress is perfect.

Green. Matt's favorite color. What would he think of this shade? I'm doing better. My mind only wanders to him ten times a day now. Yeah. It's better.

"It's gorgeous," I say on an exhale. "Where did it come from?"

"This designer is based out of New York," Julia says. "Fancy schmancy, huh?" She wiggles her eyebrows.

"It must've cost a small fortune," I mumble. The thrifter in me gets a thrill finding custom dresses and now I own one. How anyone could part with something made exclusively for them is beyond me.

The dress fits me perfectly, and even in my melancholy mood, a thin layer of fog lifts. The gold, strappy kitten heels complete the look. I give a twirl, and another layer of funk goes away. It's been a long time since I felt good about my appearance. I practically feel pretty. *Pretty girl* whispers in my head. I miss the way he called me that. I push those thoughts aside. It's about me today. The new me. The independent me. Maybe this is the start of my come back? I can't be a dud forever. My brand will never survive, and then where will I be? No, I need to step it up, play the part in order to be successful. As Sammie so dutifully reminds me, I am my company.

I give Julia a brief hug and thank her for everything. She asks for a picture, and I promise to tag her in my posts today. If I've learned anything, it's that social media can make or break you. I want to be that person who uses it for good and to lift others up. I'll start with Julia.

"Wow, Darce, you look amazeballs," a male voice says from across the room.

I turn to find Cole and Ashleigh standing in the doorway. Their smiles light up the room. Ashleigh has her phone out and is snapping pictures as I walk toward Cole's open arms.

"Hey, big brother. I wasn't expecting you here. Don't you have a game?" I cry as he wraps me tightly in his arms. It's been too long.

"It was an early afternoon game, and I wouldn't miss this for the world." He puts me at arm's length and gently wipes away my tears. "No crying. Can't have you messing up this beautiful face now, can we?"

"Don't worry, I planned for that," Julia chimes in. "She's waterproof."

We all laugh at her comment.

"We came to take the dazzling, talented, and amazing business owner to her launch party," Ashleigh says. "I'm here officially as your social media director."

"You don't have to do that, but I'm beyond grateful," I say, squeezing her hand.

"Are we ready to get this party started?" Sammie calls from the living room.

I grab a small matching clutch and throw lipstick and my phone in it. Cole reaches into his pocket and hands me a stack of business cards. They're orange with a delicate green design, partnered with a professionally created logo of interlocking Ds. Darcy Davidson Designs. They're beautiful and perfect. I add them to my bag. They've thought of everything.

"Where did these come from? Did you guys do all this?" The anonymous donor is getting the best of my curiosity.

"Nope, not us, but you know we support you, right?" Cole says. He looks into my eyes, making sure I understand. They're always in my corner. Always have been. Always will be. Whether I deserve it or not. "Ready?"

Taking a deep breath, I announce, "I'm ready."

———

I'm not ready. I'm unprepared for the valet parking, the intricate orange and green balloon arches outside the house, or the number of people entering the house. This is more than I thought and they're all here for me. This party had to cost a fortune. Who's paying for it?

"Ya'll, this is too much. How many people did you invite?" Fear takes hold. I'll just stay in the nice, air-conditioned car.

"Not that many," Sammie says. "Jay had a few contacts he wanted you to meet, some of Chance's friends, and your friends and family. I'm going to go in and make sure everything is ready." Sammie opens her door, gets out of the car, and gives a lingering look to Cole. He gives her a slight nod. Something's going on. I feel it. I'm on heightened alert. Are they afraid I'll bolt again?

"It looks like a lot of people," I say, trying to quell my nerves.

Ashleigh grabs my hands to get my attention.

"Darcy, you've got this. I've watched you work a room. This room, to be exact. You're going to be great. I won't leave your side. I promise." Her eyes don't leave mine. I trust her. I do.

The wave of emotions catches me off guard, and I feel like I'm drowning. It's more than the launch party. It's this house. The memories. The last time I was here was the last time I was truly happy. It's also the scene of my worst memory. I'm overwhelmed and feel like I'm about to pass out.

"Are you okay?" Cole asks, his tone full of worry. "You look pale."

I shake my head yes. I need to do this. I roll my shoulders and paste on a smile. I remember Chance helping me breathe in the airport. Two deep breaths and I'm better.

"I can do this," I say under my breath. With more confidence, I say, "Let's start this new chapter."

Cole steps out and helps Ashleigh and me out of the car. He offers each of us an arm and escorts us to the front door.

When we enter, it feels like coming home. The decor is just like I left it. I smile as I look around, allowing the pride to push away the fear. A large Darcy Davidson Designs logo is on the TV scrolling pictures from my expanded portfolio. It now includes this house, Lawsy's house in Atlanta, and a townhouse in the historic district. My contact information is listed and a QR code to my webpage on each picture. Ashleigh is a marketing genius.

A waiter offers us champagne, and I graciously accept. I gulp it down and take another one.

"Easy there," Cole whispers. "It's early, and I need you clear-headed."

"I know. I'm just nervous." The background music is quietly playing Taylor Swift songs by Vitamin String Quartet. The familiar tunes set to strings brings a peaceful air and I chuckle. They out did themselves with the attention to detail.

"These are your friends. Nothing to be nervous about. But we promise we've got you," Cole says as he hugs me.

"Damn girl, you look hot," Jay says as he approaches and hugs me, swinging me around.

His greeting makes me laugh. A genuine laugh. Jay has a way of washing all the nerves away. Sammie is by his side, her smile beaming.

"Thanks. You too." I'm not used to seeing him in a suit, and, damn, he looks good. "I'm glad you're here."

"Are you kidding? I wouldn't be anywhere else."

"That goes for me too, beautiful," Chance says, embracing

me and picking me a foot off the ground. He kisses my cheek and pulls me away from the group. So much for Ashleigh not leaving my side.

"Come on. Everyone is dying to see you," Chance says.

"Do I have you or Julian to thank for all this?" I wave my hand down my dress and around the room.

He chuckles, and his eyes sparkle with mischief. "Sorry, beautiful, I'm just providing the venue. The rest, well, it's a gift from someone else."

"Who? You know! Who do I need to thank?" I resort to violence and pinch his arm.

He laughs and shakes off my feeble attempt to coerce him. "Tsk, tsk. I'm like a vault. Now come on, your fans await."

He pulls me into the living room, where the crowd greets me with cheers and hugs. Harper and Lawson. Julian, Emma, and Trevor. Mom struggles to hold back her back tears. The McIntyres hug me, and Mr. Mac tells me I'm the most brilliant investment he's made in decades. It's the boost in the arm I need, reminding me I can't let him down. When Mrs. Hartman joins the circle, I can't hold back the tears any longer. She hugs me and holds me tight, whispering how proud she is.

A tissue appears at my shoulder, and Cole gives me an understanding smile. "Need a minute?" I give him a slight nod. "We'll be back," he tells the crowd, leading me up the stairs to the second living area. It's much quieter here, so everyone must be downstairs. I'm grateful for the moment away.

He leads me into the room where the French doors are open to the upper deck, the ocean breeze flowing in. The room is filled with vases of orange Gerber daisies, my favorite flower. They must've incorporated them into the party design, but I didn't notice them downstairs. Then again, I was too overwhelmed.

Cole keeps my hand at his elbow, like he's my escort, and leads me out on the deck. When we step outside, my heart stops. I let out a gasp as my feet refuse to move. Matt's eyes lock with mine, a smile filling his handsome face. His eyes sparkle with excitement.

He's in a light grey suit that fits him like a glove. His tie's pattern is an intricate and beautiful design of orange and green tangled together, reminiscent of my business cards. It's beautiful, and if I weren't so shocked, I'd examine the design in depth.

Cole reaches out to him, and I practically flinch as Cole hugs him and slaps his back. A different reaction than the last time I saw them together. This is the old duo I remember. This is how it should be.

My ears must be playing tricks on me because I think I hear him say, "She doesn't know. Good luck." I don't trust any of my senses at this point. Cole kisses me on the cheek and whispers, "Give him a chance, Darcy. He's one of the good guys," and he walks away.

I wrap my arms around my waist, willing myself to hold it together. I can't look at him, or I'll lose it. I look past him, watching the waves rolling onto the shore and rushing back out to sea. The rhythm allows me to focus on something other than Matt.

"Hey, pretty girl. You look stunning."

I can't respond. I can't. He complimented me, but all I heard was *mistake*. Several seconds tick by. I want to turn around and go downstairs, but my feet are firmly planted where they are. No matter how hard my brain tells them to move, they don't. Traitors.

"I've missed you," he says, trying again.

Mistake. The ocean keeps doing its thing. *Mistake. Mistake. Mistake.*

Seconds pass. "I'm sorry," he says with less confidence. "I shouldn't have crashed your launch party. I'm so damn proud of you. But clearly, this was a mistake. I'm sorry."

My head snaps toward him at his word choice. My eyes fill with tears, but this time, they're from anger, not sadness.

"Mistake?" I say through gritted teeth. "Mistake?!?" I practically yell at him. "Yeah, seems to be your favorite word when it comes to me, isn't it?"

He seems shocked. I'm not sure if it's because of what I said or how I said it, but either way, I've caught him by surprise. His timidness washes away, and he regains some of his conviction. He's not used to pissed off Darcy, but it's time he met her. She's been my companion for a few months now.

"What are you talking about?" He reaches out to touch me, but I step back, putting more space between us. "I don't understand."

"You told Ashleigh I was a mistake." My sadness over the past few months gives way to anger, and now I'm ready for a fight. I don't want to slink away and lick my wounds. I want him to answer for his crime of breaking my heart.

"I would never say that." He steps towards me, reaching out.

"Liar!" I yell so loud a few people look up at us from the pool deck below. I push him away, but he grabs me by the wrists when my palms hit his chest. He holds my hands to his heart. I try to pull away, but he won't let me.

"No." His tone is firm. "I NEVER said you were a mistake. You're my everything, Darcy. My everything." His eyes plead with me to listen, but I'm still in fight-or-flight mode. Since my feet refuse to move and he has my hands, fight it is.

"I saw the text, Matt. You sent it to Ashleigh during spring training. It said I was a mistake." I tug on his grip, but he doesn't let go. He lifts my hands to his mouth and gently kisses my fingers. The touch of his lips to my skin dampens my anger a little. Now even my hands are betraying me.

"No, baby, it didn't say that. I met with Ashleigh that day, and she asked me if I loved you. I told her it was just a fling. She called me a liar." He chuckles. How is this funny? "She was right. I was lying to her. Everything, Darcy. Everything. I told her it was a mistake. I meant calling us a fling. My words were a mistake. Never you. Do you think I'm the kind of guy who would use you like that?" His voice is full of emotion. Tenderness. Desperation.

His smile is gone and he looks hurt. Do I think he's the kind of guy who would use me? No. Hurt me? Yes. Because he did. To the core.

"But you ghosted me," I whisper, my fight betraying me too. It's slipping away.

"I did. And I'm sorry. I'm so fucking sorry." He pulls me into his arms. I let my hands drop to my side. "I left. It wasn't the right response. I should've faced Cole head-on. I shouldn't have kept us a secret. I was never ashamed of us. I needed time to figure out how to fix the mess." I stiffen at his use of the word mess and he notices. Holding me at arm's length, he leans down so we are eye to eye. Gah, I've missed those soulful dark eyes.

"No, we weren't a mess. We're meant to be, pretty girl. The mess was the cowardice of not talking to Cole. I didn't need his permission to be with you, but I owed him the courtesy of telling him how much I loved his sister."

My brain processes all his words, but I fixate on how he said he loved me. As in past tense?

"You loved me?"

He keeps his hand on my shoulder but gently tips my face to look into his eyes. "No," he says with force.

"Oh." Now my feet decide to catch up with my brain, and I step back. I turn to leave.

"Damnit, Darcy. Stop. I love you. Love in the present tense. Not past tense. I. LOVE. YOU!"

My feet stop my exit. I look around the room full of flowers. There must be almost two hundred flowers with every shade of orange imaginable scattered throughout the room. I begin to put all the pieces together. Cole telling me to give him a chance. The flowers. The green dress. The party. The text messages. Matt waiting for me. Giving me space. Because he loves me.

I don't turn around. I can't look at him yet. I need my wits about me.

"You love me?"

I feel his breath on my cheek. He's behind me, his head by my shoulder, his hands at my waist. "Yes, pretty girl. I love you, Darcy Marie Davidson. With my whole heart."

"When did you know you loved me?" I don't know why this is important, but I need to know. Does he love me because he lost me?

"What?"

"When? When did you know you loved me?" I say with conviction. This matters.

"I fell in love with you over the years. When did I love you so much that the thought of another man being with you would make me a murderer? I knew for sure on our fancy dinner date."

His response is unexpected. "That was before we ever slept together."

"Baby, we slept together BECAUSE I love you. Don't you get it? That's a line I'd never cross with you if love wasn't involved. Darcy, I've loved you for a long time. And I haven't stopped. Not for a minute. I love you, and if you let me, I want to show you I'll love you forever."

He loves me. Not because we had sex. Not because he was lonely. Not because he lost me. He loved me before.

I turn around, and he tightens his arms around my waist. I put my hands around his neck and pull him down to me. Our lips barely touch when I say, "I love you, Matt Hartman. I've been in love with my brother's best friend since middle school. I love you more than words can express and promise to love you more and more every day."

I barely get the words out before Matt presses his lips to mine. Our kiss is desperate, passionate, and toe-curling. I've missed him so much. I've been hollow, an empty shell, since he left. Having him in my arms, telling me he loves me, I'm so full of love I feel like I might explode. It's a tsunami of love filling me up.

I pull away and give him a quick peck.

"I" Peck.

"Love" Peck.

"You." Peck.

"Same, pretty girl. Same." He lets out a little groan. "And as much as I'd like to take you into one of these bedrooms and show you exactly how much I love you and have missed you, there's a whole party downstairs waiting for you."

"They can wait," I mumble as I kiss him again.

He laughs and steps away. "Including our parents. I put this together to launch your future career. Let's get it started."

"You? You did all this for me?"

"Well, I had a little help from our friends. But yeah, I want you to know I'm team Darcy all the way. Pretty girl, I'm your biggest fan." He's said this before, but his actions speak louder than words.

I look around the room. It's bright and a little extravagant. "How many flowers are in this room?" I wonder aloud.

He holds my face, our eyes connect. "One-hundred-seventy-four. The exact number of days I've been without you." I'm glad he's holding me because I've just turned to goo. Literal weak in the knees.

A tear escapes, and he kisses it away. I can't move. I don't want to move. I want to stay here forever, in his arms. "Come on. You're far too fabulous for me to keep all to myself. Besides, we have forever." He gives me another quick kiss.

Forever with Matt Hartman? I like the sound of that.

We walk downstairs, hand-in-hand, and the room erupts in applause. A blush heats my face. It hits me that our time upstairs wasn't as private as I imagined. Not taking it to the bedroom was the right call.

"Team True Love wins again!" Julian yells as he high-fives Chance. Chance grins at me.

Sammie runs up to me and gives us a group hug. "I'm so happy you guys worked it out. I love you both."

Matt kisses Sammie on the cheek. "Thanks for all your help."

I raise an eyebrow at her. "Help?"

"We'll talk about it later. Let's celebrate," she says.

"Yeah, we'll talk about it later," I grumble. It seems several people were working on us, and while I appreciate it, I hate being on the outside, especially when it's about me. I look around the room at the smiles, and as I make eye contact, each person raises their champagne glass to me.

Cole comes up and clasps Matt on the shoulder. "It sounded touch and go there for a bit. Glad you toughed it out. She's worth fighting for." He laughs and gently pats Matt on the cheek. "But if you ever break her heart again, I promise, I won't be team Matt next time."

"Noted. But there won't be a next time if I have anything to say about it." Matt leans over and gives me a chaste kiss.

"That may take some getting used to," Cole says. "But if I can get used to playing against you instead of with you, I can get used to this."

Cole turns his attention to me. "And he makes you happy?"

"No." Cole and Matt look at me, stunned expressions on their faces. I give them my most sincere smile. "He makes me every-thing. It's so much more than happy." Matt pulls me in tight to his side.

Matt exhales and kisses my temple. "Everything, pretty girl. Everything."

———

"Well, the party was a hit," Ashleigh announces as we sit in the living room with our friends. The last few hours passed in a blur of congratulations, social media posts, and more pictures than I recall taking. At one point, Ashleigh did a blitz campaign where everyone used her hashtag with their favorite picture of tonight and posted it on every platform. I experienced the Chance effect once before, but the Decker Connection effect? Wow! I got a gigantic number of followers in no time. Ashleigh turned off my notifications because this is work now, and boundaries are necessary. I love that girl.

The sun went down a few hours ago, and as much as I adore these gorgeous shoes, it's time to take them off. I snuggle on the couch with Matt. It's super comfortable, and I think back on the day Matt and I picked it out. The memory of the laughs we shared makes me cuddle a little closer. He holds me tight and kisses me on the top of my head.

Everyone is gone except the Decker Connection, who are settled in for the night. I smile and survey the room. We're relaxed and chilling out, exactly what Chance wanted. Yeah, I did a pretty good job.

Julian and Chance enjoy the massage chairs while Ashleigh and Cole cuddle on the big Squishmallow beanbag chair. Trevor and Emma are pouring shots in the kitchen and laughing at something Trevor said. Sam and Jay are cozy next to me and Matt. Alexander is on the deck having a heated conversation with someone, but no one seems focused on him because he's always on the phone.

"You have over two hundred thousand followers now and several DMs from influencers requesting a personal style consult. Some of Chance's friends have already reached out for apartment makeovers after they saw what you did at Lawson's place. And *The Today Show* reached out to see if you would be interested in doing a segment on trends for the fall. Girl, you are officially launched and booked!" Ashleigh is beaming with pride as she sets her phone on the table.

"Wow. I can't believe it. Thank you. Thank you, everyone. From the bottom of my heart. Ya'll believed in me when I didn't believe in myself. I'm blessed beyond measure." I didn't know I could ever feel this much love and gratitude at once. It's overwhelming, but in a good way.

Matt pulls me in a little tighter. "No, Darce, you bless us. Your sparkle lifts us all up." He kisses me on the temple.

"I'll drink to that!" Chance holds up his glass of scotch and takes another sip.

"So, what's next for you two?" Julian asks.

We both shrug.

Matt looks at me, a twinkle in his eye. "Well, we date. It'll be tough because it's the middle of the season and my travel schedule is intense. It sounds like D cubed will be slammed with clients."

"D cubed?" I ask.

"Yup, D cubed. Darcy Davison Designs." He gives me a little wink. "But we'll make time, right, pretty girl? We're lucky to be in the same city, which makes it easier."

"Yeah, about that," Alexander says as he enters from outside. His hand rubs the back of his neck. "Hey Trev, bring those shots out here for the group, would ya?"

"Sure, what's up? Everything okay?" Trevor asks. He brings a tray full of lemon drop shots, and everyone takes one.

Alexander makes me nervous because he's always intense. He's the opposite of Julian and Ashleigh. They're relaxed and casual, whereas Alexander is more buttoned up and grumpy. Maybe that's because he doesn't joke and laugh often. His job running a Major League Baseball team is high pressure and a lot of responsibility, so I get it.

Alexander clears his throat and holds up his shot glass. He looks directly at Matt, and he tenses around me. "Let's raise a glass and say congratulations to the newest member of the Carolina Reapers, Matt Hartman, starting third baseman, effective immediately."

The room erupts in cheers and congratulations. Matt is stunned. Neither of us takes our shot. He looks at me, stricken with fear.

This should be the best day of his life, and he looks terrified. It takes a second, but I realize why. We just got back together.

We're going to figure this out. And now he's leaving. I'm so excited for him and nervous for us at the same time. I love this guy so much that I'm confident we'll be okay.

I raise my shot glass high. He needs to know we're solid. We're going to be forever. "Here's to all your dreams coming true. Welcome to the show!" I throw back the shot.

Matt looks at me in disbelief. I take his face between my hands and kiss him. "We're going to be fine. Better than fine because we're forever, and my man is a Major League Baseball player. I'm so proud of you, Matt. You got this!" I kiss him again, and he kisses me back. The shock must be wearing off.

He downs his shot and looks at Alexander. "What? Why?"

Alexander grabs Chance's scotch and downs it. "Fucking Pauly just got arrested for assault and other charges. He's out. You're in. You suit up and start tomorrow against Chicago. At least we're at home for your first game. Welcome to the big leagues, kid." He gives Matt a rare smile and heads upstairs.

Ashleigh stops Alexander at the foot of the stairs. "You okay?"

"Yeah, I'm fine. It's just a shit show and PR nightmare. It pisses me off when someone tarnishes our family reputation."

"I'll help you any way you need me. You know that. I may not work for the Reapers, but they're my family, too. Just let me know, okay?"

Alexander kisses the top of her head. "Appreciate it. Love you."

"You may not realize it, but Matt might be the answer you need." He pulls out his phone and starts up the stairs, giving her a brief nod.

"Wow," Cole says. "Matt! The show, man, the show!" Cole gets up and pulls Matt into a hug. "I wish I could be there for it, but I'll be here beating your loser team tomorrow night."

"Yeah, you might stand a chance without me playing," Matt teases. Cole picks Matt up and spins him around.

Julian stands up and gives Matt one of those bro hugs.

"You'll stay at my place in Charlotte until you get settled. It's close to the stadium and in the same building as several other players. Tripp lives there, too. Unless you'd prefer the hotel the team provides," he says. He reaches into his wallet and hands Matt a key card. "I'll text you the address. And I'll review your contract and ensure they pay you well, especially since you're saving their ass." Julian chuckles. He loves making Alexander pay for the guys he represents.

"I'm so fucking happy for you," Cole says. "All your dreams are coming true."

Matt reaches his hand out to me. "My dreams are coming true." He pulls me into him and gives me a kiss that makes everyone uncomfortable, but I don't care. Matt loves me. Can it get any better than this?

Matt pulls me into the kitchen after everyone shares their congratulations.

"Darcy, I'm sorry." His smile gone, his face full of worry lines.

"Sorry for what?" I genuinely don't know why he's apologizing.

"Tonight was supposed to be all about you. This timing couldn't be worse." He leans down and places his forehead on mine, putting us eye to eye.

"Tonight is about us. From here on out, it's always about us." He nods, acknowledging my proclamation.

"Come with me?"

"What?"

"I'll understand if you don't want to, with your launch and everything. We'll make long-distance work, but I'm putting it out there. Come with me?"

Matt wants me to take the leap. It may feel fast, but I've waited to be with him practically my whole life. So much change at once, but there's only one way to face it.

"Okay, let's do it."

Yep. We're doing this thing. Together.

EPILOGUE

MATT

———

The last twenty-four hours have been crazy. Darcy and I officially became a We. We launched her new company. We got the call to the Major League. We called our parents. We said goodbye to our friends and made a hasty exit. We packed so quickly you would think we were on the run. We drove to Charlotte, finally able to be alone and talk about the months we were apart.

Darcy insisted on driving first so I could FaceTime my parents. They left the party hours before Alexander got the call changing my career. They were on high alert when they answered because late-night calls are never good. Once I assured them everything was okay, better than okay, I told them the good news. It's the first time I ever remember my dad crying. No, not crying. Sobbing. He was overcome with emotions. His son is a Major League Baseball player.

After a few moments, Mom took over the conversation and talked to me and Darcy. She told us to keep our love central.

She's worried we both have big things happening at the same time, and our relationship is fresh, tender. We assured we received her sage advice loud and clear. We want to protect what we have, too.

Tripp called to welcome me to the team and congratulated me on getting the girl. Darcy laughed as Tripp told her some Spring Break pranks they pulled on me.

We stopped at the halfway point and switched driving duties. After fifteen minutes of silence, the massiveness of the situation hits me.

"We need to talk, huh?" I ask.

"Oh," she squeaks out. "We need to talk never ends well." She tucks her knees under her chin and turns to the side window.

"Whoa, whoa, whoa, pretty girl." I reach over and put her hand in mine. I entwine our fingers and give her a reassuring squeeze. "Not like that. Not like that at all. I mean, we need to talk about all the crazy good stuff that happened today. We probably need to talk about the practicality of it all, right?"

"Oh, I thought maybe you were reconsidering now that you got called up."

I'm a little hurt she thinks I can switch her off like that, but I guess all the time I was working on getting her back, she was working on letting me go. I understand how we might be at different places when it comes to us. I vow to keep healing her damaged heart.

"Baby, if I never played another day of baseball again, today would still be one of the best days of my life. You know why? Because you told me you love me. Best part of my day, by a mile." And it's true too. Baseball is the cherry on top. It won't be around forever, but I hope Darcy will be.

"Wow. Quite the sweet talker, Matt Hartman." A slight smile peeks from her lips. Those lips I'll never get enough of.

"It's true. You were just ripped away from your family and friends on one of the biggest days of your career. I hate the timing. I want you at my first game, and that's selfish of me. I'd love it if you were at my second, third, tenth, and hundredth games too. But that may not be what's best for you. I meant it when I said I wanted to date you. I want to do all the boyfriend things with you. I need to let you know how much I love you and how amazing you are. It's not going to be easy with my schedule. And the last thing I want is to hold you back from D cubed. I want you to be successful, pretty girl. I want you to share your sparkle with so many people. So I'm good with giving you the space and time you need to grow your business and be the best damn designer on the planet. Tell me what you need because I'm a selfish bastard and will ask for all you can give me. I won't be upset or mad or anything, because you have to put D cubed in front of me. I promise."

"Seems like something you've put some thought into." She turns her attention to the darkness beyond the window.

"I have. I've been thinking about us since Ashleigh gave me hope there could be an us. Team True Love gave me homework assignments and lots of work behind the scenes. I had to work on myself and us."

"Team True Love?" She looks at me, curiosity in her eyes.

"Yeah, Chance and Julian have been cheering for us since New Year's." Hell, maybe longer? "Then later, when Cole and I sorted our shit, Team True Love got to work. There was an elite team working with me to get us together."

"Yeah, tell me about you and Cole. I heard something about an on-field incident, but I refused to search for it. I've been pretty internet silent these past few months. I figured it would be easier to avoid you in any form. For the record, it wasn't." That sadness she had when she first saw me crosses her face again.

I lift our clasped hands to my lips and kiss her knuckles, bringing a small smile to her face. She needs to hear this. She needs to know the entire story to know I'm all in when it comes to her.

She's avoided everything baseball. She was working hard to

put me behind her. I'm glad her love won out. "Well, it was our first game against the Liberties at spring training, and Cole and I had a personal and heated on-field conversation. I let him and the entire stadium know I loved you. I'm sure that's on YouTube somewhere. I heard it went viral, but I never watched it." I didn't need to watch it. I lived it. I shake my head slightly to rattle away the deep pain associated with that time and finish the story. "Anyway, we talked out our shit. Team True Love was there with advice and homework, and the rest is history." I give her a wink.

She giggles. "You told the entire stadium you loved me?"

"Yep. The stadium. The team I'm joining tomorrow. The coaching staff. Alexander Decker. Everyone." I hadn't thought about that until now. I'm not embarrassed, but maybe a little nervous I didn't make a good first impression. Hell, the locker room teasing will be relentless. Worth it? Absolutely.

She types on her phone, and then I hear the argument with Cole like it was yesterday. *I fucking love her.* She watches the short video and smiles.

"Wow."

"Yeah, not my finest moment."

"Oh, I don't know. I kinda like it. It's swoony. And over a million views, so somebody must have liked it?"

"Swoony? Doubtful. And a million views, seriously? It was a baseball miracle the benches didn't clear." I sigh.

"I'm surprised Lawsy and Harper didn't show this to me," she says as an aside.

"Fucking Lawsy," I mumble. When we met, I thought he was a little too friendly with Darcy. But then again, anyone who hugged or touched her set my nerves on edge. So that was basically a hundred people, both men and women, who irritated me today.

She giggles, and I relax a little at her laugh. I remind myself I'm with her right now, not Lawsy. "Tone down the jealousy, slugger. I think you're seeing green. They're my friends. Harper helped me create the D cubed business plan." She leans over and kisses me on the cheek. She's right. I'm jealous of anyone that got to spend time with her when I couldn't.

"I look forward to getting to know them better, then." Yeah, it's another hockey player, but if he's important to Darcy, he's also important to me.

"So, part of the creation of D cubed was to ensure I can work from anywhere. I can do a lot virtually, and when I have to travel, I can schedule it around other priorities." She bites her bottom lip, hesitant to say what's on her mind.

"What are you thinking about?"

"Well, now that I think about it, I'm not sure those girls weren't secret agents of Team True Love too. I thought I needed a storefront, offices, you know. They were insistent that I should be mobile, virtual. While it's more cost-effective, Ashleigh insisted that I never know when I'd want to pick up and move." She smiles at me. "Like now."

"Yeah, being with a baseball player requires a lot of flexibility. I'm serious when I say I love you, but I want you to consider the downside of being with me. The lifestyle of the WAGs was a big part of my pulling away from you too. This isn't a simple life. I don't want to hold you back." I squeeze our hands to emphasize my point.

"Am I officially an MLB WAG?" WAGs are wives and girl-friends. It's an exclusive club.

She's not my wife, but I'll make her that soon enough if I get my way. "You are if you want to be, pretty girl. I want to call you my girlfriend if you'll let me."

"Look at us having the DTR conversation like two adults," she teases.

"We're doing everything on a sped-up timeline." Do I want her to move in with me? Absolutely. But I mean it when I tell her it's at her pace. I never want her to be uncomfortable with us or become resentful of me because I'm the one who could get traded or moved with little notice.

"Yeah, but I'm okay with it. We aren't your typical couple. We have a lifetime together."

"We do, don't we?" I like the idea of a lifetime with Darcy Davidson. I love the idea of We.

The night wasn't what I had in mind. I thought I'd make love to my girl all night and worship her like she deserves. Instead, we barely made it to bed before we fell asleep, exhausted from the adrenaline rush and four-hour drive. I didn't realize how poorly I've been sleeping until now. Last night was the best I've slept in weeks because I had my everything in my arms.

After two rounds of morning sex, we get cleaned up and ready for the day. I have to get to the stadium early for media, uniform and equipment check, and meetings with coaches and trainers. I've got a full day ahead, but I can't think of a better way to start it than with Darcy.

The concierge calls to let us know breakfast is ready and will arrive shortly. Such is the lifestyle of the rich and famous, I guess. Julian's apartment is impressive and nicer than any five-star hotel. He's not only a skilled agent, but a fantastic friend. Letting us stay here is extremely generous and convenient, as I look out over Decker Stadium from the floor to ceiling windows in the living room.

The delivery person arrives, and he sets out a spread on the breakfast bar. There's every kind of breakfast item you can imagine: bacon, eggs, grits, coffee, tea, and cinnamon rolls the size of your head. I open the card that came with the food.

It's game day! Enjoy breakfast. You'll need your strength. *Wink, wink*
See you at the stadium.
Go Reapers!
TTL

I roll my eyes at the ridiculousness of this group.

Also included in the delivery is a white box tied with a red satin ribbon and a card for Darcy. Who's sending her gifts? The list of suspects is short, considering only a few people know where we are.

Darcy comes out of the bedroom looking like a fucking dream. She's wearing a Reapers tank top and cut-off shorts that make her legs look like they go on forever. Her eyes light up when she sees the breakfast spread.

"How thoughtful," she says as she kisses me on the cheek.

"Team True Love." I hand her the card and shrug.

She reads the card and laughs. "I like it."

"And this came for you." I hand her the box and card. She reads the card, holds it to her chest, smiles, and tucks it back into the envelope. She doesn't open the box. My curiosity gets the better of me.

"What's in the box?"

"Something. For later," she winks.

I get a little irritated. "Okay, Team True Love has crossed the line if they sent my girl lingerie. While I appreciate the sentiment, they need to stay out of our bedroom."

She giggles and seems to enjoy my annoyance. "Not lingerie. And it's not from Team True Love. Well, I don't think it is, anyway. It's from Alexander. Was he part of TTL?"

"Decker?" What the hell is my boss doing sending a gift to Darcy?

"You know what, never mind. Don't worry about it. Ohhh, doesn't that cinnamon roll look good?" She takes a swipe of the cream cheese icing and licks her finger, making eyes at me. She's so cute when she's trying to be seductive.

"I'm not worried. Just curious." I shrug because it's going to drive me crazy. I'm tired of not knowing when it comes to her. The days of need-to-know when it comes to her are over if I have anything to say about it.

"You trust me, don't you?" She puts her hands on her hips, challenging me.

"Of course, one hundred percent." And I do.

"Then chalk it up to the Decker Connection."

"The Decker Connection?"

She motions to the food, we make our plates, and sit at the kitchen table. Darcy sips her coffee and tells me about the Decker Connection. I laugh as my girl, hell yeah, my girl, spins a tale of connections, people, and family, all a part of the Decker Connection. And because my best friend fell in love with a Decker, I'm part of the Connection as well.

I conclude that a subsidiary of the Decker Connection is Team True Love, and for them, I'll be eternally grateful.

———

I walk down the tunnel towards the field, the familiar crunch of my cleats calming my nerves. I've played baseball my entire life. I've had big games before with other teams. Tonight is just another home game for the Carolina Reapers, but for me, it's my MLB debut, my childhood dream come true.

"You okay, Hartman?" Alexander Decker asks when I get to the field entrance.

The low rumble of the crowd echoes in the tunnel, making all the sounds reverberate in my head.

"Yeah, I'm good. I'm grateful for this opportunity." I barely get the words out, the emotion putting a lump in my throat.

"Just play your game tonight. You only get one debut, so enjoy it all. Besides, you've got quite a cheering section who loves you, no matter how you play. Play tonight for them. Hell, I think the entire Charleston party just came up here." He gives me a rare Alexander Decker smile and a slap on the back. "Listen, this Pauly thing is a PR nightmare. Ashleigh thinks you're exactly what we need to counter it. Just keep being you and don't let all this," he waves his hand around the stadium, "change you. The Reapers and I are depending on you."

Wow. No pressure. "Thanks. I'm a lucky bastard."

"You deserve it. And for what it's worth, I'm rooting for you and Darcy. You two are good for each other. And she's a gem."

Maybe he's part of Team True Love? Which reminds me of the gift box. "I agree. Um, what did you send her this morning?" I need to stop my raging imagination. With Darcy, I've discovered I'm extremely protective and jealous. Seeing green? Absolutely.

He laughs, probably knowing it's driving me crazy. "Honestly, it was more for you than her. Now get out there and have a good time."

More for me? I swear I'm appreciative, but if he sent something sexy to my girl, I'll have to kill my GM, Alexander fucking Decker. Probably not the best way to start my new job.

It's game time. I step out of the tunnel with my team, and the crowd behind me goes wild. I look up and see at least twenty signs for me. I smile at my support system, all cheering loudly for me. Julian, Trevor, and Ashleigh are making an obnoxious amount of noise. She has a giant picture of ten-year-old Cole and me with a word bubble that says, "So damn proud of my best friend." Mom, Dad, the McIntyres, and Mrs. Davidson all have signs proclaiming they're proud parents of number thirty-three. They are beyond supportive and I wouldn't be here without them. I continue to scan the crowd for my girl. Maybe she's already in the WAG section, but I thought she'd be with this group. Our family and friends.

Tripp claps me on the shoulder. "Ready for this, Hartman?" He pulls my attention from the cheering section, and I focus on the game. She's here. That's what matters.

I scan the field and stands, taking it all in. I've never played in a stadium this big, and it looks like a near-sell-out crowd. It's mind-blowing. I take a deep breath.

"Yeah, I'm ready. Been waiting for this my whole life."

"Hartman, get ready to field the opening pitch," my coach barks out.

I look at Tripp, confused. "Isn't that the catcher's job?" I whisper. He smiles and shrugs.

"It's a rookie thing. Joey hates chasing the bad pitches," Tripp explains.

We line up for the national anthem and Joey Samuels, the catcher, motions me to home plate as we head to the dugout. I hesitate. After all the pranks at spring training, I've learned to be on high alert around these guys.

Alexander walks to the pitcher's mound with a microphone. Not sure if this is typical pre-game fanfare, I slowly make my way to home plate. No one prepared me for this part.

"Welcome to Decker Stadium, home of the hottest baseball team in the league." The crowd goes wild and the pepper mascot does a backflip. "I'm Alexander Decker, General Manager of the Reapers. As a family-owned and managed organization, we hold family, team, and community as our highest values. They come before everything, including baseball. We expect every member of our team to uphold those values, from the grounds crew to the players to the front office. We are all held to the same standards, no exceptions. Now I know many of you saw last night's headlines about one of our players who did not uphold these values, and for that, on behalf of the organization, I apologize. When one of our team fails, we all fail." He looks around the stadium, letting the fans know he's speaking to everyone. "I'm extremely grateful to see you all here tonight and appreciate your continued support of the Reapers family." The crowd applauds again.

Alexander pauses and then looks my way, giving me a slight nod. "But tonight is also a time to celebrate new beginnings. Matt Hartman is an MLB rookie making his debut. He was our third-round draft pick last year, and we called him up from the Ghost Peppers late last night. He's an example of a leader on and off the field, and we're excited to have him join our team here in Charlotte."

As Alexander mentions my name, I stop mid-stride, halfway between the bench and home plate. I'm stunned. They don't make a fuss about everyone's first game like this. What's happening?

"Behind every guy here living out their dream, there's a team of supporters who helped him along the way. We're honored to have Matt's family and friends here tonight." Alexander motions behind the dugout, and they go nuts. "Matt represents everything we stand for, especially home and family. We're excited to host his cheering section, including the Charleston High School Pirates Baseball Team and their coach, Matt's father, Ken Hartman. Matt spent his off-season mentoring these ballplayers, hopefully growing the next generation of Reapers." The team stands to applause.

"Many of you saw a viral video from spring training where Matt had a bit of a scuffle with his best friend, Cole Davidson, of the Liberties organization. There was lots of drama and online speculation about what happened next. Did Matt get the girl, who is his best friend's and now baseball rival's sister?" The crowd laughs, and several oohs start. Yeah, my best friend's sister's a risk, but one I'd take again.

"So, in the theme of family, love, support, and to answer that burning question, allow me to invite Miss Darcy Davidson, Cole's sister, to the mound to throw out tonight's first pitch. She's a good friend of the Deckers and the Reapers. She's also an up-and-coming designer." He waves her over to the pitcher's mound. "Darcy, let's get this game started, shall we?"

She walks up to the mound from the visitor dugout, dressed like she was this morning, but now she's added an oversized, unbuttoned Reapers jersey. She's cute as hell. Her hair is in soft waves that frame her beautiful face, and she takes my breath away. Alexander hugs her, picking her up and spinning her around so her back is to me and the cameras. Then I see it. She's wearing my jersey. Hell yeah, she is. A grin spreads across my face, and my heart is full. The crowd goes wild when the cameras zoom in on her back. "How You Get the Girl" plays overhead and I can't help but laugh.

I stand behind home plate and know her pitch will hit the mark. This girl doesn't miss. She throws the ball to me, and it's a strike. Perfect. I jog up to the mound to give her the ball, shake Alexander's hand, and kiss her. I whisper in her ear, "Tonight. You, pretty girl, in nothing but that jersey."

"You got it, slugger. Now go live your dream."

"I already am," I say walking to the dugout. "Everything, pretty girl. Everything."

And just like that, I'm exactly where I belong. I found home.

WHAT'S NEXT FOR THE DECKER CONNECTION?

A PR crisis isn't the only dilemma Alexander Decker faces this season. He's the youngest General Manager in the MLB, and that comes with immense pressure. Add in being self-appointed protector of the Decker Connection, and it's no wonder everyone calls him grumpy.

When he meets a strong, independent, single mother full of sunshine and sass, he discovers not everything is as he thought, including his outlook on love and life. Game on!

Get ready to cheer him on in Living the Suite Life.

ALSO BY CHERYL CAMPBELL

Trouble at First: Decker Connection #1 Ashleigh and Cole

The Decker Connection series starts with Ashleigh and Cole ⚾

All Ashleigh Decker wants this summer is to be the social media intern for the Savannah Pajamas. Is that too much to ask? She's off to a great start until she meets a player who is nothing but trouble.

This summer league is the perfect opportunity for Cole Davidson to impress the MLB scouts. His dream to play first base for the Carolina Reapers is within his grasp. An added bonus? A beautiful intern who steals his heart.

The only problem? She's hiding her identity. Her father is the owner of the Reapers, and her overprotective older brother is the General Manager. Can Ashleigh keep her secret and the guy without jeopardizing his career?

Living the Suite Life: Decker Connection #3 Alexander and Dani

Stress and pressure come with the territory when you're the youngest General Manager in the MLB. Add in my self-appointed role as the protector of the Decker Connection, my tight-knit group of siblings and friends, and it's no wonder they say I'm grumpy.

I'm facing down a public relations nightmare after one of my players assaults someone at a local food festival, and this PR problem is about to push me over the edge. Then I meet this full-of-sunshine, rainbows from storm clouds, heart-full-of-kindness, single mother, and I'm in more trouble than I ever imagined. There's absolutely no saving me from falling now.

The Final Draft: Decker Connection #4 Julian and Harper

Julian Decker's billion-dollar sports agency represents the top athletes in the world. His charm, success and sexy blue eyes have landed him on the hottest bachelor list for the past five years. He's a hopeless romantic, with money, fame, and a rotation of beautiful women on his arm each week. Some would say he has it all. But things aren't always as they seem. Behind the flashing lights and camera clicks, Julian has deep-seated trust issues and a secret he keeps hidden, even from his closest friends in the Decker Connection.

Harper Cartwright is tired of being known as "the hockey player's sister" and is ready to forge her own path. With her master's degree in hand, she's headed to New York to learn from the best and make her author dreams come true. It's a whole new ball game for her. A new city. A NHL goalie roommate and his adorable dog. An intense and demanding writing program. She has a lot on her plate. Harper's handling all these life challenges until she encounters Julian Decker, a handsome playboy with a panty-dropping smile. His intense pursuit of her has Harper excited and wary, especially after she discovers his secret.

LET'S CONNECT

Cheryl loves connecting with readers and talking about the Deckers. Join her in the conversation. Follow for sneak peeks and behind the scenes fun.

And don't forget to leave a review on Amazon 😊

Cheryl Campbell Facebook Cheryl Campbell Author

Cheryl Campbell Instagram @Cheryl_Campbell_Author

Cheryl Campbell TikTok @cherylcampbellbooks

CherylCampbellbooks@gmail.com

Want to hear the Sliding Into Home Playlist? Check it out on Spotify.

Spotify - The Decker Connection: Sliding Into Home

www.ingramcontent.com/pod-product-compliance
Lightning Source LLC
Chambersburg PA
CBHW050021120726
47903CB00006B/1862